RILEY WEAVER
NEEDS A DATE TO THE
GAYBUTANTE BALL

JASON JUNE

HARPER TEEN

An Imprint of HarperCollinsPublishers

Also by Jason June

Jay's Gay Agenda
Out of the Blue

HarperTeen is an imprint of HarperCollins Publishers.
Riley Weaver Needs a Date to the Gaybutante Ball
Copyright © 2023 by Jason June
All rights reserved. Printed in the United States of America.
No part of this book may be used or reproduced in any
manner whatsoever without written permission except in
the case of brief quotations embodied in critical articles and
reviews. For information address HarperCollins Children's
Books, a division of HarperCollins Publishers, 195 Broadway,
New York, NY 10007.
www.epicreads.com
Library of Congress Control Number: 2023930684
ISBN 978-0-06-326003-0
Typography by David DeWitt
23 24 25 26 27 LBC 5 4 3 2 1
First Edition

To Megan, for seeing something in my words
and introducing me as a Gaybutante to the
world. I wouldn't be here without you.

A Note to the Reader

First off, thank you so much for picking up this copy of *Riley Weaver Needs a Date to the Gaybutante Ball*. Before you dive in, I want to take a second to explain that within these pages, you'll be reading from Riley's perspective as he discovers how liberating and limiting labels regarding gender and sexuality can be. In this journey, Riley encounters language that is femmephobic, homophobic, and transphobic. Over the course of the novel, Riley explores how this negativity affects him and others in the queer community, as well as examines his own role and fellow queer people's role in glorifying certain gender presentations over others, intentionally or otherwise. While overall this is a lighthearted story, these extra layers may be hard to read for some, so please don't feel any pressure to read until you are ready. So much love to you, and remember, no matter how you identify, you are beautiful.

Love,
    Jason June

**Excerpt from Episode 1—*Riley Weaver Needs a
Date to the Gaybutante Ball*: "How It Started"**

Let's start at the very beginning. A very good place to
start.

My name is Riley Weaver, and I'm a junior at Mountain
Pass High. Yes, the Mountain Pass High of Gaybutante
Society fame. That lucky school an hour outside Seattle
that fate decided would be forever linked to the much-
flashier New York City, Atlanta, and Los Angeles branches
when the four GS founders met at a Maine summer camp
in 2002. It was four years before I was even born, but
their creation of the buzziest society for LGBTQIA+ teens
would trickle down and affect my life now, more than
twenty years later.

Here's the first thing you should know about me: I want
in. I want to join the ranks of the Gaybutante Society and
make a mark like so many Gaybutantes before me who

have gone on to become artists, actors, singers, politicians, activists, you name it. I will become part of this year's class of queer tastemakers and have so many interview subjects for what will hopefully one day become my number one podcast. I like to talk a lot, and the only thing I like more is hearing other people talk and share their stories. But for this podcast, my very first podcasting endeavor, I'm going to be sharing my story as I complete each of the tasks required to be deemed a Gaybutante: Service, Hosting, Mentorship, and General Gay Chaos. I figure I'll go after that last one first and get started with the chaos.

Which leads to the second tidbit you should know about me: I'm femme. I like to wear feminine clothes (and don't you dare call them women's clothes, because clothing doesn't have genitals), I dabble with makeup most days, and of course by "dabble" I mean eyes, cheeks, bronzer, highlighter, the whole shebang.

Gender-wise, I'm still figuring things out. I'm not trans, but I don't consider myself cisgender, since "boy" and all the expectations that come with it don't always fit. I do still go by he/him pronouns. I feel sort of like a dot somewhere in the middle of that line connecting the two ends of man and woman, rather than somewhere outside of that binary entirely, so saying I'm nonbinary doesn't feel quite right, and I don't want to take away from the people who know for sure that nonbinary is the term that best describes them. But my best friend and producer of this podcast, known here very creatively as Producer, says

I shouldn't worry too much about labels. But I feel like I should address my identity, genderly speaking, since that's a key aspect of this podcast and my mission to get into the Gaybutante Society. Say hi, Producer.

Hi, folks. Producer over here, he/him, and if anybody sends an email to the show with questions or advice for Riley, I'll be the one relaying the info.

Thanks, P. So, to recap, the two things I know for sure are that I'm outwardly and inwardly femme, and that I'm gay. Which apparently is the problem. At least according to The Jock.

Quick sidenote before we begin: names have been changed to protect the identity of those involved and to protect the future earnings of yours truly because I don't want to get sued on some bogus defamation charge, even though everything I'm saying here is one hundred percent true, and if the truth happens to make anyone look like an asshole, that's on them, sweetie.

Okay, now that we have that covered, let me tell you why I, Riley Weaver, need a date to the Gaybutante Ball.

Chapter 1

Nothing makes my leg jiggle harder than gay impatience. It shakes up and down with anxious anticipation as I scan the quad for any Gaybutante faces.

"We're two weeks into the year and they haven't made a move. *When* are they going to announce the season?" I feel my silver hair bounce back and forth as my head bobs from side to side.

"*How* they're going to do it is what I'm most concerned about," Sabrina says, her head staying perfectly still so she looks way less like a chaotic gay chicken than I do. But her eyes swing left and right, and she's got that slight flush she always gets whenever she's excited. Her white cheeks look mildly sunburned and her smattering of freckles stands out.

4

"There's definitely not going to be explosions this time," Nick says. "Ms. Hassbend burst a blood vessel in her eye from screaming so hard after last year's rainbow confetti cannons."

Nick doesn't take his eyes off his phone, most likely watching some behind-the-scenes footage of one of his favorite movies. It's just his bright blue Afro and a sliver of his dark brown forehead visible over the top of his phone. Nick may be a part of the queer alphabet soup, but he's not down for the intense attention Gaybutantes get. He's the only out queer junior who's decided not to throw his hat in the ring, and he really hams up the disinterest. But despite his outward indifference, I know he's just as invested in how the Gaybutante Society will announce the season.

"What's that?" Sabrina throws her arm in front of me like she's my dad driving his truck and slamming on the brakes. My turkey sandwich lands with a wet slap on the damp cement under my bench, but it's fine. I can't eat. Not knowing we're *this close* to the big reveal.

Sabrina's eager eyes fall. "Never mind. It was just a seagull."

"*You two* are going to burst a blood vessel if you don't chill," Nick says, nonchalantly skipping an ad on whatever it is he's watching.

"Oh, come on, just because you don't want in doesn't mean you're not curious too," I say, playfully tapping Nick with the toe of my bootie. "Your production-obsessed heart can't help but appreciate all the time and effort it takes to coordinate these things."

I nudge his phone down, and a small smile pushes up his round cheeks. "Okay, fine. You're right. But I'm not going to waste my breath talking about what's going to happen until it actually happens." He finally puts his phone on the table and grabs one of my hands, the sparkling silver polish on my nails going really well with the glistening navy blue on his. Nick holds out his other hand, and Sabrina places her polish-free fingers in it.

"Deep breaths," Nick says.

As one, we inhale for four beats, exhale for five. It was this trick I read about on the internet when I had jitters before my second stint as the morning announcements announcer in seventh grade. It wasn't that I was nervous; I was too excited. I had so much adrenaline the first day that I recited the school news way too fast. I sounded like I'd had a thousand energy drinks or something. So I needed to figure out how to slow myself down, and this helped. The trick has stuck ever since, and Nick is usually the one to start it nowadays, since Sabrina and I get carried away with our excitement pretty damn quickly.

"Thanks, Nick," I say through my exhale. "You're the most important wheel of this tricycle, keeping us grounded. I don't know what we'd do without y—OH MY GOD, IT'S HAPPENING!"

Three flashes of red light burst in the distance over Nick's shoulder. In any normal town, this could be a number of things: a stoplight, a radio tower, brake lights.

But this is Mountain Pass, a tiny town up in the Cascades, where the only thing you can see is a billion evergreen trees and the reflection of the highest peak in the mountain range—Mount Rainier—glistening in Peak Lake. Not to mention it's a hazy day in mid-September, so to see any light in the sky and not just gray cloud cover *means something.*

Every head of the juniors and seniors lunching in the quad snaps to the sky as my scream echoes through the space. Nobody's alarmed—they're all used to me screaming about something by now after eleven years of school together—but they all know to pay attention. If I'm screaming, it means I'm screaming about something good.

The three red flashes zoom above the trees and become three solid dots, quickly followed by dozens more. They zip through the air and form a red arch.

"Drones," Nick says, calm and cool and like we aren't about to have the big reveal I've been waiting for my entire life. "Neat."

He's right. The drones' metallic gray bodies and whirring fans lift the glowing orbs attached to them into the air. This has to be the work of Paola Burgos, bisexual Puerto Rican goddess of drone art and a Mountain Pass Gaybutante who graduated in 2016. She's been hired for drone performances all over the world and is rumored to be working on a piece for the next Olympics.

"Neat?" Sabrina says, incredulous. "Our lives are about to change forever and all you can say is *neat*?"

Nick shrugs, that small smile getting even bigger. His favorite pastime is messing with us when Sabrina and I are getting all worked up about something.

"Rainbow!" somebody shrieks behind me. "It's definitely a rainbow!"

We all *ooh* and *aah* as more and more drones add to the lineup, a row of orange arching beneath the red, then yellow, then green, and so on. Little bursts of white even gather at the ends to look like clouds. Then, as one, the drones whiz through the air, a mechanic dance routine that forms a word blinking in all the colors of the rainbow.

GAYBUTANTES

They flip and turn and re-form once more.

ARE YOU READY?

They zip into word after word, the anticipation bubbling inside me with each one.

THE

SEASON

STARTS

NOW

It's brilliant, it's gorgeous, and everyone has their phones pointed at it. The Gaybutante Society social accounts must be blowing up right now with the Mountain Pass High announcement of the season.

I zip open my neon-orange cross body and take out my compact. I do a quick once-over. After trying approximately a million different brands, I've finally found the right foundation that won't shine, flake, or cake over any stubborn stubble spots. Everything's still in place. My lilac eye shadow hasn't smudged, I have just the tiniest amount of oil that a little blotting paper will soak up in a sec, and my silver swoops of hair are still chicly disheveled even after my chaotic chicken bob.

I'm ready all right.

PEAK PARK 3PM

The drones give us the location of our first Gaybutante Society meeting, then blink out of existence, falling into the trees where Paola is sure to be waiting with her assistants and apprentices to pack it all away. It's a lot of work for sixty seconds of art.

But that's the Gaybutante Society for you. It doesn't matter how much time it takes to make something come together as long as it makes a mark, a lasting impression on your audience's life. And the number of successful Gaybutantes speaks to how much that effort pays off. I mean, the group has spawned four Billboard Hot 100–charting artists, two mayors, one congressperson, one *Fiercest of Them All* runner-up, an Academy Award nominee, a three-time Tony-nominated actor, the inventor of an indestructible steel heel, I-can't-even-count-how-many social media stars, and the nation's first nonbinary dating show lead on a broadcast network. And that's just off the top of my head. The wildest part is the group has an agreement that once you start earning a living wage, you donate 3 percent of whatever you earn to pay for future Gaybutante events *and* all members' health care. And it's worked! It's like a union except they all get to work in whatever field they want and share the love to the group that's supported them along the way if any of them make it big. It's fabulous.

Here's hoping that in just a few months, I'll be among their ranks and the group can add "host of the nation's most downloaded podcast" among their alumni accomplishments. I mean, yeah, that's a pretty lofty goal there, especially considering people's obsessions with true crime podcasts, but a girl can dream. I've been waiting for just the right theme to launch a podcast of my own that will truly stand out, and I'm hoping inspiration will strike soon. But in the meantime, I've learned the interviewing ropes hosting my own Q&A hour with Mountain Pass residents for our local radio station, KMPK, The Peak. I talk with my guests for an hour, getting deep into their lives and why they love Mountain Pass, but that's all going on a brief hiatus while I commit my whole heart and soul to the Gaybutante season.

"It's all happening!" Sabrina turns to me, a glimmer of hope in her eyes, or maybe that's just the last of the drones reflecting in them before the little machines are lost to the forest. "I'm making vet science sexy again!"

"That's right you are," I say, and throw my arm over Sabrina's shoulders. She wants to let the STEM gays out there know that they have just as much a place in the Gaybutante Society as any artist or politically minded member. She wants to become a veterinarian, and other than a few shirtless male dog doctors on social media, she doesn't think that vet science gets the attention it deserves. Plus, it's very male dominated. She's ready to spark the drive for girls everywhere to become a vet. She could definitely do that on her own, but the Gaybutante Society jump-starts things for their members, seeing as how they have a combined following of *millions* of people. One share from, say, an Oscar-nominated member or one of our chart-topping musician alums creating a playlist to soothe your cat on the way to Sabrina's animal clinic and *bam!* People know who you are.

"You'll be the face of animal medicine before you know it. And with the help of the GS, folks will be freaking *flocking* to get into veterinary school. They'll be *pawing* down your door to join your lesbian-led vet clinic."

"Okay, let's not go overboard," Sabrina deadpans.

"All I'm trying to say is, this is going to be the best year yet." I spare her from *People will be* hounding *you for advice*.

Nick's forehead furrows. "But what if you don't get in?"

I clutch my nonexistent pearls and gasp. "Nick! Why would you say such a thing?"

"All I'm saying is it seems dangerous to hinge your happiness on whether or not this one group of people accepts you."

My mouth falls open, and I blink my extension-enhanced eyelashes at him. I look at Sabrina. She looks at me. We look at Nick together.

"It's not like it's hard to get in," Sabrina says.

"Yeah. It's really just making sure the folks who try out are actually willing to put in some effort. We don't just sit around and *hang out*. We do charity, we throw parties, we plan gay shenanigans. Anybody who shows they can do the work is accepted. And as many people as want in will get in as long as they try. We're shoo-ins."

Nick nods. "You've just got to be prepared for things to not go as planned. You two get your hopes up about everything, and when a wrench gets thrown in there . . ." He trails off, and I know we're all imagining the time Sabrina and I *both* melted down when she didn't get chosen for her equine therapy internship last summer. "I don't want either of you to get hurt."

"Somebody's feeling ominous today," Sabrina says with a scowl, fidgeting with her dirty blond ponytail.

"No, no—don't go nervous ponytail pulling on me," Nick says. "I'm just saying to be realistic. Life can throw curveballs at you, right? Just be happy with yourselves and know no matter what happens with the Gaybutantes, you are each a part of my heart and always have a place in *my* society."

"Niiiiiick," I say. "What are you, a tree? Because that was *sappy*. And I loved it."

Nick rubs his hand over his face, which he always does when he's embarrassed. His skin is so dark that most people can't tell when he blushes, but his habit of instantly trying to wipe away the warmth in his cheeks is just as blatant. He can't take a compliment or any open adoration, which is simultaneously frustrating and adorable. I picked this up from all the time we've spent together, walking the woods behind my house, or zip-lining through the course my dad runs on our property. Mountain Pass might be this little idyllic town, but there's not really much to do, so you just kind of end up talking to each other. A lot. And any time I pay Nick a compliment or get as sappy on him as he gets on us, he sort of shuts down. Like right now, where he picks up his phone and leaves the conversation.

"Riley, you don't seriously think you're going to become a podcast host with puns like that, do you?" Sabrina asks, bumping me with her shoulder.

"Just you wait," I say. "Pun man's trash is another man's treasure."

Everyone's eyes are on us as we leave Mountain Pass High and walk through Main Street to head to Peak Park. Mountain Pass is one of those annoyingly quaint towns with the high school, middle school, and elementary school sitting at one end with a perfect view of the lake, and then a stroll through the old-school brick building town takes you to the park where everybody can partake in said lake's freaking freezing—I mean, perfect and pristine—waters. Seriously, you walk through this town and supposedly it's like you've gone back in time. There's the Mountain Pass Café, the Mountain Pass Cinema (complete with one screen), the Mountain Pass Bed &

Breakfast in which the owner, Tim Clammette, tells everybody about who's staying there and why. There's a lot of Mountain Pass camaraderie here, and, like, hardcore loyalty, which is why you really won't find anything without *Mountain Pass* somewhere in the name.

Thanks to the Gaybutante Society, the town has kind of been put on the map as this home to influential queer folks. So, we get a lot of artsy-type tourists, and the town is pretty LGBTQ-friendly. Which was nice when I came out as gay and femme my freshman year and started wearing a ton of high-waisted pants and booties and throwing on a face of makeup (my looks that first year were *atrocious*, but you've got to start somewhere, right?). Nobody really batted an eye—they congratulated me on getting a step closer to knowing who I am in my heart and asked if they could give me a supportive hug (it gets very lovey-dovey here). But, instead of people judging you for your gender expression or sexuality, once you come out, you get questions about the Gaybutante Society and what sort of mark you're hoping to make on the world. It's weirdly a lot of pressure. You come out and instantly all eyes are on you. Not because anyone thinks you're abhorrent or an abomination, but because people expect big things out of you from the jump. It's wild.

The only problem with that is I don't just have big things expected of me from the town—I get it from my family too. See, the thing is, I'm cursed. Or blessed, depending on how you look at it. My mom's family, the Haydens, have been in Mountain Pass since the start. Like, since 1916 when the city was founded and known for logging. Great-Great-Grandpa Hayden was the first mayor of the town, Great-Great-Grandma Hayden opened the library, Great-Great-Uncle Bobby opened the Mountain Pass Saloon—and it's still owned by my mom's cousins, even though they live down in California now. Everything is just . . . great. Except Mom expects me to stay in the town, not just because she's taken after Great-Great-Gpa and is the mayor herself, but because after my grandparents died and her cousins moved away, we're the only Hayden descendants left. Meanwhile, I want out.

It's not that I don't love it here. Mountain Passers are amazing, and thanks to my radio show, I know a whole lot about a good chunk of them. But I'll eventually run out of new folks to talk to. I just want more than what this tiny place can offer. I want to meet more people, hear more stories, see as much of the world as I can. It's weird to live in a sort of quaint, Hallmark-movie paradise yet know in your heart it's not enough.

But unlike most Mountain Pass Gaybutantes, the pressure on me to stay and never experience anything else is intense, thanks to my mom. The owner of the radio station, Wilhelmina Zanos, has already told me I can take over the business once I get my degree in broadcast journalism and she retires. So, Mom thinks life is perfectly planned out for me, and I can carry on the Hayden tradition of boosting up Mountain Pass. This is why the Gaybutantes are so important. If their platform can make my name big enough *outside* Mountain Pass, I'll have a solid case to convince her that I need to go see the world. With a large enough following, she'll realize that other plans can be just as safe and reliable and Hayden-pride-creating as a job waiting for me back home.

From the wide-eyed looks of Tim Clammette, and Jasmyn Ngoza, the cinema owner, and the lead barista / café owner, Roz Bianchi, and just about everyone else in town whose excited gazes follow us twelve Gaybutante Hopefuls as we walk down the street, it seems like other people believe a fabulous future could be in store for me too. I don't want to let them down. I don't want to let *me* down.

"Look at them all, Cliff. They're so cute. Our little gaybies."

The current senior Gaybutantes are just as pumped, apparently. They stand in front of the lake in Peak Park, the reflection of Mount Rainier glistening on the surface as the water gently laps against the shore. The soothing sound does nothing to slow the pounding of my heart as we take the last step out of the parking lot and my pre-Gaybutante life. The fact that Sabrina and I haven't said a word to each other this entire walk is saying something. The fact that *none of us* Hopefuls have said anything shows just how seriously we all take this.

Front and center in the Gaybutante crowd is Lonny Bu—Korean American pansexual crocheting whiz whose Etsy store is going to solidly fund her college education with the most intricately designed sweaters, scarves, and hats that I've ever seen. Next to her is Cliff with the cleft chin—white, gay, essentially a high school version of Superman who, word on the street is, has already been approached by *multiple* modeling agencies to sign with them, but he insists on waiting until he graduates. Behind them are the eleven other senior Gaybutantes, as well as Paola Burgos. I can't stop staring at her, and I'm resisting every urge in my body to leap forward and ask her to follow me back to the radio station so I can record a banger of a return episode once my show kicks back up in the spring.

"Lonny, we know who they are," Cliff says. "They're juniors. We've all been going to school together practically our whole lives."

"I know," Lonny replies, her eyes getting wider with each passing second. "I'm just seeing them differently now that they're one of us."

I get exactly what she's saying. That's one of the weird things about the Gaybutante Society: once people get in, they take on this celebrity status. Most of us have known each other our whole lives. Mountain Pass is a town of only about ten thousand people, and there's not even four hundred kids in all of Mountain Pass High. So, at some point, you've been in a class, or on a band trip, or on a sports team (minus yours truly; I do *not* athlete) with just about everyone in the school. But when the world takes note of that familiar face, you suddenly see them in a whole new light. Sure, it's not like the Gaybutante Society is this huge unstoppable force, and not everyone goes on to superstardom or anything, but the odds seem greater that you'll affect the world once you join. So, when Lonny went from winning every art competition in Mountain Pass to suddenly having a TikTok following of 1.1 million, you're like, *whoa*. You know? And most of the Gaybutantes in front of us have similar stories, or even if they don't have a talent to showcase quite yet, they're noticed by association.

It's intoxicating.

"Anyway," Lonny says, the pattern on her sweater almost an exact replica of the Peak Lake scene behind her, "we're here for a very specific reason. To start the Gaybutante season."

I cheer loudly, but I'm literally the only one.

My cheeks instantly blaze, and I know for sure my layer of blush is too light to do anything to hide it.

"Yes, good, Riley," Cliff says, directing a megawatt smile my way, and I'm positive my blush gets even blushier. He's said my name probably a hundred times before, but today it just hits different. "We want excitement! This is the Gaybutante Society! It's not your senior seminar or something. Let loose! Don't be so serious."

Sabrina laughs nervously, then whoops, and a few other people clap weakly. They're all too anxious to know if anything they're doing is right or cool or Gaybutante worthy, even though the seniors are all looking at us like they can't wait to spend the rest of our lives together.

"You'll get the nerves out soon, I promise," Lonny says, and the Gaybutantes behind her laugh knowingly. "We were all there once too. But let's get to business." Her sweet, wide-eyed expression drops, and she's super serious. It's totally at odds with the happy crocheted products she's wearing. "Cliff, if you would."

Cliff reaches into a rainbow, knit knapsack and pulls out journals, complete with custom Lonny-crocheted covers that each read *Gaybutante Hopeful* followed by our names in gorgeous cursive. He walks among the crowd of twelve and hands a journal to everyone, each of us getting our own custom color combination. Mine has an orange background and purple cursive, one of my favorite color combos. It completely matches the color scheme of my outfit and eye shadow, like we planned it or something.

"Sabrina Heiss." Cliff hands her a teal journal with black cursive writing, and when she turns it over, there's a little paw print knit into the back. It matches the scrubs she often leaves school in to help at her parents' vet clinic. I flip mine over to find a microphone—but not a singer's mic, a broadcasting mic—and practically want to faint. I'm in love with the Gaybutantes already for paying such close attention to us and knowing all the things we like and anticipating who would show up. Some might read it as stalker-y, but I think it's cute.

"Inside you'll find your four main requirements for entry into the Gaybutante Society," Lonny says. As one, we all open our journals to find this page:

So, you want to be a Gaybutante?
Welcome to the first day of your journey toward that fabulous goal!

But what is a Gaybutante?
A person who is anywhere in our LGBTQIA+ spectrum of rainbow awesomeness who wants to make a mark on the world; someone who doesn't want to sit on the sidelines but be noticed and do good in the process.

Our four main Pillars of Gay Excellence are:
1. Service—It's always better to give' than receive (well, *charity*-wise)
2. Hosting—Gays live for a party (Pride, Halloween, the Met Gala, you name it)
3. Mentorship—Be the Obi-Wan to a queer Anakin in need (try not to create any Darth Gayders in the process)
4. General Gay Chaos—Be loud, be proud, and make them taste the rainbow (get people talking, but don't do anything illegal)

Your mission to be accepted into the Gaybutante Society is to show us an example of each of our pillars, proving you have what it takes to hold the Gaybutante mantle. It's not all fun and games in the GS (although there's a Pride parade's worth of that), it's hard work too, and you need to rise to the occasion.

Over the next twelve weeks you must complete fifteen hours of community service; host an epic party for current and Hopeful Gaybutantes; find any queer teen that needs a helping hand and actually help them; and finally (or firstly, if this is your favorite), cause any sort of gay chaos in any manner you see fit.

Every Hopeful who completes these tasks will be accepted. There is no scoring. This is only pass/fail, and we want our Gaybutante Family to be as big as possible.

Gaily yours,
The Gaybutantes of Mountain Pass High

"Feel free to use the rest of the pages for brainstorming and inspiration for your tasks," Cliff says. "Or better yet, journal your experiences through this whole process. I find writing my thoughts on paper helps me calm down."

Lonny puts a playful finger through one of Cliff's belt loops and pulls him toward her. "That's Cliff, for you. Always in his thoughts. You think he's going to be this supermodel—which he probably is—but just you wait. He's going to be a poet."

Cliff blushes and it's inordinately charming to see someone so hot get so flustered from a sweet compliment.

"Anyway." Cliff clears his throat and absentmindedly scratches his neck, making his bicep bulge. How can someone make simple moving seem so attractive? "All four tasks need to be approved by a senior Gaybutante. Don't worry—we aren't going to say no to most things, unless it's seriously against the law or could cause harm to another person or out them. We just need someone to have a heads-up, so we know you're actually making headway on the four pillars and are putting in the work it takes to be a part of the group."

"And of course, you've got to give us a heads-up to your PARTAY!" Lonny shouts, her voice echoing across the lake. It breaks the tension in all of us newbies, and we finally laugh. "That's probably the most important of all the pillars."

"Except for service. It's most important that we give back," Cliff says, very seriously. Then his face breaks and he adds, "But yeah, the parties are epic."

Sabrina elbows me and whispers, "I'm going to need your help with that one. Like, lots of help. Where am I going to host it? The elk operating room at the clinic? Come on."

I can tell by how seriously scrunched her scowl is that she's worried she'll never live up to Gaybutante party standards. Their parties are legendary. At least, that's what their social media accounts show, like beach bashes for the Gaybutantes in LA, a rooftop soiree complete with aerial acts in Atlanta, a rented-out subway in NYC. Mountain Pass's parties have been all over the Pacific Northwest, from an enchanted forest setup on Mount Rainier to a tucked-away log cabin in the San Juan Islands. You can't attend unless you're a part of the group, something about controlling the crowd but also making sure everyone who attends has everyone else's back. The debauchery is all PG on social media, but rumors are the parties can get deliciously wild. But it's just rumor, because the GS eliminates all proof that could get any of them in trouble. No evidence of getting too drunk or flashing each other or anything like that has ever been made public. Can you tell that I haven't really been to many wild parties? It's because I've been saving myself for the GS and figure anything else would just be a waste of time and a colossal disappointment. But even though I've never been to an epic party, I've been throwing ideas at Sabrina for what I could do *for years*.

"I've got you, lady." I tap my temple. "There's enough wild ideas in here for the both of us. And you have to promise there's a stray cat or something I can help out with at your clinic."

Sabrina's parents run a veterinary office and animal rehabilitation center that's a pretty popular spot to take injured animals found in the Cascades. Between her parents and her older sisters, Melissa and Clarissa (Sabrina's mom is a serious fangirl of Melissa Joan Hart), the Mountain Pass Veterinarian and Animal Rehab is well staffed, but there's bound to be some spare animal around that I can help with and knock out my Service portion of getting into the Society. This is how it's supposed to be: Sabrina and me having each other's backs through this entire process. After dreaming about this since we both came out freshman year, I can't believe we're finally doing it.

"I'm sure there'll be some bobcat that shows up with porcupine quills in its face soon."

"I said *cat*, Sabrina, not bobcat."

She gives me an *Are you kidding me* scowl. "Which do you think is more common in the forest?"

"Just give me a call when something *without* claws *or* teeth *or* antlers that could pierce me through the heart needs help."

"So, you're looking for what? A slug?"

"Maybe something less slimy. And cuter. Shouldn't be hard to find."

"Yeah, okay, I'll get right on that."

Lonny and Cliff finish answering any remaining questions, then Cliff delivers the most key bit of information yet. "This all culminates in the Gaybutante Ball, as you're all familiar. All four branches of the GS come together to debut their newest crop of inductees, and this year Mountain Pass is hosting. We've already booked a ferry to take us around the Sound while each of you has the opportunity to parade your best Gaybutante looks on the bow of the ship. And just like the debutante balls that inspired us, you'll need an escort. This is the only party where non-Gaybutantes are allowed to accompany you. *No pressure* whatsoever on who you want your escort to be, but I am saying that currently five members have gone on to marry their escort, so choose wisely."

"But also if romance and/or sex isn't your thing, that's just as loved and accepted in the Society. Friends or family make great escorts!" Lonny chimes in. "Well, for the Ball, not *escort* escorts."

With that, everyone goes apeshit. There's only twelve of us Hopefuls, thirteen senior Gaybutantes, and Paola taking it all in, but you'd think the whole town was here. I glance over my shoulder to find that there actually is a pretty sizable crowd of Mountain Passers gathered in the parking lot. They're just as eagerly discussing everything we're getting the rundown on. Some even have their phones out, the pictures of this year's Mountain Pass Hopefuls sure to go up on social media in no time. I'm simultaneously pumped to start getting my name out there and freaked out about it. I mean, sure, I love to put together a femme look, and they're usually pretty attention grabbing, but that doesn't necessarily mean I want people examining *me* all the time. I'd rather focus on other people; I want to be this world-renowned podcaster to get to know *others*, not to have all eyes on me.

But when people start seeing me as a potential Gaybutante, they're going to start picking me apart. And gays commenting on other gays can be vicious. It's one of the things that happens every year: the Hopefuls get dragged through the mud for their talents, their looks, their sexualities, their genders. Definitely not by everybody, but by a very vocal minority who wants to make it clear that so-and-so does *not* represent the entire gay community or their gender or any group that they happen to share a label with. The lousy thing about Mountain Pass and its super supportive community is it hasn't really prepared us for that kind of hate. I know it's something I need to get used to as someone who wants a public-facing job, but still. What kind of things are people going to say when they find out Riley Weaver wants into the Gaybutante Society?

Turns out, I don't have to wait long to find out.

Chapter 2

"Yeah, no, there is no way you're going to take Carter as your escort—he is just *way too girly*. So feminine, he shouldn't even get to call himself gay. He's practically a girl."

Okay, hi, record scratch.

I skid to a stop so hard in the parking lot that I'm pretty sure a chunk came out of the heel of my bootie. If Sabrina were beside me, I'd look at her like, *Did I hear what I think I just heard?* But she had to race off to the animal clinic since she wants to work there at least two hours a night. It's like if she doesn't get time in with a limping coyote or a broken-winged owl she'd combust or something. Normally I'm all about that and love to support her vet goals, but right now, I wish I had backup when I confront this outrageously heteronormative comment.

Skylar Jefferson—baseball superstar from Crestview High who Wilhelmina had me interview at KMPK last spring because he's *that good*—leans against his blue pickup truck. He's white, has shaggy brown hair, and is constantly showing off muscular arms that always look like they're trying to break the seams on his V-neck tees.

Skylar's talking to Adam Paramus, white, gay Gaybutante Hopeful who has a way with CGI. He's already made a few shorts following an alien and a dinosaur that have racked up a pretty good amount of hits on YouTube. He's close with Skylar because they both play on the same club baseball team. I always thought Adam was a nice guy.

But how he can stomach what Skylar is saying right now is beyond me.

"Excuse me, what?" I stomp over to Skylar and, yep, I've definitely lost a chunk in my heel. I bob down an extra inch anytime my right foot hits the ground. But I don't care if the hobble makes me look any less intimidating—I can't let a comment like this slide. Besides, it's the interviewer in me that needs to get to the bottom of this.

"Oh, come on, Riley, you know I don't mean anything by it," Skylar says, giving me some smug smirk like I'm blowing this way out of proportion.

"You didn't mean anything by stating that femme guys can't be gay because we're too feminine? It definitely sounds like you meant something by that. Something exclusionary and gross."

"I'm not trying to exclude you from anything," Skylar says, that smug expression not budging a bit. "In fact, I'm saying that you should get your own letter in the queer alphabet entirely. Gay guys are into guys because they want to be with *guys*. It's not my fault if I don't want to be with someone who looks and acts and dresses like a girl."

"Someone who looks and acts and dresses like *me*, you mean?"

Skylar puts a hand on my shoulder and my whole body wants to recoil. But I also don't want him to think he has any sort of upper hand on me, so I don't move a muscle. "Riley, come on, you're coming at me hard. This isn't anything against you. This is just about preferences. And all I'm saying is gay guys don't prefer femme people. They like *guys*. It's why they're gay. It's why I'm gay! It's why you're gay too—right, Adam?"

Adam just stands there and doesn't say anything. He looks back and forth between me and Skylar. I can see him wanting to side with one of his closest friends, but he also knows how bogus said friend's take is.

"Adam, don't chicken out on me now. Have you ever gone out with a guy who wears makeup before?"

"Well . . . no," Adam says, looking awkwardly at the asphalt.

"And when you're going through Pornhub, are you ever looking for guys with false eyelashes and painted nails?"

A fire burns in my belly at Skylar picking out two things I very much have.

"Dude!" Adam shouts, and punches Skylar in the shoulder.

"Have you?" Skylar says through a laugh. A very derisive, very prick-ish laugh.

"I guess not." Adam's face is redder than a pack of Red Vines, like he hates to admit that his truth is in line with what Skylar's saying.

I cross my arms, making sure that my perfectly polished, sparkling silver almond manicure shows while I tap my fingers indignantly against my arms. "Listen. It's one thing to have a preference for the type of energies or bodies *you're* attracted to. It's a whole other thing to think that you can speak for the entire population of gay guys out there."

Skylar crosses his arms right back, clearly mocking me. "What do you even know about it? You don't date. I thought you were, like, sexless or something."

"Okay, wow, that's pretty presumptuous." Sure, I haven't dated around much, but it just hasn't been a priority. I definitely know the type of person I'd want to have sex with when the time is right, but I don't owe Skylar that. And even if I didn't want to have sex, that's not a bad thing, despite how he makes it sound.

"I'm honestly doing you a favor," Skylar says. "If nobody tells you this, you'll be in for a rude awakening when you finally date. *If* you date, I should say."

"God, you sure think highly of yourself. Nobody asked for your take. Just hook up with whoever it feels right to hook up with without shitting on femme people everywhere."

A look of sympathy finally appears on Skylar's face. Maybe we're getting somewhere. See, this is why I would be a good interviewer. I'd be able to change hearts and minds for the better, like I'm about to do with Skylar right now.

"Riley, I'm so sorry."

I knew it.

"I'm sorry to be the one to have to tell you this hard truth." That look of sympathy isn't sympathy at all. It's annoying, obnoxious, blatant condescension, turning me into a seething ball of anger. "But all guys who are into guys think this. And you need to accept that fact so you can go into the dating pool knowing what you're in for. I'm just trying to help you out. Besides, you wouldn't even call yourself a guy anyway, right? What are you so upset about?"

I don't know how to respond. It's not that he's right about me, but it's not that he's wrong either. If a person came over right now and said to me, Skylar, and Adam, "Hey, guys!" and meant it in the "Hey, group of people who have penises" way, it wouldn't upset me. It wouldn't feel wrong or not me. Same as how when Sabrina and I walk into a store or a restaurant together and people only see me from the back and say, "Hi, ladies!" meaning "Hi, duo of humans who have vaginas," that doesn't feel wrong either. That feminine energy that people are capturing in the word *ladies* feels right. It's not about genitals for me. But it always is for other people.

"You're completely missing the point," I say. "It's not about my gender. It's about the fact that I identify as gay, and you're taking it upon yourself to say what everyone else who says they're gay likes and doesn't like, or should look and act like, but I'm right here in front of you saying I'm a gay person who doesn't look or act like you. It's like you don't even see me."

"I see you perfectly, Riley, which *is* the point." He is such a freaking mansplainer, and he's not even right! "You're femme, and the type of guy who wants somebody like you isn't exactly *gay*. They're something else. Maybe it's pan, maybe it's bi because they're into your femininity, who knows. All I'm saying is, nobody like me is ever going to be attracted to somebody like you."

Adam sucks in a breath, like he's been stung or punched. But any points he gets for recognizing how shitty Skylar's being are null. I'm done with Adam just sitting on the sidelines and making me take this. Couldn't he chime in and stick up for me? Especially as a fellow Gaybutante Hopeful? Having each other's backs is what this group is all about.

"So, you think there is no gay guy out there who would ever want to be with me?"

Skylar shrugs. "Yeah, that's what I'm saying. No gay guy would want to be with someone who looks like a woman."

"I've already hooked up with one," I say. "Over the summer when I visited my cousin. His name was Phil and he lives in Portland."

Skylar rolls his eyes. "You get how fake that sounds, right? How do I know you didn't just make that guy up?"

I really want to take my perfectly manicured nails and stab Skylar's eyes out. That would definitely be some General Gay Chaos. But the Gaybutantes specifically say we can't do anything illegal, and I'm pretty sure assault is illegal, even if Skylar deserves it. I just really want to make him eat it right now, and I'm not going to ask my cousin Kristina for Phil's number so I can call him when we haven't spoken for two months just so he can tell some stranger that I gave him a hand job. But if Phil was out there and ready to do that with me, I know there have got to be guys closer to home who'd also want in on some Riley action.

That's when it hits me. Like one of Sabrina's wild bobcats clawing into my chest and hitting my heart.

I *can* prove Skylar wrong.

"Let's bet on it," I say, my own smug smile matching Skylar's.

"Bet on it?" he repeats. "What do you mean?"

"I bet that I can get a guy to ask me to be my escort to the Gaybutante Ball."

Skylar throws his hands up in exasperation. "Well, of course you could. It could just be some big ole pity party and you tell this guy that I said some harsh truths to you and he feels so bad that he asks you to the Ball."

"I won't tell whoever I date about the bet. I won't tell them about what you said. And I won't ask them to be my escort either. It'll entirely come from them, unprompted by me or anyone else, and show you that gay guys who like femme guys exist."

"They've got to be gay masc guys or it doesn't count. And they've got to be cis. All you noncis kids stick together, and I don't want you cheating this bet just so you can win. Yes, trans guys are guys, but I'm specifically saying here that guys with dicks want other guys with dicks or they wouldn't call themselves gay. It's just how it is!"

Would it really be that bad if I clawed his eyes out? He's not only taking a dump on femme folks, but on trans and gender nonconforming people everywhere. Who does he think he is to belittle every person out there who's not cis? I mean, my one brief sexual encounter over the summer was with a masculine guy who happened to be cis, but that doesn't mean there haven't been trans guys or non-binary people or other femmes who I'm attracted to. Mostly I know that I haven't found myself attracted to ladies, which is why I call myself gay, but I'm still figuring all this out.

My overriding stubbornness and that Libra need for justice makes it so my blood boils when Skylar categorically says cis people could never like me. What about my noncis siblings who might hear this shit from him? I can't let him go on spouting these ignorant takes. I've got to prove him wrong before he says this to someone who will truly be hurt.

"Okay, fine," I say. "Someone who says he's cis and masc and *traditionally* boy acting." I let my voice drip with sarcasm because there's nothing traditional at all about the way our society makes boys act. It's entirely forced. The manliest men used to wear curly wigs, paint their faces for the back row, and wear chunky heels!

Skylar's eyes narrow as he goes over my proposal.

"And what do I get if I win?"

Crap. I hadn't thought that far. I don't have anything I could give him. Based on this conversation, I doubt he'd be interested in my collection of eye shadow palettes. My dad runs a zip-lining company on our property, but he lets kids use the course for free pretty much whenever they want, so a lifetime pass to the place is out.

But then I take in Skylar's perfectly pristine blue Ram 1500. Skylar's leaning against it in a crisp, white V-neck shirt, and his Diesel jeans are distressed just enough to look cool. Skylar has money, so I'd guess that something material is not what he wants. He'll want *stakes*. Big ones.

"If you're right, I'll pull out of the Gaybutante Society before I can be inducted."

The words are out of my mouth before I can stop them. For the briefest second, my stomach turns with dread. If Skylar's right, there goes any chance of having the GS help me reach my dreams. I'll be pressured to stay in Mountain Pass by my family, hosting my same radio hour listened to by the eight or so people in town who still don't know how streaming works.

But that's only *if* Skylar is right. And there's no way he's going to be right.

"Riley, come on." Adam finally speaks up. "You don't have to do that. This is dumb. You shouldn't give up the Society just becau—"

Skylar snaps up a hand to cut Adam off. "And what if—I can't believe I'm even saying this—what if I'm wrong?" He mouths that last word like it tastes bad. "Which there's no way I'm going to be, but let's entertain the idea for a second."

"It's only fair if the stakes for you are just as big as they are for me," I say. My eyes land on the blue duffel bags in the bed of Skylar's truck, emblazoned with *Crestview Baseball* and the school's logo of an angry T. rex. *This* will make things interesting.

"If I win, you have to quit the baseball team. You can't play spring semester, or next year. Club *and* school teams. A total baseball blackout until we graduate."

Skylar's eyes go wide, and for a second I think he's going to back out. He actually recoils, and I know exactly what's going through his head. Skylar has always been, and still is, the best. Scouts are going to be coming to games this spring, and all of the Seattle suburb division talk is he's going to be recruited to some top college, all-expenses-paid, because—even if he is a colossal douche—he's that good. He'll be pro before you know it.

But not if he loses this bet.

Skylar doesn't move a muscle, his eyebrow cocked, silent. Maybe I made the stakes too big, and we can all back out now, nobody's life on the line. Adam holds his breath. But then it comes out in a groan when Skylar pushes off the truck, his hand extended, that smug look back on his face.

"It's a bet," he says. His hand hangs there between us. He's got his own perfect manicure and smooth skin without a callus in sight, even though he's using them hours on end, handling balls all day.

Baseballs, that is.

I realize I'm staring too long, and somehow Skylar's expression gets even smugger. I can't let him win. I can't let him think that he has any right to belittle femme people or boldly declare that I have no love life with a gay guy in the future.

I put my hand in his, maybe trying to scratch him just a little with my nails.

"It's a bet," I echo. And with that, we look each other in the eye, grim determination set on both our faces. Because our futures hang in the balance. His baseball career, my podcast stardom.

My ticket out of here.

There's no way I'm going to lose.

Chapter 3

A very unusual feeling of dread washes over me when I pull up into the carport outside our house. Normally I get this feeling of pride when I drive in. We live on *acres and acres* of land, passed down by Mom's family, that Dad turned into our zip-lining course. When you first make it down the half-mile dirt driveway, you come upon the Lookout, the restaurant and bar and check-in station Dad runs for Mountain Pass Zip Line, or for folks who just want a bite to eat and a gorgeous mountain view. It's done up in this whole modern-meets-log-cabin vibe, concrete floor but perfectly polished wooden beams. The house, another half mile down the drive, is tucked away where you can't see it from the Lookout but done in that same style, only homier. It's got extra touches like little wooden bench nooks filled with pillows where you can read in front of iron-framed windows. The kicker is that both buildings were designed by Mom, an architect by trade, but she's put her design work on hold during her four-year term as mayor. So, the whole property feels like this marker of my parents' hard work and how you can make your dreams a reality when you set your mind to it.

But now I might have blown my dreams the fuck up. I was such an idiot to bet my whole life on finding a date! This property might turn from my home to my prison if I'm stuck here for the rest of my life because the only gig I could get was the one simply handed down to me in Mountain Pass.

"Gah!" I scream, and slam on my horn, which makes another scream happen outside my door.

"Holy hell, Riley. Jesus!" Mom's getting out of her car beside me, a hand clutched over her heaving chest. "You scared the living shit out of me."

She may be mayor, but she always swears in moments of extreme emotion. It's one of my favorite things about her.

I climb out of my car. "Sorry, Mom. Didn't see you there."

"Well, pay more attention next time. Goddamn!" She takes a beat and her face instantly transforms from freaked the fuck out to concerned parent. "Want to talk about it?"

"It's just . . ." Toxic masculinity, extreme jock assholery, a douchebag-enforced prison of gender rules. ". . . boy drama."

Mom throws the side door open way more forcefully than is needed. "Who is he? I'll go Mama Bear on his ass!"

"Down, Grizzly," Dad hollers over the sizzle of melting butter. He's always trying out new recipes to put on the Lookout menu and thinks any problem can be solved with food. Seeing my face, he quickly goes about constructing a sandwich from the ingredients in his pan that I know he's going to hand to me in three . . . two . . . one . . . "Ham and turkey melt with Brie and caramelized onion."

I have zero appetite right now, but I know Dad will only hound me if I don't give it a try. I shove a bite into my mouth and say through masticated meat, "Izgud."

"Feel better?" Dad asks.

"Mmm."

Dad beams, then saunters back to the kitchen to cook. That's the thing with Dad. He is the most supportive and loving guy out there—he even tried walking in a few pairs of heels until he almost twisted an ankle—but he's basically my polar opposite. He's not good at talking things out *at all*. He'd rather just cook and feed and eat his way into a good mood, but then nothing ever really gets solved.

Mom, of course, knows this, after having been with the guy for twenty-seven years. She sets down the vintage briefcase I bought her to celebrate her mayoral win, laces her fingers through mine, and says, "Come on. Step into my office."

Said office is just a few steps away, through the sliding door that leads out onto the expansive pine deck that she designed, giving us the perfect view of treetops stretching throughout the Cascades. The breeze blowing past my cheeks helps whip away some of the hot anger at Skylar that's still boiling just beneath the surface.

Some. But definitely not all.

"Okay," Mom says when we sit in our locally built Adirondack chairs. "Feral mother ways of payback aside, how can I help?"

Here's where Mom and I are so much alike. She'll talk to anyone about *anything*. It's how she won the mayoral election. She held twice-weekly town hall meetings during her candidacy so she could hear from anybody who had anything they needed to get off their chest about how Mountain Pass could improve. She even walked door-to-door to be sure she could hear from those who couldn't make the meetings. I get my constant need to talk and learn more about people from her. But the weird thing is, I still don't feel like I could ever tell her about wanting to leave Mountain Pass. About how this town just isn't enough.

And because of that, I shrug and say, "It's nothing."

Mom gets this knowing grin. "Okay, I get it. Sometimes you've got to spread your wings and not have your *boring old mom* swoop in and save the day. But just remember this." Mom places a loving hand on mine. "Someday all these problems will be behind you and you'll be running this town. It's in your blood."

And there it is. That pressure to stay. If I bring up the bet now, she's for sure going to say *It doesn't matter if you win or lose. Gaybutante or not, you've got your place here in Mountain Pass.*

"NICHOLAS!" Dad's voice bellows from the kitchen, and I love that even in his cooking excitement he respects that only Sabrina and I get to call Nick, Nick. "Come here and eat this!"

Saved by the bestie.

"You know you could have just walked away, right?"

Typical Nick. Always coming in with the simple truth. He even takes a big chomp into a Double Stuf Oreo for emphasis. And right about now I want to toss those Oreos over the edge of this zip-lining platform so they splat against the ground fifty feet below. Nick, Sabrina, and I usually come up here to make our plans for world domination or to vent. I'm going for a combo of the two, and today I need blind loyalty, not blatant facts. But that's more Sabrina's area. Nick is more the type of guy who looks at a problem from every angle before making a judgment call.

"Okay, yes, that's something I could have considered," I say, smacking the latest Oreo he picks up into the pack, but then I feel bad, so I pinch it between two silver nails and hand it back. "But that wasn't an option. How can I just let this guy go along and spread so much hate and misinformation about femmes and femininity and gay people?"

Nick chews his Oreo slowly, the crunch of wafer combining with the sounds of birds and the wind blowing through the pine trees. Nick does this when he's about to say something profound. He takes his time to find the right wording, and Sabrina and I know not to rush the process.

"You've got to know what battles to pick, Riley. Because those microaggressions and just blatant *aggression* aggressions are going to happen all the time. It's practically daily that I come across someone in fandom circles saying something awful about being Black or pan or both like me, and if I was fighting back every single time, I wouldn't have an ounce of strength for any joy whatsoever. I know we live in this sort of queer paradise in Mountain Pass, but the whole world out there has a lot of rough edges, and it hurts when they rub against you. Most of the time, people don't want to be told they're wrong, or that they're hurting someone, or their viewpoint needs to change. It sounds like Skylar is one of those people."

"Well, I can't back out now," I say. "I already kind of rushed into the situation. I made a bet."

Nick looks me dead in the eye and says, "So what? Skylar can't make you pull out of the running for the Gaybutante Society. And you can't make him drop baseball. It's just a matter of pride now between both of you. You can still walk away."

"But what if I don't want to?"

As soon as I say it, I know for sure that I don't want to back out. It's one of my favorite parts about talking with people and why I want to be the ultimate interviewer. Sometimes what people say makes you genuinely react, words pop out of your mouth, and it's such a human moment.

"Is that what you want?" Nick asks. "To risk it all? To risk your future in the GS and your ticket out of here just to prove some asshole wrong?"

All these thoughts about conversations connecting people make me realize this doesn't just have to be about proving *one* asshole wrong. This can be to show the world that there are gay guys out there who like femme people. Who don't need such strict heteronormative masc-for-masc-only ideas to find love and attraction.

I grab my lilac Telfar bag and grab my Gaybutante journal to furiously write *PROVE THE ASSHOLES WRONG* next to General Gay Chaos. Sure, I don't know where to go from here, but at least it's a start. I slam the book shut, and in my overzealousness, the journal falls from my lap and flips onto its back. The perfectly Lonny-stitched mic stares up at me, and everything clicks into place.

"This is it!" I say. "My very first podcast! It'll spread all sorts of Gay Chaos as I show that there are so many ways you can be gay and it's not one-guy-fits-all. I'll document the whole search for my first boyfriend to not only prove Skylar wrong, but also to show femme people everywhere that love is out there for us. In the real world. That it exists, we exist, and gay guys exist who were meant to be our soul mates." I grimace. "Okay, maybe that's too far—

maybe I don't know if soul mates are a thing—but I do know love is a thing, and I know I deserve it."

Nick lets loose his small smile, that subtle signal that he agrees with what I'm saying. Love is totally Nick's thing. He might be an action movie fanatic, but in real life, he gets all googly-eyed for romance. It's why he was so heartbroken over the summer after he and Grayson Emery broke up in June. Grayson had just graduated a year early because they're like, brilliant, and they didn't think it made sense to continue a long-distance relationship. We spent many, many, *many* days up here in the trees with Nick crying about the loss. He usually keeps his emotions close to his chest, but I was glad he felt safe enough with me to let it all out like that.

"You do deserve it," Nick says. "I'm in."

"In for what?"

Nick gives me a very pointed look, but the corners of his mouth never droop. "You and I both know you're terrible when it comes to technology." It's true. Wilhelmina had to write a step-by-step guide for me to learn how to go live at KMPK, and I have to look at it *every single time* I host my radio hour. "You're going to need somebody to edit this thing so we can upload it. So, I'll be your producer." It's what he's best at, getting very Virgo on us all the time and having lists and plans and the knowledge and expertise to put those plans into action. He's going to be a movie producer when we get out of school, the name Nicholas

Maynard rolling in all kinds of credits. It's another reason it surprises folks that he doesn't want into the Society when there are so many Hollywood connections there. But the whole public persona thing is not his jam, especially considering how terrible trolls can be to all of us once Hopefuls are announced, but our Gaybutantes of color most of all. The GS hires somebody to report hateful comments on official Gaybutante accounts, but they can't read everything twenty-four seven. Something gross always slips through, and Nick doesn't want anything to do with that. He doesn't even have any social media at all. I totally get it, and my soul breaks that colossal dickheads can ruin parts of life that are supposed to be fun and about connection. It's time to fight back against the dickheads!

My heart instantly floats that Nick wants to use his producer skills to help me out, and I know it's super cheesy, but I really do have the best friends in the universe. Then Nick's words from before float next to my heart, making it drop right back down.

"What about the assholes out there who might come for us?" I ask. "You've already had to deal with that in your fandom forums and I don't want to add more shit to your plate."

Nick picks up two Oreos, keeping one for himself and handing me the other. "Yeah, no, I'm definitely not going to put my face on this. I won't fight this fight *for* you, but I'm happy to stand beside you, behind the scenes, just be a supportive voice. I can field emails, weed out any bad ones so you don't get affected by their energy. Or if you want to stand up to the haters, I've got your back. Just like you were there for me all summer after Grayson. I mean, the amount you spent on tissues alone. I owe you one."

"You owe me nothing, Nick. I'll be there for you through anything. Always."

"Always," he repeats.

With that, we clink our cookies together, sealing the deal.

"So," Nick says through his bite, "what are you going to call the show?"

I blurt out the first thing that comes to mind. "*Riley Weaver Needs a Date to the Gaybutante Ball.*"

Nick gives it some thought, his nine-months'-pregnant pause causing me all kinds of anxiety, making me click my nails together nervously.

"It's a little long, don't you think?" he finally says.

"Yeah. But it feels good."

"All right, then." Nick stands up and dusts off his hands. He reaches down to pull me with him. "Let's get started."

Excerpt from Episode 1—*Riley Weaver Needs a Date to the Gaybutante Ball*: "How It Started"

Why put myself through all this shit just because one lousy asshole that I don't even really know decided it was his duty to tell me that I'll never find love from another gay person?

Because even though I've never met another gay femme in real life, I know I'm not the only one who will ever hear that being femme somehow makes you less gay or less deserving of a partner. It's also not the first time I've heard that. You see it all the time online. It's wild how many gay guys will go out of their way to crap all over anyone else who identifies as gay but displays their gender differently from them, different from the cis mainstream. Is it the majority of gay people? I don't think so. But it's definitely a very loud little speck of demons. And it's my duty as a podcaster to expose the truth on this gross subculture and debunk them once and for all.

To give hard and fast truth that there is love out there for us.

But I promise every episode won't be heavy. This is going to be fun! This is going to be General Gay Chaos! Because I'm going to share with you, in each new episode, the dates I go on to find THE ONE. And this isn't going to be one of those highly picked over, very fake, public-facing persona things. I'll give you the real deal, nitty-gritty take on what it's like to date as a gay femme person.

Maybe there will be a guy somewhere in my journey that you think is a favorite, that you're rooting for. Maybe there will be a guy I like that you think is totally wrong for me. Maybe you actually think a lot like The Jock and assume femme penis-havers could never be called gay, but you're here to be educated and see what happens. Whatever you think, that's okay—well, maybe not okay and just downright wrong—but you can let us hear your thoughts through emails, social media, you name it. We'll have all these chaotic gay opinions, and what's more chaotically gay than shouting out those opinions for the world to hear? This will be fun. I know I already said that, but maybe I'm trying to convince myself too. It will be a blast! And by the time the Ball rolls around on December second, I'd better have somebody ask to be my escort because I really can't lose this bet.

So, want to see who wins?

Stick around and find out what happens in each episode of Riley Weaver Needs a Date to the Gaybutante Ball.

Chapter 4

The weird thing about living in a town with ten thousand residents is that everybody knows each other. So, when you're suddenly available and looking for a partner, you've got to kind of present yourself. Peacocking. Strutting around with your tail feathers out, putting on this air that you're no longer looking at some guy next to you like the friend you've known since they had a meltdown when they cracked their macaroni necklace in kindergarten, but like a person who you want to get to know in entirely new, lip-locked, potentially someday-naked ways.

The problem for me is I constantly look like I'm peacocking. Like, my go-to booties are typically leopard print, my rain jackets are usually some shade of neon, and I very, very, very rarely go to school without a blend of at least four colors from various beauty influencers' palettes on my face. So, getting a guy I've known all my life to look at me like they might want me is going to take some not-so-subtle signals on my part. Verbal signals. Basically, just blatantly saying, "Hey, let's go out on a date." Because nothing in my bet with Skylar says I can't ask a guy out, I just have to be sure that he is the one to ask to be my escort to the Gaybutante Ball. Which, now that I think of it, some guys might assume that's kind of presumptuous, but if they just ask to be my boyfriend instead, then it's sort of implied that they'd also be the one presenting me to gay society for the first time, right?

So, now, where to meet the guys?

I mull it over before bed that night, jotting down all the ideas that come to mind in my new Gaybutante journal. It's important that it's not at school because the second someone thinks they're getting even a whiff of flirtation, anyone in their vicinity immediately pays attention. It's like some spotlight from the top of the Cascades blares down on you and everyone watches. It's too much pressure on one of my potential escorts. Too much attention could scare a guy away before I even get a chance to ask him out. And then if I'm turned down by enough guys in such a public way, I might get this reputation of being undatable, and then Skylar will think he's right and my lack of dates will definitely get me out of the Gaybutante Society. This has to be done with care, and I need to go to the spots that are known for churning out the most couples.

First, the Mountain Pass Gay Pickleball League. This town has all kinds of LGBTQIA+ groups thanks to its Gaybutante link, many of which are amped up by guys from Seattle or nearby suburbs. That means there's potential for love from somebody who's not a local and has seen me as just a friend or classmate all these years. Sure, it's a sport, but not like body checking or anything. Plus, I'd be lying if I said I didn't like the idea of seeing some gays get hot and sweaty. So that's a must.

Next, the Mountain Pass Café Open Mic Night. It's the last Friday of every month, which is about three weeks away, where up-and-coming singers and poets flock to the town. It's a spot that's totally known for making sparks fly. I mean think of it, the next number-one-hit maker up on that stage crooning his love to some unknown crush, and then we lock eyes and everyone in the room just knows that person he's singing about is me.

If for some reason neither of those come up with any possible dates, there's also the Mountain Pass Gay Teen Bird Watchers. It's another group where a lot of nearby Seattleites pop in because you get some serious bird views up in these mountains. Bald eagles, a plethora of falcons, so many owls that think it's their mission to keep me up at night by hooting right outside my window. But those owls would suddenly become way less annoying and inordinately cute if one of these gay bird aficionados were to come over and hear that who-who and could immediately name what species it was and thought it was a sign from the avian gods that we're supposed to be together. It'd be a hoot.

So, there we have it. Three scenarios over the next three-ish weeks where I'll hopefully find a guy who's into me. Plus, I'll have twelve Gaybutante Hopeful–hosted parties to go to this semester, and if the GS trend continues, a couple or two always forms at one of those. Maybe I'll be one of the lucky partygoers who realizes the love of their life is right there next to them, and then this escort train will really be rolling.

Okay, wow, that totally sounds like I'm starting some new brothel idea. Not that I'm here to shame sex work at all—that just totally puts a whole new spin on my story. Note to self: never write the phrase "escort train" again.

"I mean, if this seems like too much trouble, I could just *accidentally* unleash this bobcat in Skylar's backyard as soon as she recovers from her porcupine quill removal." Sabrina gives her loving-mother eyes to said feline in question who's sleeping with a bandaged muzzle in her cage. "How's that for General Gay Chaos?"

While I appreciate her instinct to come to my defense, I imagine that plan would have a hard time getting approval. "I think the Gaybutantes would say that classifies as dangerous and/or illegal."

"Speaking of which, have you gotten the go-ahead from Lonny yet?" Nick stands about as close to the door as he can get. He says that these cages look too flimsy to hold real live wild animals. I always try to keep my body between Nick and whatever animal is freaking him out. It probably wouldn't do much in case the critter ever did go feral, but I want Nick to know I'd rather they eat me alive than him.

"Just about an hour ago," I say. I stopped by Lonny's studio—this yarn-filled shed in her backyard—just before coming to Sabrina's family's clinic. She approved the podcast! She also wanted me to tell her The Jock's identity so she could stab his eyes out with a crochet hook, but just like with Nick, I don't need other folks fighting my battles. *I'm* going to be the one to make Skylar eat his words, and a pileup on him would just distract from me being proven right. It's been three days since the Gaybutantes announced the season and Skylar made me fume from his femme hate. I wonder how many days it'll be until Skylar regrets ever having made this bet.

But Lonny did give me a word of warning. The GS image has been tightly controlled by the Society itself. They only show snapshots of perfectly planned parties, soul-boosting philanthropy, or epic General Gay Chaos like that time a couple years ago when Carlos Ramirez created a parade of unicorns by leading a herd of costumed horses from their mom's ranch through Mountain Pass's Main Street. (They're now the host of a couture pet-grooming competition reality series and the creator of animal-safe, cruelty-free, at-home pet dyes.) But with my plan to document my whole experience of being a Gaybutante Hopeful from start to finish, it's more of a peek inside than has ever been done before, outside of the GS-created documentary about the process (now streaming on Hulu). Even that was more of a highlight reel of the best hosting gigs, the brightest Gaybutante Ball outfits, and the most heartwarming charity stories. It's all queer people thriving. My podcast will be more of an in-the-moment experience, broadcasting my worries and fears along with my potential successes and love connections. Lonny (rightly) told me the podcast would be *un*approved if I outed anybody (which, of course, I would never), or if my detailing any love connections at a Gaybutante party unwillingly put any other member's love life on blast or affected their image. The number one rule above all is that a Gaybutante always has another Gaybutante's back. I've got to be on my p's and q's—but still deliver a true, heartfelt podcast for my listeners—or else this is going to bite me in the ass harder than this bobcat could if she were truly awake. I can't get sloppy and have this thing cause so much Gay Chaos that I chaotically end my own mission.

"Shit, babe, your post is getting some serious numbers! Riley, if your podcast gets this many listeners, you're going to be the two most popular Hopefuls of the whole season."

Sabrina's girlfriend, Cassidy, is our cheerleader from not so afar. She goes to school in the city and is channeling her jealousy that she can't join the Gaybutante Society into good by being our unwavering support. She's holding her phone out in her olive-tone hands, beaming from ear to ear as Sabrina's first video for her Service pillar plays on loop.

Sabrina's in a full face of makeup that I did for her—complete with this neon leopard print look I threw on her eyes—looking gorge as she extracts a few quills from the pleasantly sedated bobcat. She's right up in the cat's face, the feline's outrageously sharp teeth gleaming under the overhead lights, but Sabrina doesn't hesitate for a second. She's gentle and tender, cooing to the bobcat while looking hot as hell, and her mom cheers her on while Sabrina removes each prick expertly. Cassidy filmed the video yesterday while I hung out in the waiting room with Nick, because while it doesn't bother me when this kitty is in a cage, I did not want to see what she could do if she happened to wake up midoperation. But watching this footage back now? Sabrina is fucking fierce.

"Wait, seriously?" Sabrina snatches the phone from Cassidy's hand and I crowd over her shoulder. The video has over five hundred likes and more than four thousand views. Sure, it's not viral status, but it's more attention than any of her posts—or mine, for that matter—have ever received. It was boosted along by the fact that the Mountain Pass GS account shared it just after Sabrina posted.

But honestly, reminders about how many people are watching us—not just at school and in Mountain Pass, but throughout the country—does slightly turn my determination for vindication into nerves. After the rundown at the park, Jesse Morganstern snapped a group photo and quick videos of us to introduce the Hopefuls to the Gaybutante accounts on every app out there. I already got about a hundred new followers on each in just one night. I know it's not many, but to have that happen in a span of about twelve hours is intimidating.

This is what I've always wanted, though. A platform to launch my podcasts and create connection, human to human, one conversation at a time. These aren't nerves of wanting to go back on that dream at all. They're more like *It's about to finally happen and I don't want to screw it up* nerves. And anticipation that I'm finally starting to build a following that will hopefully become sizable enough to convince Mom I've got more going on than just what's happening in this tiny town.

"This is wild!" Sabrina looks like she could scale a wall. "I never thought people would actually watch this stuff before. I mean, you're always the attention grabber, Riley—but this? Holy shit! It's got to be because of this themed look."

I shake my head. "Nuh uh, this is because of how epically badass you are with your head practically in that bobcat's mouth! I deserve zero credit."

Sabrina sighs all wistfully. "If we can keep this up, these videos might actually save an animal's life. I'm so pumped that Lonny approved this as my Service pillar. If people watch because they think it's fun, but actually *learn* something about how to alert the professionals who can help injured animals, that would be amazing."

"And all those shirtless vets will be taking a back seat to *my girl!*" Cassidy pulls Sabrina in for a long, epic kiss.

I glance at Nick. This sort of PDA used to bother him, especially in the weeks after the Grayson breakup. It's not that he was jealous or mad—more that he wouldn't get to have that with G anymore, and it stung for a while. He says he's good now, but I'm not so sure, the way his small smile gets even smaller whenever he sees Sabrina and Cassidy kiss. I clack my way over to him, careful not to lose my footing in these heels on this slippery linoleum floor just in case I fall into a cage and accidentally release some rabies-recovering raccoon.

"How you doing?" I ask.

"I'm fine if I just stay back here, far, far away from that killer cat. Note to self: I will *not* be able to work on any productions with animals larger than a Pomeranian."

"You know that's not what I'm talking about."

His eyes dart to Sabrina and Cassidy, who are still deep in their kiss.

"I'm happy for my friend."

"Okay, wow, I've never heard a lingering *but* that big before."

Nick rolls his eyes pointedly. "That was cringe, lady."

"It was, wasn't it?" I drape my arm over his shoulders. "It's okay if it still hurts. Healing takes time. Especially when you were together for nearly two years. And sorry for sounding like a cliché couples therapist."

"Can I tell you something?"

"You know you never have to ask, Nick."

"It's gonna make me sound awful, and I don't want you to take this the wrong way."

That instantly makes me nervous. I swallow down the metallic taste of dread to ask, "What is it?"

"I'm sick of being the one with nothing relationship-wise going on." He gives one more hurried look at Sabrina, who's now leaning back into Cassidy's arms. Based on the hickey-level-bordering neck nuzzling going on, I think C likes the makeover I gave Rina too. "Between them and now your podcast, I'm surrounded by all this romance that I'm not a part of. I'm used to you being the single one." Nick's eyes pop wide the second after he says it. "No offense."

"What could be offensive about the facts? I *was* always the single one. I'm still the single one."

"Yeah, but you won't be for long. You and I both know what a catch you are, and I'm happy for you that you want to date now. But I don't want to get left behind."

"Aw, Nick." I squeeze him as tight as my little noodle arms will allow. "You never have to worry about that. And if it's too much to handle, you know I can do this podcast on my own. I don't want to pour salt in the wound."

"But it's been over three months," Nick says, sounding more frustrated than I've ever heard him sound before. "When will this stop hurting?"

I wish I could give him any advice, but I don't know from experience. Phil was just a sweet and horny guy who felt safe to experience something with that we both hadn't done before. So, it didn't hurt when we parted ways after that two and a half minutes of a good time.

All I can do for Nick is shrug. "I'm not sure."

Nick sighs. "I'm not backing out on the podcast. But if you come across any potential partners in your dating adventures that you think might be good for me, send 'em my way, will you?"

I've never really had to play wingwoman before. Sabrina is always so confident when it comes to dating, and Nick and Grayson happened so organically that it was like they'd always been dating. But they say that you attract the energies you put out there, and while I'm broadcasting to the world—literally and metaphorically—how I'm ready for love, it wouldn't hurt to add an extra heaping of good vibes for Nick too.

I pull back so I can look Nick dead in the eye. "Absolutely."

There's that small smile again.

"So, you're, like, really diving in, huh?" Sabrina looks at me from head to toe, taking in my pastel-pink crop top, purple leggings, and neon-orange tennis shoes. "Just take it easy on your first day. You're not super sporty and you haven't broken those shoes in *at all*. Even with socks, you're bound to get blisters."

"Thanks, Mom," I say, giving a significant eye roll. I did not ask her to come along to pickleball just so I could sit in the passenger side of her family's Bronco (complete with an airbrushed design of some fierce falcon on the side advertising their vet clinic) and give me more things to worry about than just meeting a boy. I need pep-talk Rina!

"What? I'm just trying to be realistic." Sabrina tugs on her ponytail. "Remember that time I tried to play soccer with Cassidy to make her think I was cute and we had so much in common? I could barely stand on my feet for a week, they hurt so bad. Don't make my mistakes."

"Why are you nervous?" Nick asks from the back seat.

I whip around. "I'm not nervous. Not in the slightest. I'm just ready to prove to a masc asshole that he's simply a masc asshole, that's all."

"Not you," Nick says, doing that thing where he can have a whole conversation while focused on something else entirely, this time on the laptop propped in his lap. "Sabrina. You get all cautionary when you're anxious. And you're tugging on your hair."

Sabrina drops her ponytail and crosses her arms over her own workout gear. One arms hits her chest perfectly so that the *Just Do It* logo now reads *Just D,* which seems oddly appropriate before I get started on my journey to find a man.

"I'm not nervous," she says.

Nick finally looks up from his computer to give Sabrina a silent stare.

"Okay, fine. It's just that"—she points at Nick's laptop—"are you sure you want to do this? I mean, we've already gotten so much attention since the Gaybutante posts went live, I'd hate for this to get the *wrong kind* of attention."

"You mean *you've* gotten a lot of attention," I say with a playful push. Cassidy called it: Sabrina is by far the most popular of the Mountain Pass Gaybutante Hopefuls, if you go by social media response. People really connected with Sabrina's bobcat video and are eating up her behind-the-scenes footage of the animal center. And by people, I mean ladies. Ladies crushing on her. *Hard.* She's already gotten a few DMs from girls at nearby high schools asking her out, and this happened in just a matter of *three days.* It's all innocent enough, but I know from how epically wide her grin gets every time we talk about it that she's loving the spotlight. It's about damn time the world saw how great she is.

"Stooooop!" Sabrina says, pushing me back. Her face gets über-red, her freckles standing out loud and proud. But still, she's beaming.

"I'm just saying," Sabrina goes on when her face cools off, "I feel like your attention could turn from good to bad pretty quickly, don't you think? We're lucky we have the GS moderators on their accounts to take down any trolls, but since this is *your* podcast, *you're* going to have to deal with the trolls directly. Are you sure you want that? Especially when you're challenging what it really means to be gay, and you *know* how the gays get. They can really come after their own."

She's not wrong. When Nick and I first told this idea to Sabrina, she could name eight internet squabbles between gays off the top of her head. All of them were about who gets to call themselves queer and what it means to be *insert any letter of the LGBTQIA+ alphabet soup here* and how so-and-so didn't fit X letter because they didn't have the "right" characteristics.

"We already went over this," I say, but I link my fingers with Sabrina's so she knows that I know she's not trying to be a wet blanket. "There is no one way to be gay, and if a few jerks have to let it be known they don't like the way *I'm* gay, at least other femmes will know they aren't alone. That's what this is all about. Femme power in the face of our haters!"

Sabrina nods once, uncharacteristically quiet.

"And it's live," Nick says from the back. He turns the computer to face us. Our podcast logo beams out from the screen. In the perfect orange and purple color scheme it reads RILEY WEAVER NEEDS A DATE TO THE GAY-BUTANTE BALL, complete with a fan art illustration of me done by a Gaybutante follower after the Hopeful Introduction Post (used with permission and a one-hundred-dollar commission fee, of course). A little Play symbol is underneath, meaning anybody at any moment could listen to my story and go on this journey with me as I find my first boyfriend. As we watch, the total listens count goes from zero to one.

"AH!" Sabrina and I scream together. I even leap over the stick shift and squeeze her. "It's happening!" Sabrina shouts.

"It's real!" I yell.

Now it's Nick's turn to roll his eyes. "You two are so dramatic. And you're not going to have any more episodes to get all dramatic over if you don't, you know, start dating."

We agreed we'd just upload episodes as the material comes in, so there's no pressure to meet an arbitrary deadline and force dates when there's no spark to begin with. While this is for an audience, the goal is for me to actually end up with a boyfriend who can be my escort, so I can't let the pressure of getting episodes out there affect that.

"You're right," I say. I take a deep breath—four in, five out—and grab the door handle. "Let's go meet the man of my dreams."

The Mountain Pass Rec Center is *the* location in town for anything active. Its outdoor offerings include soccer fields, a baseball diamond, and tennis courts. The latter happen to have happy yellow lines painted in them to mark off the special space where my gay love story could finally take off:

The pickleball courts.

It's a typical gloomy mid-September afternoon, but the crowd in front of me is anything but gloomy. People *turn out* for the Mountain Pass Gay Pickleball League. There's any number of bright shorts, shirts, knee-high socks, and a lot of rainbow sweatbands. Gladys and Dora—the town's most adorable elderly lesbian couple—split the group into age brackets, and when I see there are around two dozen of us in the teen group, and that sixteen of those are guys from outside Mountain Pass, my spirits get about as high as Mount Rainier. That's a whole lot of gays to possibly make a connection with. This whole finding-a-date thing could be way easier than I thought.

"Oh my god, eyes on Hottie in court one," Sabrina says under her breath. She elbows me in the ribs and motions toward the edge of the teen group where just about everyone is flocking to one guy in particular. He's probably six-foot-three, white with a tan that says he just got back from somewhere with way more sun than we get here, and hands so big, he could engulf mine in one of his own.

"Wow. Do we know him?" I look to Nick and he shakes his head. Same thing for Sabrina. Then Sabrina's eyes practically bug out of her skull.

"There's no way this is possible, but he's looking right at you."

"*No way this is possible?* Ouch." I cling onto Nick's arm to keep me upright while I handle the verbal blow dealt by one slice of my bestie sandwich.

"No, not like that. Just like, it seems against all odds that the *first* cute guy we see is the one who's going to ask you out. You are a *total* catch," she says, then pulls me back toward her so she can squeeze the life out of me. Supportively, that is. "I just didn't think things would happen so fast."

"You should go over and talk to him," Nick says, plucking a piece of fluff off my shoulder and readjusting a stray lock of silver hair. He knows just how I like it, so he's literally the only person I'd trust to do this. When it's perfectly in place, Nick takes in his handiwork with that small smile before finally patting my arm. "You're beautiful."

"All right," I say, glancing over Nick's shoulder to where Hottie is definitely watching me. "Here I go."

It's like one of those slo-mo movie moments. Everyone turns to look as I make my way through the crowd. The ones I know from MPH give me a wave or a smile, and I beam back. After each "hello," my eyes snap over to Out-of-Town Hottie, and every time, he's looking right at me. He gives me an up-down, has his lips quirked in the sweetest smile, and even fiddles with the waistband of his basketball shorts nervously. It's so cute. *I'm making him nervous.*

The closer I get, the more I can't stop thinking about this guy on my arm at the Gaybutante Ball. Skylar is going to eat it. Like, his jaw will be so far dropped to the ground that I could fit just about anything into his smug maw. Hottie here is even more athletic-looking than Skylar is, and with him as my boyfriend, it will prove once and for all that Skylar has no idea what he's talking about in regard to what gay guys do or do not like.

"Hey," I say, and I want to give myself points for how smooth I sound. No anxious, out-of-breath fast-talker here. Those calming breaths actually work and are making me seem *hot.* "I'm Riley."

"Hi, Riley," Hottie says, and he puts out one of his huge honking hands to shake. Just like I imagined, it completely engulfs mine, and I can't stop thinking about him rubbing those hands all over me. "I'm Ricky."

Riley and Ricky—holy crap, how cute do our names sound together?

"Nice to meet you, Ricky," I say, and I can't stop smiling and looking up at him through my extra-curly eyelashes. Flirty to the max.

Ricky smiles back and fidgets with his waistband again. He is *adorable*.

"I know we just met," Ricky starts, "but can I ask you something?"

"You just did," I say with a laugh and playfully smack his arm.

Ricky chuckles in return and it makes my heart flutter. He has the most perfect laugh.

"But of course you can," I add. "Ask me anything."

Then my heart flutters even faster. If he prefaced this with "I know we just met," does that mean he's already feeling these flirtatious sparks and wants to ask me on a date within the first *two minutes* of talking? Consider this bet won and my love life set!

"I was just wondering . . ." Ricky trails off, bites his lip, and flicks the waist of his shorts over and over. Finally, he leans in slowly, and for the briefest second I think he's going to kiss me. But then, "I was just wondering where you put your—" His eyes flash to my crotch. "You know. Your junk. In those leggings. There's not a trace of your balls and I'm just like, *how*?"

Turns out it won't be Skylar's mouth that falls to the floor. It's mine.

Excerpt from Episode 2—*Riley Weaver Needs a Date to the Gaybutante Ball*: "Dropping Balls"

So instead of thinking about the Gaybutante Ball, or pickle-balls for that matter, Pickle Hottie was thinking about mine.

I'd like to say this is the first time that's ever happened, but when you're femme and have a penis, people are obsessed with your dick. Like, obsessed *obsessed*. Just because I wear high-waisted pants or skin-tight leggings. I've been asked so many times by well-meaning friends, oblivious family, and inappropriately curious strangers where I put "my junk," as Pickle Hottie so eloquently put it.

What I always want to say is, You realize you're thinking about my genitals, right? There are two of us standing here and only one of us is asking the other about their balls, yet I'm the one who it's implied is the weirdo because I'm wearing clothes that society has said are for females only? *It's so messed up!*

Fortunately, Gladys blew her earsplitting whistle at just the right time and saved me from having to address Pickle Hottie's question. She kept throwing references to balls in practically every sentence, at which PH would nervously glance at me and I would glare at him, and I'd let him fidget with the waistband of his shorts as much as he freaking wanted. The strange thing is, the waistband fidgeting turned to full-on junk adjusting like he thought the lack of a bulge on my end meant he had to check and make sure his was still there. Ugh.

For the record—because I know so many of you are now wondering the exact same thing PH was—there are a multitude of ways you can position your balls to fit into feminine clothing. It's not hard in the slightest. Okay, wow, poor word choice. It's not difficult at all. There are all kinds of underwear made to position you so you're not peacocking your actual cock and can keep things PG. Look it up. Start with gaffs.

There was one other unfortunate observation I made while swatting pickleballs: I didn't get any attention from the other gays there. But you know who did? You guessed it: Pickle Hottie. The longer we played, the glistenier his muscles got, and that caught every masculine-energy-loving individual's attention at the Rec Center. Not a single look my way. Which did make me worry. What if what The Jock said is true? What if, when presented with a sweating, muscular, Greek-god-looking guy next to crop top–wearing me—who, let's face it, has about as much athletic ability as the three-legged skunk that keeps ending up at the animal rehab—gay guys will pick the traditionally masc guy every time? What if I really don't stand a chance?

Just to be clear, I want to make sure you all know I'm not saying there is anything wrong with having a body or a gender presentation like PH or The Jock. You can be a cis guy, you can be athletic, you can be Dude City, and that's beautiful. You be you. Just let me be me, too. But it wouldn't hurt to get a bit of physical attention for this lil femme either, you know what I mean?

I think the takeaway here is to not look for a boyfriend at sporting events. It's stacking the cards against me, and if I'm going to win this bet, I've got to find guys who are into more than sweat and scoring and balls.

Sports balls. They can still be into my balls. Gah! Now I'm the one who's doing it!

Chapter 5

"He did *not* ask you about your balls!"

Lonny screams it across the quad, her brightly knit sweater featuring a clown juggling all kinds of rainbow-colored balls very on theme for this conversation. Maybe she even planned to wear the outfit specifically for this talk about my podcast, and rather than getting embarrassed that we're bringing up my business in front of the entire junior-senior lunch crowd, I'm touched that she's already listened to the episode. Nick and I only uploaded it last night at, like, midnight.

"He did!" Sabrina says when Lonny saunters up to our table. "Can you believe it? What is going on with people?" She goes back to scrolling through her phone, which she's been doing nonstop since she uploaded her own new video, this time mending a broken wing on a hawk. "I can't keep up with these DMs. 'Come over here, girl, and mend my broken heart.'" She wants to sound exasperated, but she can't stop the smile breaking across her face. She pops over to her bobcat video and screams, "OH MY GOD!"

"What?!" I snatch her phone. "What is it?"

"R-read that last comment."

> You sure are great with cats. You could come over and get cozy with my kitty anytime you want.

I look at Nick. He looks at me. Then we both lock eyes with Sabrina.

And burst out laughing.

"What kind of pickup line is that?" I yell.

"Who is that supposed to work on?" Nick asks, wiping away tears. "Literally who would sign up for a date after that?"

Sabrina holds a stitch in her side. "Thank god she just said *kitty* and didn't take it a step further."

I look at her, deadpan. "Yep. She showed some serious restraint."

Which only makes us lose it harder.

Lonny gives her own knowing smile. "Getting a lot of attention already, huh?" She takes the empty seat next to me as we finally start to catch our breath. "There's one in every class."

"One what?" I ask.

"One Hopeful who the world has deemed the certified hottie. As you can expect, it was Cliff last year. The DMs got so bad, and shall I say . . . *intimate*, that he had to make all his accounts private for a while. We can only do so much on the Gaybutante end reporting the comments and stuff, so it's up to you to let us know how you're coping with everything. If it gets to be too much, we're always here to talk."

Sabrina's face lights up and she suddenly gets all bashful. "I know this most recent one was too overboard, and I should find all these other comments and DMs overwhelming, but I, uh . . . I actually kind of like it."

"Ain't nothing wrong with that," Lonny says. "Having people say they're attracted to you can feel empowering for some of us."

I wish I could say I knew that from experience myself, but here we are with me having to field questions about my dick placement instead of people salivating over their phones to tell me how hot I am.

"I didn't even realize that about Cliff," I say, trying to get my mind off the fact that it may *never* be me getting that attention, stuck here in Mountain Pass as everybody's favorite sexless femme neighbor forever. I've been following Cliff since freshman year when I first saw a raindrop perfectly slide down that surreal dip in his cleft chin. Plus, Cliff's got that happy Mountain Pass attitude of following anybody who goes to MPH whether he knows you well or not, so the drama he was going through never really registered to the rest of the student population.

Lonny shrugs. "He kind of just deals with it now. He's got his thumb constantly hovering over the block button."

"When I said I wanted to make science seem sexy to ladies, I never thought people were going to say *I'm* the sexy lady."

Nick hovers his hand over Sabrina's phone so that she finally looks up. Then, he plucks it from her fingers.

"I'm doing this for your own good," he says, and places her phone in the front pocket of his messenger bag. "You're obsessing."

"I am not," Sabrina says.

"What does Cassidy think about all this attention?" Nick asks.

Sabrina's freckles jump out even more as her flush deepens. "I haven't really brought it up."

Nick just nods, pensive. Somehow, he has a way of making all his facial movements seem nonjudgmental too, while I've got a scowl on my face so big, my forehead hurts.

"But it's not like she can't see most of the comments herself," Sabrina insists. "They're right there on my posts. Besides, it's only been a few days. I'm sure all this will die down, and why make an issue out of something when I would never act on these comments to begin with. I'm a one-woman gal. Cassidy knows that."

"Just be sure that so much doesn't go unsaid that she jumps to conclusions," Nick says calmly.

"Anyway," Lonny says, putting a sympathetic hand over mine. "I really came over here to run something by you."

She reaches into her knapsack and pulls out a knitted ball about the size of a baseball. It's beige, with big, bulging eyes and brown fringe coming out the top like hair.

"Stress balls!" Lonny says excitedly. "Or Stress Heads is more like it. The newest addition to my Etsy shop, thanks to the inspiration from your podcast episode last night with all that ball talk. Completely customizable to resemble the person you want to get your stress out on the most! Based on your description, I thought this little bugger would resemble Pickleball Prick. That totally should have been the name you gave him, by the way."

Now that I look closer, it does look an awful lot like Ricky. I grab the ball and squeeze, its buggy eyes bulging from its skull even more. "It's perfect!"

"I figure if you come across any more assholes like that guy, you can pulverize this and get all the feelings out. Speaking of feelings, your podcast is *good*. I'm going through all the emotions with you: the conviction, the attraction, the anger. I didn't realize it would get so personal so quickly. Challenging notions of what it means to be gay like that, and examining it from the jump? It's definitely going to cause General Gay Chaos."

"I'm not so sure about that," I say. "I'm not Sabrina getting people running to my comments. How many listeners do we have now, Nick?"

Nick cringes.

"Just say it."

He can barely look me in the eye. "Twenty-six."

Twenty-six. That's the entire MPH Gaybutante Society and the Hopefuls (myself included), plus Nick.

"See what I mean? I'm not really getting a lot of reach here." I posted the cover image for the podcast and it got a few likes, but apparently none of my 433 followers who don't know me took the time to listen to it yet.

"Well, that's really what I'm here to talk to you about. I wanted to gauge how you're feeling after that run-in with Ricky. If you're already feeling too exposed, we can approve a totally different Gay Chaos for you. But if you really want to get some reach, we could share it on GS socials." She motions toward Sabrina. "You've seen how people can go a little wild in the comments, so I didn't want to put the spotlight on your show unless you were ready for the potential backlash. Or overzealous fans, as in Sabrina's case."

I glance at Nick, but he's got that pensive look again, this time letting me be the one to draw my own conclusions without his initial reaction swaying me. Sabrina, however, is staring at the front pocket of Nick's messenger bag, like if she tried hard enough, she could telekinetically get her phone to float to her hand and bask in her new attention some more. That's what I really need: attention. If this podcast gets lots of it, and I get more people clamoring for Riley content, I'll have the perfect evidence to convince Mom I've got to leave Mountain Pass to give the people what they want. There's just not enough *newness* in this town to really run a successful show. A successful anything. The majority of Mountain Pass Gaybutantes have moved away to make their mark. I think there's, like, three total MPH Gaybutante alumni that still live here. Lonny's offering me the chance to become big enough to leave this town too.

"Let's do it," I say. I find Nick's eyes again, and he's got that small smile on his face, so I know he approves of this decision. "I already knew we might get some heat from this. How can I change anyone's opinions on femme folks if nobody hears it?"

Lonny shows me the tweet she's got cued up.

> You've gotta hear the episode of Riley Weaver Needs a Date to the Gaybutante Ball that inspired my latest creations: Stress Heads. It's really *balls* to the wall!

I take a peek at her follower count: 15.7 thousand. If even 1 percent of her followers listened to the episode, that'd boost my listener count like five times over. And don't even get me started on what would happen if she shares this on her other social accounts.

It's time to really take the leap.

"Share away."

"Do I need to lock up your phone too?" Nick holds his hand out, motioning with his fingers for me to give it over. "You and Sabrina have been doomscrolling for the past seven days, and I'm starting to forget what y'all's eyes look like."

"Okay, fine, you're right." But I refresh the listener count one more time. 4,388. Seven days since Lonny tweeted about my podcast and that's where we're at. But I haven't uploaded a new episode since, hence tonight's mission to find somebody to kiss me.

"Besides," Nick adds when I slide my phone into my clutch. "This is a party and you're not going to catch anybody's attention if you keep staring at that thing."

I know I'm going overboard on screen time, but that phone has been my personal cheerleading squad for the past week. I've gotten nothing but support so far, which has been surprising. Maybe that's just because most of the listeners are followers of the Gaybutante Society, so they're full of all kinds of queer camaraderie. Either way, it's been nice to know that so many people *want* me to find a boyfriend and aren't Team Skylar. Their little digital voices echo in mind, mostly the two or three (okay, *two* because I remember them very vividly) guys who said they'd date me in a heartbeat. If those internet strangers would date me, somebody in the real world will too.

"Not to sound too dad-ish right now, but you two know the drill." Nick alternates his gaze between me next to him in the front seat of his Toyota Camry and Sabrina in the rearview mirror, who's obsessively stroking her ponytail. "Call me if you need me to bail you out for any reason. Riley, if you find somebody you like, but they go too far too fast, I got you."

Um, excuse him. "You make it sound like I haven't done anything before, but if the way things ended with Phil are any indication—"

Nick plugs his ears. "I'm not sex-shaming, but I've heard about just how *messy* that hand job was and I don't need to relive it!"

Sabrina throws her palm in between our seats to give me a high five, and the resounding slap supplies the little confidence boost I need. Because, even if Phil's happy ending made it *very* clear how much he liked what went down, what if I wasn't great at making out beforehand? What if I wasn't actually a very good kisser, and Phil just put up with it to get to the end goal?

"I'm just saying," Nick goes on, "for *both* of you, if you need an out, I'm it. If you need someone to drive you home after the night, I'm it. We don't need this podcast to end in some drunk-driving tragedy."

"Got it." Sabrina reaches around Nick's seat and hugs him from behind. "I wish you could come with us. I don't think it's too late to say you want in on the season so you can join."

Nick shakes his head. "Yeah, no. I love you, but even my two best friends in it isn't enough to make me risk the wrath of racist assholes online. I don't know how Antoine does it, but good for him. And for most of the folks in the Atlanta delegation. I'm rooting for them."

Sabrina squeezes him harder, while I get in on the hug.

"I'd kick all those bigoted douchebags' asses," Sabrina says.

"It'll take a long time," Nick says. "But I'm good. I'm going to make hit movies with Black casts as soon as I'm out of this place, and I'm confident I can do it on my own. Well, without the Gaybutantes anyway. But I'm happy y'all's dreams are coming true. Now get out of here."

He shoos us off him, the movement of his now-neon-green Afro reflecting in the windshield, a blinking Green Means Go that makes me fling open the door, ready to hopefully make a connection at my first-ever party. It's a surprisingly clear night too, no clouds in the sky, the stars twinkling down on me like sparkling omens of good things to come. Yes, that is corny as hell, but I am *ready*.

"Let's get this party started," I sing. I kiss Nick on the cheek, and he awkwardly clears his throat like he always does because he doesn't know how to take affection even though he told me it *does* make him feel nice inside.

I leap from the car. Sabrina is a little slower in her exit, but when she makes her way around the back and I take her arm to steady myself in these black stiletto boots, she lets out an excited squeal.

"Our first party," she says, and bounces a bit on her toes. "We're really doing this. Can you believe it?"

"Honestly, I think you're gonna be the belle of the ball," I say. "Considering how much attention you're already getting. It's not just lusty ladies living for your videos. The Gaybutantes too."

Sabrina blows a raspberry. "Come on, most of my attention is just from anonymous horndogs online." But then a devilish grin takes over her face. "Although it does feel pretty nice. My plan is *working*. I feel like celebrating!"

Sabrina leads the way, me seriously regretting my shoe choice (not really—I'd *never* regret a heel—but sometimes they just aren't practical) as we make our way through Antoine Gregory's field. He and his family live on a farm on the outskirts of town, a clear field surrounded by forested peaks on all sides. His parents run one of the top Black-owned furniture companies in the country, and he's taken after them with his woodworking skills, creating armoires and tables and all sorts of furniture with his bare hands.

Tonight, he's put those skills to use. A huge pine table sits in the center of the field, a couple dozen chairs around it, each unique yet somehow perfectly matching. Most are filled with Gaybutantes and Hopefuls. They're laughing, some drinking wine from the plethora of Franzia boxes in front of them, all underneath fake-vine-covered trellises, no doubt made by Antoine as well. In the center of the table are charcuterie trays like you've never seen, piled with meats and cheeses. There's even a cow wandering the field, like maybe this cheese came from the Gregory farm itself, but since we're all Mountain Passers, we know this cheese is store-bought from the Mountain Pass Creamery, owned and operated by Dennis Pak from the Gaybutante class of 2006.

"This is fucking fabulous," I say.

"So classy," Sabrina adds, then gulps. I already know what she's thinking.

"Don't worry. Everyone brings their own flair to their hosting gig, and this is *so* Antoine. We'll find a way to make yours feel like you."

Sabrina puts her head against my shoulder, this thing she likes to do when I'm towering over her in heels and she doesn't have the right words to express her thanks. Normally, I lay my head on top of hers and it's this sweet bestie moment, but tonight, this is the time my right heel sinks into the moist land of Antoine's property.

"Holy shit!" I wobble and find out just how appropriate that exclamation is because my left foot—instinctually slamming down to regain my balance—lands smack in a mushy cow pie. "Ah!" My foot slips out from under me, and I'm careening toward the ground. I know before it happens that with my right heel still stuck in the mud, my ankle is going to snap. Sprained at best.

But just as I feel the pressure build in my right ankle, a pair of hands yanks me upright. Even though I'm wearing a long-sleeved sparkling-silver turtleneck bodysuit, I can feel the person's calluses through the fabric. In one fluid movement, I'm lifted up, my boot unsucks from the earth, and I'm looking into the smiling deep brown eyes of Antoine.

"You just saved me from never being able to wear heels again!" I say. "Or, at the very least, the three to six months while my ankle recovered. And I'd be *devastated* to not be able to wear them during Gaybutante season."

Antoine laughs, the low, deep chuckle vibrating through me with his hands now on my waist and mine on his biceps. Correction: his *seriously bulging* biceps. Lifting all that wood to make furniture has really filled him out. Why have I not noticed that before? Maybe it's because I can still picture him making log cabins out of Popsicle sticks in the fifth grade, but now, having literally fallen into his arms, I'm like, *hubba-hubba.*

Antoine's gaze travels down my body, head to toe. He takes in my outfit, and the upturned corners of his eyes never fall, his smile never once wavers. My silver hair is perfectly coifed, my bodysuit is catching the light, and my black jeans with their sequined tuxedo stripes down the sides hug my hips in all the right places. It's femme, it's warm for this fifty-some-odd-degree night, and Antoine's up-down doesn't give a second of Skylar-esque toxically masculine judgment or creepy weird Ricky vibes with his stare lingering on my crotch.

Then his eyes hit my shoes.

"Well, shit," he says.

"Crap." It's going to be my *shoes* that throw him off? My favorite accessory of all time? Maybe this isn't going to be as destined as I thought.

"That's what I'm saying," Antoine says.

"What?"

He points down to my boots. The left is covered in cow poop.

"Oh! Shit!" I say it with a surprising amount of glee that makes me, Antoine, and Sabrina all crack up. "Oh, no, wait, *shit*. Not the feces kind. These things are suede and that is *not* going to come out."

This is not how I pictured entering my first party, let alone my first *Gaybutante* party. Hobbling in one-heeled thanks to falling victim to a cow mine.

"Actually, I think I have something that can help." Antoine motions toward my shoe. "May I?"

"Are you actually volunteering to remove my cow-crap-encrusted footwear?"

"I just figured if you did it yourself, you might fall over again. The ground's a little unsteady here, huh?"

"You're my hero," I swoon dramatically, which only makes him laugh more. I place a hand on Sabrina's shoulder to steady myself and stick out my left foot. Antoine unzips it and holds the black suede boot delicately between his long pointer finger and thumb. Staring at his hand makes me envision what it would feel like to have it running up my arm again, and I get goose bumps. The good kind.

Antoine nods to the table, where the Gaybutantes and Hopefuls are getting increasingly rowdy. "Why don't you two join the fun and I'll be right back."

"'Kay" is all I can manage while he dashes off to the barn. I hobble over to the rest of the group, using Sabrina as a makeshift bestie crutch.

"Did. You. See. That?" Sabrina emphasizes each word as we sit down. She grabs two empty plastic wineglasses and fills them from the nearest box of white zinfandel. "I mean, the way he bounded over to you at just the right time. It was too perfect; he *had* to have been watching us arrive. Almost like he was waiting specifically for you to get here. And the way he stared into your eyes!"

She hands me a glass and we cheers. "So, I didn't imagine all that? It was real?"

"Oh, it was real, baby!" She holds her glass up into the air and shouts, "To love!" before taking a giant swig.

"That's what I'm talking about," Lonny says from across the table. "It's why the Gaybutantes were made." Lonny stands up on her chair, holds her glass straight to the sky, and screams, "To love!"

"TO LOVE!" Our shouts echo all around as we chug our drinks, and I don't know if it's the sweet wine or the sweet lovefest, but I suddenly know without a doubt that romance is just around the corner.

Or maybe it's because of the way Antoine saunters across the field with long, confident strides, looking right at me. He's got my boot in one hand, a small bottle and a cloth in the other. His eyes never once leave my face, like he's not worried at all if he slips in a cow pie of his own. He seems more concerned with getting to check me out for as long as possible.

"Okay, lady, you got to get."

Sabrina follows my gaze while taking another swallow

from her glass. She nods. "Got it. I don't want to ruin your cool. I should go FaceTime Cassidy anyway. She's bummed non-Gaybutantes aren't invited."

A brief yet surprising fire of indignation burns in my belly that Sabrina has to be worrying about her girlfriend when this is *her* Gaybutante season. But it's extinguished the second Antoine plops into Sabrina's free chair.

"Hi." He's breathless. Am I making him nervous or is he catching his breath because he just hustled to the barn and back? For me. He hustled for me.

"Hi," I say, and I can't stop smiling. It makes my cheeks hurt, my hand instinctively pressing against my face. Antoine glances up at my fingers, gently places my boot on the table (which thankfully has no leftover cow poop on it and only a slight discoloration on the bottom), then takes my hand in his own.

We're already holding hands!

"Hold this steady, would you?" Antoine asks as he places my hand on the shoe. "I promise I already wiped off the gross shit."

"You got it."

Antoine's hands leave mine, and my fingers already feel off without the skin-to-skin contact. He pours a bit of whatever is in the bottle onto the cloth, a sharp smell making my nose hairs burn and my mouth water.

"What is that?" I ask.

"White vinegar. We use it on suede for stains all the time, and I thought I could give you a little tutorial." Then, even though I'm already holding the shoe steady from the top, Antoine places his hand on mine, pressing down.

I catch Antoine's eye and he smirks. "You know. Just to be sure that shoe is nice and still," he says.

"Yeah. Definitely."

"So, to clean your shoe, just take a fresh cloth, put some white vinegar on it, and wipe the spot until most of the discoloration goes away." Using firm, even strokes, Antoine caresses my boot, looking into my eyes the whole time. His swipes are long, drawn out, and I can practically feel his hand doing the same thing to my arm, my leg, my back.

I get lost in the hypnotic movement of his fingers guiding the cloth until I finally hear him say, "Like that?"

"Yeah, I like that."

Antoine laughs, loud, and it snaps me out of my hot-boy trance. "I said, would you like to try that?"

My face instantly bursts into flames and I'm hoping the mood lighting of these lit trellises hides it all. "Oh my god. Yes! Yes, I can try that!"

I grab the cloth from Antoine's hands and hide my face behind it, but I huff in a whiff of extrapotent vinegar and cough up a lung. Antoine pats my back and then—just like I imagined—starts running his hand up and down my spine. It sucks the air out of me, and suddenly I'm not coughing anymore, but I *am* being stroked by Antoine.

"Better?" he asks.

"Much."

I take a few swipes at my boot to try to get my mind off the fact that Antoine is touching me and doesn't seem intent on stopping anytime soon.

"That's enough," Antoine says, nodding toward my shoe. "Now we just have to let it dry. Little-known fact is suede can totally get wet. It's Pacific Northwest–proof: just wash it with water and vinegar, and you're good to go."

"Who knew?"

Antoine grins, then slides his hand over my shoulder, down my arm, and to my palm, where he absentmindedly traces the lines on my skin. I'd be shocked if my love line wasn't changing shape as we speak to spell *Antoine.*

"What do you think of my party?" He uses his free hand to grab a glass and take a gulp of wine. I've never seen anything sexier than the way his Adam's apple bobs up and down. My mouth goes dry, and I take a swig of my own. It slides down into my belly, warm and comforting, and I remember that this is my time to shine. I can't get so worked up over bulging-biceped-sexy-calloused-furniture-artiste Antoine that I forget how to function and ruin the moment before it even gets started.

"It's beautiful. Classy." I run my finger along the edge of the pine table, hoping Antoine wonders what it'd be like for me to run it along his body. "Did you make this?"

He nods. "It was the first solo project Dad let me do. It's good, right?"

"So good."

I break into another toothy smile as Antoine looks into my eyes. I know I'm blushing based on the way his gaze travels down to my cheeks, but it only makes him smirk more.

"You are so cute," he says. He takes my hand that's still absentmindedly stroking his wood. I mean, *the wood*, of the table, and laces his fingers through mine. He pulls me closer, gently, using just the right amount of pressure until our faces are only inches apart.

"Can I kiss you?" he asks.

This is really happening.

"Of course," I breathe.

In another heartbeat, he presses his lips against mine. He's firm, soft, not a second of tongue, which makes it almost that much more special. He's not trying to go too fast—just seeing where this moment can take us. I taste a bit of the sweet wine on his lips, and my heart flutters thinking about doing this for the rest of the semester. And hopefully longer if Antoine wants. This bet is won, baby!

"ANTOINE, this is fabulous!"

Antoine snaps back, drops my hand, and launches from the chair in point-two seconds. He flies over to the newcomer, at the far end of the table. It's Patrick Abadi, senior Gaybutante, gay, Pakistani American, climate change activist who Antoine is now holding hands with. Just seconds after holding mine. They laugh and sway into each other, gabbing back and forth until I hear Antoine echo to Patrick what he literally just said to me.

"You are so cute." Then he pulls him in and they kiss.

Same firmness, confidence, no tongue.

The *exact* same kiss he just gave me.

Suddenly, a plastic cup blocks my vision.

"Refills!" Sabrina sings.

"Perfect timing." I take the glass and down it in two huge gulps.

"Whoa, wait a minute. Slow down there, cowboy." *Cowboy?* Sabrina's own buzz must be kicking in. Even still, she has enough of her wits about her to be all protective, pointing at my empty cup. "We're pretty new to this. Don't go getting all wasted on me at our first real party." She waves her hands in front of my apparently distraught face. "What's happening here?"

I motion toward Antoine and Patrick, who've now let go, but Antoine has his arm draped all over Cliff, leaning his head against Cliff's shoulder, now rubbing *his* back.

Sabrina's eyes go wide, and even though she's tipsy, I can see everything click into place. "Oh nooooooo."

"He was giving me so much attention. But apparently, he does that for everybody."

Sabrina plops down into Antoine's empty seat, hard. She laughs with the impact, then waves her hand over her face, her smile turning into a drunk yet cute, thin-lipped straight line. "No, sorry. This is serious." She puts a consoling hand on my knee. "Babe, maybe Antoine is just a total flirt."

"He's never flirted with me before! We've known each other since kindergarten."

"Well, *you're* sort of having a romantic awakening this year. He could be too."

"But he was such a gentleman. He got all close and sweet and asked if it was okay to kiss. It was so intimate!"

Sabrina hoists her glass into the air and screams, "Consent for the win!"

The Gaybutantes all go wild at that, cheering and yelling, "CONSENT!" so loud that it echoes through the mountains like Mother Nature is wholeheartedly backing us up. As she should.

But healthy-relationship behavior aside, this night is not going as planned. I slap my hand over my eyes and moan. "Why am I such an idiot? Of course it wouldn't be that easy."

"Who hasn't got caught up in a hottie giving us some attention every now and then?" Sabrina says with a mischievous grin.

"Easy for you to say! You've got ladies knocking down your DM door, all while having the perfect girlfriend in real life!"

"It'll happen for you to, Ri. Trust me."

Music starts blaring through the field. Lexi Hasseldorf—white, trans, lesbian goth-rock goddess—has busted out her electric guitar.

Sabrina bends over and rips my other boot from my foot, then pulls me up. "Less worrying, more dancing!"

Excerpt from Episode 3—*Riley Weaver Needs a Date to the Gaybutante Ball*: "Falling for Flirts"

This whole time I thought the obstacles might just be guys who aren't into femmes. But the first Gaybutante Hopeful bash made me realize there's run-of-the-mill dating pitfalls I could easily fall into as well.

First and foremost: flirts.

And it wasn't until Forest Flirt was playing with my fingers, pulling me into him, pressing his lips against mine that I realized how badly my body is ready to start a relationship. I mean, it all felt right. I don't know if it's because I'm really committing to this bet with my whole being, or if trying to find my first boyfriend/escort coincidentally lined up with the time my body was like, Yeah, you're ready, lady. Either way, I can't let all my feelings get in the way of finding a guy who actually would want to take me to the Gaybutante Ball, not just kiss for ten seconds and call it a day.

This isn't to say that flirting or casually hooking up is wrong. No sex-shaming here on Riley Weaver for a single second. But it is to say that I don't want to scare anyone away from potentially seeing me as datable or escortable if word gets around that I'm just kissing everybody willy-nilly. This has to be a delicate balancing act of letting guys know that I want to be kissed, but that I need more too. Now I just have to figure out how to send those signals without coming across too clingy.

Putting yourself out there is so much harder than I thought. With my one and only hookup, it was just a look and then we were behind a tree. How do I, you know, make it clear I want to date?

Anybody have any tips? Send them to RileyWeaver NeedsADate@gmail.com.

In the meantime, just because he isn't looking for a relationship doesn't mean I can't still think about that kiss with Forest Flirt, right?

Because it was a really nice kiss.

Chapter 6

"If you weren't hosting this thing, I don't think we'd ever find a table," Nick says, edging his way between the packed two-tops, trying to clear enough space so that I don't knock anybody over with this pack full of recording equipment I'm lugging around. It's the monthly Mountain Pass Café Open Mic Night, and I thought I could use this event to up the podcast production in more ways than one.

First, I can record a little bit of the background noise and performances, giving a bit of an audio edge to the next *RWNADTTGB* episode. (Wow that's a lot of letters, isn't it?). Second, I asked Roz Bianchi if I could host it tonight, so I'd get face-to-face time with every performer, one of which I'd hopefully feel sparks with and could ask on a proper date. Roz was all about it, and thank god too, because we have a table right in front of the stage with a little handwritten name card resting on top with RILEY WEAVER across it in black Sharpie. Now I'll have an excellent view of any crooning cuties, and they'll be able to ask for me by name if they want to chat after the show.

Nick and I make quick work of setting up the microphone when Roz—white, midfifties with spiked shining gray hair—carries a tray full of her signature Mountain Pass Peppermint Lattes to the table next to us. It's like she has eyes in the back of her head because she's able to perfectly hand out each drink with different milks to their respective owners while looking directly at me.

"Head on back to the breakroom, Riley," she says in her gravelly voice. "The performers are ready and you can get their names and determine the lineup. These orders always stop when they start, so I need them up on that stage ASAP. Working that frother is making my arthritis act up again and these old bones need a break."

"On it, Roz!" I lean against Nick's shoulder. "Be right back! Save my spot!"

I hop up on the tiny six-by-six-foot stage, since I'm not convinced I'll be able to squeeze by any more tables without knocking them over. This place has completely filled up, more so than usual. Not an empty seat in the house, with people standing by all the available wall space. But when I glance back at my table, I see Nick's face clearly while he fiddles with some of the recording equipment. He's got that slight smile like he always does whenever he's content and happy, and he's rarely happier than when he's using any kind of tech. It's freaking adorable. And since I can see his face perfectly, I know that whoever's up onstage will see *me* perfectly too. If we had been even one row of tables back, the thickness of the crowd and their bulky coats could have blocked me from view. I'll be locking eyes with some hot performer, *for sure*. Now all I have to do is meet them.

I book it down the tiny brick hallway that leads to the restrooms and the breakroom. Framed posters from past Mountain Passers who've performed at Roz's café and gone on to superstardom (many of them Gaybutantes) line the wall, and I imagine all of them are belting out love songs leading me to this fateful moment. I grasp the scuffed bronze doorknob and know that as soon as I open this door, I'm going to meet the person who will be asking to be my Gaybutante Ball escort. I turn the handle, let the door swing open, and find . . .

A girl. With more people crammed into the room behind her, but it's so packed in this little breakroom that I can't even see the tiny folding table I know is back here. I used it when I interviewed Ransom Beckett—Mountain Pass Gaybutante class of 2015 and lead singer of the boy band Heart Murmur—when he came here for a locals-only private show. All I can really make out in the cramped space is the long dark hair of the girl in front of the doorway.

My heart drops. Not that I don't think girls are amazing, it's just . . . not what I'm going for romantically right now.

"Excuse me, everybody—hi!" I call over the girl's shoulder. "I'm Riley Weaver, and I'm going to be introducing all of you. I just want to get the lineup and make sure I'm pronouncing everybody's name right. If I could just get in here." I gently tap the girl to squeeze by. She turns around and my heart immediately kick-starts, beating a million miles a minute.

She's not a girl at all, but a very, very, *very* attractive boy, with light brown skin, dark eyes, and the most thick, gorgeous dark hair I've ever seen. A flare of shame swirls in my gut. Even though I count myself in the noncis brigade, I can still sometimes get caught up in the prison house of gender rules when seeing other people. I shouldn't be so quick to determine someone's gender before really knowing more about them, especially considering my whole podcast is about how one size of gender and attraction does not fit all.

I realize I'm staring when Gorgeous finally waves, causing his beautiful hair to swish back and forth, reaching so far down that it swings just above his butt. Which happens to look great in his jeans.

"Hey," he says. "Sorry, let me just try to . . ." I finally notice the guitar case that this hottie has propped up against his leg. He gingerly picks it up like it's the most precious jewel in the world, holds it high above his head so it doesn't knock into anybody or anything, and awkwardly shuffles along until he's pressed up against a metal rack full of reusable coffee cups. He knocks his shin against it, not enough to cause him pain, but enough to get a tower of sixteen-ounce cups to lean over and rest against his butt.

"I'd offer to help, but this room is packed so tight that I'm worried one wrong move will make me much closer to your derriere than either of us anticipated." *Derriere*? Seriously?

But Gorgeous laughs, his hair swaying side to side as his shoulders shake. "Yeah, I think we should at least save that for the second performance." He twerks his butt just so, and the cup tower rights itself. The move is simultaneously cute and sexy as hell, and now I seriously can't stop thinking about his ass. "I'm Daniel Stone. Last on that sign-up sheet." He nods toward the center of the room, where a few more musicians and poets get as far out of the way as they can so that I can see a clipboard with everybody's name on it.

I start to awkwardly edge through the crowd when I'm snatched back.

"Whoa, hang on!" Daniel has pulled me back into his gloriously firm chest. "You were going to crash into Ronda's cello, and I could see your life flash before my eyes. Not that we know each other. I just know it wouldn't have ended well for you."

He nods over to Ronda, who's about seven feet tall with extremely large biceps that could beat me into a pulp. She menacingly cracks her knuckles to boot.

"Nobody messes with my cello," she growls, then hands me the clipboard. "We've gotta get out of this room. Just announce us in the order we signed up."

"Right," I say. There's clearly no arguing with Ronda. I right myself off Daniel's chest and read the names out loud really quickly to make sure I'm getting all nine right. Then we file out of the room in order. The only problem is, Daniel is last in line, while I have to be up front announcing each new act. But maybe this could give me time to do some research. If I glom onto him too quickly, it might come across as desperate. If I give him space and wait until the second half of the acts to talk with him some more, I could find that perfect balance of mysterious yet available.

This time when I walk out onstage, the entire room goes quiet. All eyes are on me, and I get that thrill of tingles down my spine whenever I get to talk with a crowd. They say public speaking is the number one fear, but for me, public speaking is *life*.

"Hello, all you gorgeous people! Welcome to the Mountain Pass Café Open Mic Night." The room erupts in whistles and cheers. "For those of you who don't know me, I'm Riley Weaver, and I'll be introducing each act. We've got a great mix of poets, singers, and artists of all kinds. First up, it's the poetic stylings of Cherry Macrini."

I hop down to my table and plop next to Nick. "I think we've got a guy here that might be a potential escort."

"Mountain Passer?" Nick asks.

I shake my head. "I haven't seen him around. I've got to do some sleuthing." I position the recording equipment so it hides my phone while Cherry launches into her poem, "Recycled Heart."

"Here's the thing about recycled products.

They're always used.

Used, abused, confused, and bruised.

Here's the thing about my heart.

It's been misused, refused, recused, bambooz-led . . ."

It sounds like it's going to be a long one, which is perfect to find out more about Daniel. I look him up on socials and find out all the bullet points: Daniel Stone, junior at Snoqualmie High, about half an hour away, singer-songwriter, member of the Willapa tribe of the Chinook Indian Nation, and jackpot, he's gay. Most of his posts are videos of him singing, and I'd listen to every last one of them right now if it wasn't for the fact that Cherry's going on about how whoever misused her heart was obtrusive and elusive, seductive and reductive.

"That's him?" Nick whispers.

He takes my phone and scrolls through Daniel's posts, nodding like *Yeah, he seems great.* Then, "Look," he mouths, pointing to the back of the stage, but behind the recording equipment so nobody can see. I follow the direction of his finger to find Daniel peaking over the shoulder of the next performer.

And he's looking right at me.

The room bursts into applause, signaling the end of Cherry's poem.

"That's my cue," I say, and hop up onstage, a smile beaming across my face. Not because hosting duties require it, but because I've locked eyes with Daniel, who smiles back and adorably blushes before his eyes drift behind me.

I introduce the next act and the next and the next, all the while glancing at the hallway where Daniel waits, biding my time until it's the exact right moment to strike up a conversation. We exchange stupid smiles, a back-and-forth of giggles and blushes, until I finally make my move after giving the fifth act—a mime from Seattle—the stage. Instead of heading back to my seat, I inch my way down the hall, squeezing past Ronda's cello to sidle up next to Daniel.

"Halfway through," I say. "You getting nervous?"

Daniel gives this confident smirk that's inordinately sexy. "No way. Music is my life." He gently pats the guitar strapped to his back. "We've basically melded into one being by now."

I tap my boot against the cement floor. "That's how I feel about my shoes."

Daniel laughs, low so it doesn't carry down the hall into the café, and it's so intimate. Like we're sharing a secret together.

"They look great," he says, pointing at my toes. "I think I'd crash and burn anytime I tried to put on a pair of heels. I'm impressed."

This is absolutely perfect. He's already appreciating my femme fashions from the jump. It's the end of September now. If we start dating soon, we've still got over two months until the Gaybutante Ball. The timing is perfect for us to develop a solid relationship where even if we weren't official boyfriends, we'd have to be close enough that he'd want to escort me while I'm inducted as an official member of the GS. Then I'll have a cute boy, official GS status, and my ticket out of here when I graduate!

"Tha—"

"SHHHHHHHHHH!" Ronda whips around so quickly, it scares the shit out of me. I even squeal a bit. Daniel lets out the loudest laugh, but it thankfully coincides with the exact moment the audience cheers for our mime, whose Parisian accordion music has just ended and who is now waving and hamming it up.

"You'd be totally safe in a horror movie," Daniel says, just before I make my way up to introduce the next performer. "One shriek like that and the axe murderer would think you're way too adorable to kill. You might be the cutest scared person I've ever seen."

I can barely read the next act's name with my thoughts jumbled over Daniel calling me *cute*. But as I make my way back into the hallway, Ronda's glare makes it very clear I shouldn't say a single word until the open mic night is over. It's not so bad waiting through the next couple acts, though. Daniel keeps brushing up against me in this small hallway, and I swear he keeps giving me these nervous glances. It looks like he's working up the courage to ask me something, and I want to just tell him right then and there that *yes*, I'd love to go on a date with him. Because that's definitely what he's going to ask.

We finally get the chance to talk when Ronda goes onstage, leaving just me and Daniel waiting in the wings.

"So, I wanted to ask you—"

"I would love to—"

We both rush into our hushed conversation at the same time, making us laugh.

"Oh god, we've got to be quiet or else we're going to get the wrath of Ronda," I whisper.

Daniel shakes with silent chuckles. "That is a fight we will lose," he says.

"What were you going to ask me?"

Daniel steps closer so we're not even an inch apart. He must be able to feel my heart beating against my chest.

"I wanted to ask . . ." He hesitates, his perfectly minty breath warm against my face, but in a way that's not at all clammy or gross.

"Yes?"

His eyes dart out to the café, to my empty chair. "I was wondering about your friend? The one with the recording equipment and the green hair?"

"Nick?" I don't even whisper it, then slap my hand over my mouth.

"Sure, Nick. I haven't met him before," Daniel whispers. I want to tell him that only close friends call him

Nick—everyone else gets Nicholas. But apparently this is taking a lot of nerve for Daniel to ask because he barrels on. "Which is where you come in. Do you think you could introduce us after the show? He is *so* my type. He's got eccentric-nerd vibes going for him and yeah. I'd love to say hi."

A whole storm of mixed emotions rages inside me. I got my hopes up on Daniel *way too fast*. Another Mountain Pass outing that has failed to find me a guy means I'm three weeks into the Gaybutante season and haven't made any headway on this bet. But I can't very well try to convince Daniel that he should be interested in *me* over Nick. That's not how attraction works; you can't convince somebody that they're not feeling what they're definitely feeling. And that would make me a terrible best friend. Not to mention this is exactly what Nick asked for: me to keep a lookout for any partners who would be great for him. There's no bigger clue than someone telling you, "Hey, I'm into your friend Nick." This is perfect to get Nick's relationship ball rolling again.

I only kind of slightly wish that it was my relationship ball first.

"No, yeah, that's great," I say, my voice inordinately high, but I'm trying to hide my disappointment here. "Of course. I'd be happy to."

"Great!" Daniel beams, but eventually it wavers. "Um, I think it's my time to go up."

I finally tune in to reality to hear confused chatter as the audience wonders what the lull's about.

"Oh crap!" I jump on stage, my boots landing on the platform way too hard, a clumsy clunk accompanying my nervous laughter. "Sorry about that, folks. Last but not least, please put your hands together for Daniel Stone!"

I take my seat as the crowd completely loses it. That must be why the café is so packed tonight. Daniel did post about this performance to his pretty impressive 10.3 thousand followers, so all these folks must've come to hear him sing. But, despite the adoring fans—one of whom is a white guy with tears in his eyes and platinum-blond hair wearing a *Get Stoned* T-shirt with Daniel's face on it— Daniel can't take his eyes off Nick.

Nick notices and that small smile is back. I know he's blushing because he can't stop ducking behind the recording equipment and trying to nonchalantly wipe the warmth from his face. I have to admit, it's really cute, and even if I'm nowhere near finding a date for the Gaybutante Ball, I've got to be happy for him.

"What's going on?" Nick whispers after the seventeenth eye catch.

"He wants to ask you out," I say.

"Wait. What?" His smile falters. "What about you?"

"What about me?" I say, leaning my head against Nick's shoulder. "This one's not about Riley. Daniel straight up told me he's *super* into you."

Nick's eyes wander back onstage. "Really?"

Daniel sings his last note, an ethereal *Me and youuuuuu* in which he stares directly at Nick. It's exactly the scenario I pictured for myself. But if I can't have it, at least somebody I love is getting all the attention.

"Really," I say.

Ten seconds later, I'm introducing my best friend (as *Nicholas*) to my latest failed date, but the way they keep giving awkward smiles and laughs at each other keeps the jealousy at bay. I help Roz clean up while they get to talking and the crowd files out. The longer they talk, the more confident they seem, their laughs louder, Daniel nervously fiddling with a strand of hair that Nick can't stop giving puppy dog eyes at. It's genuinely sweet, and most of those feelings of bitterness at the universe for not making this night work out the way I planned fade. Who knows? Maybe Daniel has a musician friend he can introduce me to, and Nick and I will be double-dating. Plot twist!

As Nick and Daniel get deeper into their convo, I've got to find something to do so I'm not just the friend twiddling their thumbs on the sidelines. Instinctively, I swipe open my phone, and the algorithm puts Sabrina's posts front and center (as it should). All that time she puts in at the clinic has really paid off in terms of content. In addition to the bobcat and injured-hawk videos, there's one of her bottle-feeding a baby deer, one demonstrating what to do in case you find a fallen chick out of its nest, and another of her giving a bath to an adorable stray dog that keeps shaking and soaking her in suds. In each video, she's wearing a look either painted by me or created while I coached her through FaceTime.

She has thousands of views on each, so many likes, and dozens of comments from her adoring fans telling her how beautiful she is, how helpful her videos are, how she is the dream girl for so many ladies out there.

All those comments are 100 percent correct, and it's exactly what we always hoped for: totally killing our Gaybutante season. Except, only one of us is doing the killing.

And it's definitely not me.

Excerpt from Episode 4—*Riley Weaver Needs a Date to the Gaybutante Ball*: "Single on the Sidelines"

That bitterness that started to fade? It solidly came roaring back.

It's not that I'm not happy for my friends. I know how important being in a relationship is to Producer, and I really am glad that the escapades for this podcast brought us into the path of a guy who might be right for him. And Killer Cat Lady, she really deserves all this attention.

But, can't I get a little love too? The Mountain Pass Gay Teen Bird Watchers was another bust with no love in the air. Well, at least, not for me. The birds flitting through the trees got a lot of love from their fans, but nothing for Riley.

For my friends, however, that's a different story. It's like, I'm the one broadcasting to the universe that I'd like some love to float my way, while my friends are just doing their own thing and WHAM! Here's another lady for you who's going to profess her undying love in your DMs. BOOM! Here's a hot singer who is going to breeze right over all my signals and land right on my bestie with his head buried in a laptop.

It's not that I was already in love with Sexy Singer or Forest Flirt or Pickle Hottie. It would be all kinds of hard-core levels of creep if I fell for them in one conversation. It's about finding love when I least expect it. Somehow, that seems to be happening to all the people around me while I just have to sit back and watch from the sidelines.

Which made my brain sink even further into this rabbit hole. Have I been on the sidelines all along and just didn't realize it? As in, is The Jock right and no guy wants to date me because they do see me as something other than gay, as someone they could never be interested in because I'm too femme? All along I thought I never really found anybody interested in me because I wasn't interested in them and wasn't quite ready for romance in general. But maybe I've had it all wrong. Maybe nobody's ever wanted me from the jump, you know?

All this time, I'd watch other people date, even my own best friends, and be completely happy for them. I wanted them to find love but didn't need it for myself. I've never really felt like I was lacking something.

Until now.

Chapter 7

"You know that's not true, right?" Nick says it suddenly as we walk through Main Street, on our way for coffee at the café like we do every Sunday morning. He says it fast, out of the blue, like he's been having this whole conversation in his head that I haven't been a part of.

"What isn't?"

I open the door and Sabrina waves us down from our usual table, tucked into Cassidy's side. Cassidy, however, doesn't look up. She has her right arm draped over Sabrina, but she's got her phone in her left hand, and she's staring at it with the deepest scowl on her face.

"The part where you're too femme." Nick goes on like he hasn't noticed how royally pissed Cassidy looks, which is weird because Nick notices everything. "You have so much going for you. They're the things people see when they first look at you: your fashion sense, your epic makeup looks, your perfect hair. But then there are the internal qualities—the most important qualities—that I think your femininity makes shine: you listen to people, you have a really open heart, you'll let people literally cry on your shoulder if they need it. Someone would kill to be with you."

"I appreciate you having my back on this, Nick, but name one person who's ever tried to date me." Nick opens his mouth, but I jump in with, "And Phil doesn't count."

Nick's mouth snaps shut.

"See? Nobody." Cassidy doesn't look up when we sit at the table. Weirdly, Sabrina doesn't seem to catch her girl-friend's mood either. Instead, she just slides our drinks across—an Americano with cinnamon powder for Nick, an oat milk hazelnut latte for me.

"You're not going to believe this," Sabrina says, her words rushed and jumbling together with excitement. "Lonny says I'm officially the most-followed new Gaybutante. Of any of the Hopefuls in *any* of the cities! Over artists and singers and actors and activists. Not that I don't want them to have success, but—" She slaps her hands on the table and I have to catch my cup before it tips over. "This plan is working! Vet science is sexy again!" She twirls her phone to show us how her following is nearing six digits.

Personally, I haven't been keeping up with social media. After the episode featuring my failure with Antoine, the comments of people telling me I'd eventually find a date were making me feel worse. I decided to use one of those timed-posts apps to throw up new content, like when another podcast episode comes out or I want to show off a new look I put together. Besides, people's comments are bound to turn soon. I don't know that my fragile heart can take any negative feedback right now when I've got enough doubt swirling in my head already. Nick's kept me posted that our unique listener count is nearing the five-digit territory, which seems wild, but who knows if any of them want to tear me down.

But I don't need to mention any of this to Sabrina and take away from this moment. We should be celebrating. I expect her go-to cheerleader, Cassidy, to lead the bulk of it because, like, that's her job as girlfriend. And maybe because all this Sabrina success is stinging just a little.

Cassidy, however, hasn't looked up from her phone once.

"Hey, lady." I gently tap the table with my cup in front of Cassidy. "What's wrong?"

She finally meets my eyes. There's no more scowl there. There are tears.

"Cassidy?"

Sabrina glances up at the worry in my voice, and her eyes instantly go wide when she takes in her girlfriend. "Babe!" She flings her phone and it clatters to the floor, but Sabrina couldn't care less. She wraps her arms around Cassidy and pulls her head into her chest.

"What's wrong?"

"Mm dowrkk mmm abroo."

"Uh, Rina?" Nick says. "I think you're smothering her in your boobs."

The second Sabrina lifts Cassidy, Cassidy wails, "I'm so mad at you!"

"At me?" Sabrina looks like she's been slapped. "What did I do?"

"This!" Cassidy holds up her phone as if that explains everything.

"She . . . called you?" I try.

Nick puts his hand over mine. "That's not it. She's upset about all the comments."

He doesn't say it with blame at all. It's just a statement of fact.

Cassidy points at Nick and nods like a bobblehead. "Exactly! Someone else sees my point."

Sabrina's taking a while to catch up. She looks back and forth between Nick and Cassidy before finally saying, "Wait. You're mad at *me* that people like my videos?"

"Like your videos?" Cassidy lurches from the table to grab Sabrina's phone and unlocks it. She opens up her girlfriend's social media and points out all the girls who've slid into her DMs. "This is so much more than liking videos. They're going out of their way to message you, and you haven't deleted a single one!"

A flare of anger bursts in my gut toward Cassidy. She's acting like Sabrina's kept this all a secret, but Sabrina's never held anything back from her in their entire relationship. Cassidy knows the code to Sabrina's phone, for crying out loud.

"Sabrina is the most trustworthy person you know!" I can't keep my bestie defense instincts from kicking in.

"I'm not saying she's not trustworthy, I'm saying—"

"Do you think I asked for this?" Sabrina snaps. Although, it's really more of a yell. It's the first time I've heard her get like this. Even in her past breakups, when she had a right to be mad, she sort of had a *life goes on* mentality. None of us are used to Sabrina getting mad. Anxious, sure. Sad, yes. But so mad she'd snap? Never. Nick and I share a nervous glance. We've got to be able to provide solid bestie backup if this goes off the rails.

"A-asked for what?" Even Cassidy is so caught off guard that she stutters.

"Asked for all these girls messaging me, trying to date me, mentioning my *kitty*?" Sabrina's voice is a frantic whisper now as eyes in the café focus on our table.

"No, of course not," Cassidy whispers back. But she isn't frantic. She's quiet like she's hurt. But Sabrina hasn't *done* anything. "That's not what I'm saying."

"Then what are you saying?" I snip.

"I'm saying you like it, Sabrina!" Cassidy's tears start flowing right after she says it, and now I really feel guilty for being such a jerk. Because Cassidy's not wrong entirely. Sabrina *does* like it, but I know she wouldn't ever act on it. "I'm saying it makes me nervous how many girls are falling for you. What's to stop you from falling for them back? What's to stop you from finding someone better?"

That sucks the air from our table. She says it with so much sincerity and genuine worry that my anger melts away. And from the tears silently slipping down Rina's cheeks, I know hers has too.

"Oh, babe!" She pulls her girlfriend in again, the two of them crying into each other's shoulders. "I didn't know. You've been so supportive about everything; I didn't see that this bothered you."

"I didn't want to be a wet blanket and ruin your season," Cassidy says. "I know you've dreamed about this for a long time. I wanted to be there for you."

As if on cue, an alarm on Cassidy's phone goes off. She silences it and says, "That's your signal to head to your next Gaybutante event. I didn't want you to be late in case you three got caught up in your conversation. Like you always do."

God, she really is the most supportive girlfriend ever.

Sabrina kisses her over and over and over. I peek at Nick, but this time his small smile doesn't falter. With Daniel in the picture, maybe the girls' constant PDA doesn't affect him so much anymore. But now I'm starting to feel the sting that Nick felt before. Not that I don't want Cassidy and Sabrina to be affectionate—more that I want someone to be affectionate with me.

"You're not a wet blanket at all," Sabrina says. "You want me to delete these messages? I'm on it." She swipes her phone open and starts hammering on the screen, knocking out DM after DM.

Cassidy laughs, a bit of snot landing on her upper lip. "You don't have to do it right this second."

"No, I don't ever want you to feel like this again," Sabrina says, keeping at it until Cassidy softly lowers Sabrina's phone so they can stare all lovey-dovey into each other's eyes.

"You should go," Cassidy says. "You can't be late for the party. Sorry I blew up at you."

Sabrina gives her a long kiss before finally pulling away to say, "You have nothing to be sorry for. I'm sorry I went off on you."

That bit of me that felt the defensive flare wants to say *Uh, this isn't your fault, Rina. Cassidy shouldn't blow up like that*, but I think that would derail the moment.

Instead, I try to lighten the mood and say, "All that time around wild animals was bound to make her a little feral."

Sabrina curls her fingers and swipes at the air. "Rawr."

"I have an idea," Nick says, and of course he does. He always knows how to make an actionable plan. "We've gotten a little caught up in our life goals. Why don't we make some time to all hang out?"

Nick's an angel for not pointing out that said *goals* revolve around the Society, but if we dance around that point, we might end up here again. So I add, "With the one rule that we won't bring up the Gaybutantes." I lock eyes with Cassidy. "We promise. How about Wednesday?"

Nick frowns. "Um, I can't. Sorry. Date with Daniel."

"Ah!" Sabrina hops in her seat and bashes her knee against the table. "Shit! It's happening!" Even through her teeth gritted in pain, you can tell she's pumped.

Nick shifts around awkwardly. "It's just a first date."

"But it's your first date since, like, your heart was broken!" Sabrina says.

"Ouch," Nick says, a little defensively.

"No, no, I just mean this is good. This is progress!"

"You know we expect a full report, and you can't leave out any details," I add, pushing past the tug at my heart to play the part of Supportive Best Friend and not Increasingly Jealous Asshole. "The gritty kind. How he smells, if there's trash in his car, all of it."

Nick rolls his eyes. "I know, I know. But let's move on. How about Thursday?"

Sabrina shakes her head. "Shift at the clinic and then Cassidy has a game on Friday in Bellingham. But then there's Homecoming Saturday!"

"We were always going to go to that together," I say.

Sabrina glares. "That doesn't make it any less of a hangout."

I throw my hands up defensively. "I was just saying. So we'll start solidly hanging out more at Homecoming and go from there. No more blowups, right?"

Everyone knows that this is directed at Cassidy without me having to say it. She at least gives a little *my bad* blush and says, "No more blowups."

Nick puts his hand on the table, palm up, fingers beckoning. I put mine in his, and Sabrina throws hers on mine. I nudge Cassidy with my heel. "Get in here, lady."

Cassidy puts her hand on top, and together we breathe in for four, out for five.

But as we exhale, I see the smile on Cassidy's face falter. I don't think we've heard the end of this.

The shoreline of Peak Lake has been completely transformed. Five tables seating five have been dotted along it, and each is done up in a completely macabre tea setting. Black teapots with green sludge dripping down their sides, silverware crafted to look like it's made of bones, and tea sandwiches and petit fours shaped like eyeballs and fingers and poisonous frogs.

"Welcome to the MortaliTea Party!" Malachi Schultes—Black, bi, baker extraordinaire (that's a lot of alliteration)—shouts to the crowd when we're all seated. "We've been working so hard to get our pillars done that we look like death, so I figure we might as well eat like it too. Major thanks to my mentor and soon-to-be fellow Gaybutante, Lexi, for the inspiration." Goth-tastic Lexi doesn't crack a smile, but her cheeks do get a bit pink with the attention. "Now dig in, and don't worry. Despite appearances, nothing you see before you will bite back."

Everyone laughs except for me. Because my heart has stopped.

"Shit, Sabrina. Mentors!" I say under my breath. "I haven't thought about that at all." I whip out my Gaybutante journal, which I always keep in my bag just in case inspiration strikes. I've been so focused on my podcast that I haven't even given the other pillars a thought. Fortunately, I already know what I'm going to do for Hosting—I just have to wait for Dad to give me the best day I can use his zip-lining course. My pages for Mentorship and Service, however, are totally blank. "What am I going to do?"

I was hoping for that to be more of an internal struggle, but of course my overly dramatic ass had to moan that loudly. Cliff and Lonny, sitting across from us, whip around.

"Trouble on the Hopeful front?" Lonny asks, taking in my journal splayed open to blank pages.

"Listen, you're not even a month into this thing," Cliff says. "Don't stress."

"Have you met us?" Sabrina asks. "All we do is stress."

"Mentees are going to be easy to find," Cliff says. "I mean, it's Mountain Pass. It's so gay. Half of you Hopefuls were our mentees last year."

I clear my throat awkwardly. I wasn't one of them, and Sabrina wasn't either. She didn't really mind because she was off being mentored by her parents at the clinic while I . . . I was kind of bothered by it.

Lonny doesn't skip a beat, her eyes meeting mine sympathetically. "You already seemed to have everything worked out. Your femme fierceness, your confidence in your radio show, your ability to never stutter while interviewing student council candidates." Wow, Lonny is the world's greatest empath because she sure knows how to boost my confidence right back up. "Your name was definitely thrown around as a potential mentee, but we all agreed you had your shit together. And you were too busy Doctor Dolittle-ing, Sabrina."

Rina shrugs. "Fair."

Lonny grabs an eyeball from the blood-decorated three-tier cake tray in front of her and pops it into her mouth. "Mmm, red velvet. Anyway," she goes on, mouth full, "you two have already smashed your first pillars, so don't freak out. Sabrina, your Service is *taking over*. And Riley, the *chaos* of that podcast. Those comments! Truly chaotic."

I take a gulp of tea from my skull cup. "Chaotic. Right."

Cliff cocks his head to the side, the world's hottest puppy. "Wait, you haven't seen?"

Nothing gets past these two. I guess membership in the Gaybutantes gives you queer spidey senses.

"I haven't looked in a while," I admit. "I can get kind of a one-track mind." I motion to the empty pillar pages in front of me. "As you can tell. I've been so focused on finding a man that everything else kind of fell off the face of the earth."

"It's about damn time somebody else has chaos in their comments for once," Sabrina says, then her eyes light up.

"Hey! Does that mean I can count my videos as the Chaos pillar too?"

Lonny and Cliff share a look, then nod together, perfectly in sync. "Approved!" they say. I guess mannerisms also kind of rub off on each other when you're Gaybutantes.

Sabrina beams while my stomach churns. She's officially halfway done with her pillars while I guess I've done one? I might as well see for myself.

I pull up my TikTok and it has officially gone over ten thousand followers. I want to celebrate how that's a good start toward proving to Mom I can make it outside Mountain Pass, but I'm too nervous to see what these new followers have to say. I suck in a fortifying breath before opening the video about my latest episode and scrolling through the comments. The first are great:

You'll find a date, Riley, don't worry.

You are so cute! I can't believe you haven't been scooped up

Then there's what I expected:

#TeamJock

Shut up and die, creep

Stop saying youre gay and just admit it! You want to be a woman!

And then there are the comments that completely take my breath away:

You're that self-hating that you have to make this douchebag think his opinion matters?

U R upholding cis supremacy by doing this!

Femmes don't need to prove themselves! We don't need you making it seem like we do!

I jolt up from the table so hard that my tea spills. But I don't care. My heart is racing too fast. I have to get out of here.

"Riley!" Sabrina follows after me. "Where are you going?"

"I, um. I think my oat milk this morning was spoiled or something."

It's an insult to Roz and the Mountain Pass Café legacy. We all know she would never serve spoiled milk. But everyone's appetite is going to be spoiled if I don't leave because I am for sure going to vomit.

I make it to the parking lot and steady myself against the nearest car, chest heaving, trying to get in as much of the mountain air as I can to settle my stomach.

"Riley!"

It's not Sabrina. It's not Lonny. It's the last person I want to see.

Skylar. The Jock in the flesh.

He hops out of his truck, the same one I leaned on without really looking. Adam gets out of the passenger's side, I guess hitching a ride and showing up to Malachi's hosting gig late.

"Just the *gal* I was looking for!" The way Skylar says it is *not* like he's appreciating my femininity. He's saying it to make fun of me.

"What do you want?"

He pops up on the balls of his feet like an excited little kid.

"I just wanted to thank you for making this the easiest bet ever," he says. "Making a podcast about our whole bet so that anybody who listens to it *can't* be your escort? It's too good. I'm sending it out to everybody I know because it's *such* a great listen. Already, like, twenty single gay friends of mine have started tuning in."

My stomach is this close to pouring out its contents, but I can't let Skylar see me sweat.

"That's surprising," I say.

"What is?" Maybe Malachi's macabre decor is getting to me, but I swear Skylar's *s* comes out like the evil hiss of a snake. A speck of spit lands on my face.

I flick it from my cheek and say, "That you'd even have two friends, let alone twenty. Glad to hear you're such a fan."

And with that, I stomp off, ducking behind a dumpster, where I finally let loose everything that's been dying to come out.

Excerpt from Episode 5—*Riley Weaver Needs a Date to the Gaybutante Ball:* "Shooting Myself in the Femme Foot"

That's when it hit me like a one-two punch:

My podcast could be working against me in more ways than one.

This is our fifth episode. We have a total of 15,657—

15,658 as of four seconds ago.

Thanks, Producer. 15,658 unique listeners, and if any of them are in the Pacific Northwest and gay (which, not to assume, but I'm guessing most of you are queer since so many of you found me through Gaybutante posts), that means they can't be considered as potential escorts. Why? Because they will know about the bet between me and The Jock. A key condition is that they don't give me a pity date, or a helping hand, so to speak. The journey to an escort needs to be entirely organic and unforced by the bet in any way whatsoever. So, I've got to figure out if potential dates have listened to the podcast already, but do it in a way that won't pique their interest so that if we do start dating, they don't listen and learn about the bet they weren't supposed to know about to begin with.

Gah, this is confusing! One little hint to a guy I like could ruin the whole thing. It's like the butterfly effect but very gay. Although something called the butterfly effect already sounds pretty gay, doesn't it?

All jokes aside, this shit is serious. Even more serious to me? That some of you think I'm doing the exact opposite of helping out gender nonconforming folks by doing this podcast. This all started with me trying to prove a cis guy wrong, but in doing that am I saying that cis opinions matter the most? I definitely don't think that, and I don't want it to come across that I do. The whole point of this podcast is to show femme people and the entire world that there is no type of person who categorically will not date us. Nobody gets to predetermine our love lives, and that's what I'm setting out to prove.

I'm failing at it so far, but thankfully, Producer says I got some great advice in a recent email. P?

Hey, everybody. So, this message comes from Meet-CuteMama206 and they write: "Riley! I love hearing about your dates and I'm rooting for you to win the bet. Toxic masculinity can suck it! But may I offer you some friendly, albeit unsolicited, advice? In your last episode, you said your dates don't hinge on the person you're dating specifically. You're just trying to

find one person there is a brief connection with and go from there, but it could be any person. Respectfully, I think that's the problem. You don't care who clicks with you, just that there's a click. But then, that doesn't make your potential suitor feel very special, does it? Why would a guy want to keep dating when they don't feel like The One, but just anyone? Said with so much love and all the positive vibes! Xo, MeetCuteMama206."

Wow, coming in hot with the truth. But, MeetCuteMama, I think you're right. I needed a little bit of tough love. I've been so bent on finding any guy that will look at me with just the slightest bit of interest that I'm not sending any signals about what makes them special and why I'm interested. I'm starting to think that this connection can't be triggered in one small accidental meetup. It's gotten me nowhere the better part of the past month, and time is slipping.

So, it's time for Act Two of this escort hunt. I need to take the next few weeks to actually connect with a person before we decide to take any steps into romance. And make sure in all that time that the topic of this podcast or my bet never comes up.

But if this next step doesn't work? I'll have really shot myself in the foot. The Gaybutante Ball will be here before you know it.

Chapter 8

"**W**hy aren't you dressed yet, Riley? We're going to be late!"

Sabrina grabs a beautifully curled lock (that I styled for her) and gives it a pull.

"Okay, first off, don't mess up all my hard work." I get up from my vanity and gently pull Sabrina's hand from her hair. "Second, it's called a jumpsuit. All I have to do is step inside and zip up. We're going to be fine. Besides, we do *not* want to be the first people to show up to Homecoming. That's for, like, freshmen. Let's play it cool. Fashionably late."

"There's no such thing," Sabrina says. "Late is late."

"This isn't about being late at all, is it?" Nick chimes in from behind his phone where he's watching BTS footage of *Jurassic Park*. "It's about making sure Cassidy feels like you only have eyes for her, and your first opportunity to go to a party with her in weeks since it's not Gaybutante-hosted."

"Okay, wow, yes, that's exactly what this is about," Sabrina says. She turns to me, her fingers wandering back up to her hair. "Why can't you be more like Nick? He at least tries to calm me down while you are just—"

"Making you look perfect so that you can take all the pictures you want and post them everywhere for the world to remember you do, in fact, have a girlfriend and are unavailable to all those thirsty DMs?" I say with an overly put-on grin. I do not need her taking out her relationship worries on me right now.

Fortunately, Sabrina takes the hint. "Yes, you're right." She takes a deep breath—four in, five out—before giving me apologetic eyes. "My bad."

"I know it's a lot. Don't worry about it." Although, to be honest, I'm at my boiling point of hearing about Sabrina's relationship and all the woe is me, I'm-getting-too-many-people-thinking-I'm-hot drama. I can't get *one* person to think that and it's freaking me the fuck out.

At least Nick didn't ditch me to go to the dance with Daniel. He's going with me this year because he always has, even letting me be the "temporary third, but non-sexually" when he went with Grayson last year. Sabrina's always had a girlfriend at Homecoming, and she gets so tied up in experiencing dances with her partner that she has no time to remember the rest of her friends. I definitely don't blame her or anything—about half the school treats these high school milestones as romantic moments, and the rest of us just want to party with our friends. Sabrina 100 percent falls into the former, while Nick and I have always been the latter, and I couldn't be more thankful to Nick because of that.

Ding-dong.

"That's Cassidy!" Sabrina screams. "Be right back!" Her steps bang all the way through the house as she bolts out of my room and heads down the stairs.

I walk over to the bed and plop next to Nick, but my silk lilac pajamas are so slick that I nearly slide off.

"Oh shit!" I squeal, and latch onto Nick so I don't topple down and face-plant. If I smear my makeup on the rug and have to start over, Sabrina will absolutely kill me.

Nick hardly even moves, nonchalantly clicking to a new video like I didn't just leave nail marks in his skin from grabbing him so hard.

"You all right?" he asks.

"Yeah." I gingerly settle myself next to Nick. "Just trying to avoid death by Rina."

Nick nods once and turns the volume up on his phone. My favorite part about our friendship is that our silences are never uncomfortable. That's the mark of a true best friend: that you can be totally okay not saying anything. With his attention on his phone, I've got a moment to give him a once-over. He's in a black suit, a white V-neck underneath that's hugging him in all the right places, and his hair dyed bright red. He's repping our school's black, red, and white colors expertly, but what I'm noticing most is how perfectly the suit fits him. He's usually just a jeans-and-a-T-shirt kind of guy, but dressed up like this? He looks *good*. Really good. I mean, he's always worn a suit at Homecoming before, but he didn't fill it out quite like he does this year. And I feel bad that he has to waste all this good-lookingness on me.

"You know you could have brought Daniel, right?" I say it even though in my heart of hearts it would have stung to see both of my besties distracted by their dates. But sometimes you have to lie for the greater good, or to talk yourself out of your totally unreasonable jealousy. "I'm okay being the temporary third. I've done it before."

Nick gets that small smile and sets his phone down. "I know. It's just kind of new. I thought maybe asking him to Homecoming so fast would be laying it on a little thick. We've only been on two dates."

"Two! When was the second?" He's being unusually secretive about this guy. Normally we tell each other everything. Even if Nick isn't as verbose or, like, erratically excitable as Sabrina and me, he'd still tell us if he went out with somebody.

"Last night," he says. "I took Daniel to a *Star Trek* marathon at the theater."

Movie marathons at the theater? That's what we usually do. It's when Nick gets the most adorably little-kid excited, not able to stop himself from speculating how each shot was put together, or what kind of special effects or man power and budget it took to make. I have a hard time sitting through movies myself, more used to the span of YouTube makeup tutorials. But Nick's chattiness always makes it worth it. I love seeing how his face lights up when he's talking about something he's truly passionate about. I'm bummed that I missed out on that.

But then again, this isn't about me. Nick's on a mission to be in a relationship again, and I've got to support that.

"Ooh yes, perfect make-out opportunity. Did you guys smooch the whole time? Did his kisses take you to a galaxy far, far away?"

"That's *Star Wars*, not *Star Trek*."

"The question still stands. There was tongue, wasn't there?"

Nick picks his phone back up and wipes at his face.

"I'll take that as a *yes*," I say.

"There may have been some kissing."

"Jesus, Nick. You sound like it was a job interview."

He shrugs just as Sabrina and Cassidy burst through the door. They go together perfectly. Sabrina is in this wine-red dress, her hair bouncing around her shoulders in luscious curls. Cassidy's got on a suit in matching red, a sprig of baby's breath behind her ear, and her dark brown pixie cut dusted with glitter.

"I don't care that we weren't on the court, I formally declare you Queen and Queen of Homecoming!" I say.

Cassidy lunges for the bed and throws her arms over me and Nick. I fall backward, but Cassidy's got me pinned under her body weight, so I don't worry about sliding off.

"I'm so happy we're all here together!" she says. "It's nice to have a second of normalcy and not all, Gaybutante this and Gaybutante that."

"No! No!" Sabrina jumps into the pile of mushiness happening on the bed. "No talking about that for the entire night. We had a deal, remember?" She pulls Cassidy into her and gives her a giant kiss, right on top of me and Nick. "This night is all about you, babe."

"Okay, hi. I don't need to be present for any baby making," I say.

Sabrina shoves my shoulder (in a good way) while Cassidy says, "I don't think it works like that."

"Go change already so we can get out of here." Sabrina flings me into my bathroom, where my red (Mountain Passers really commit to school spirit) long-sleeved jumpsuit is waiting. It's got shoulder pads for days, has the perfectly placed cutouts right over my ribs, is sequined from top to bottom, and has the cutest gold belt. Sealing the deal are designer black boots that I basically had to beg my mom to let me spend my savings on. But they're totally worth it.

"Hey, somebody zip me up, will you?"

The door creaks open and Nick pokes his head inside with his hand placed over his eyes. "Everybody decent?"

"Come on, you've seen me in way worse stages of undress than this." And really, he has. Wardrobe malfunctions were a total thing when I first started dressing femme, and Nick has basically seen me in as little as a hand around my nethers while we figured out how to sew, tape, and tuck until things were just right. "But you will see my back. Scandalous!"

Nick pulls his hand away when I turn around. He tenderly touches my shoulder, then slides the gold zipper until it's at the nape of my neck. I look at him in the mirror; his gaze is locked on the bit of exposed skin on my sides.

"If you get cold, you can wear my jacket," he says.

I pull him in for a one-armed hug. "Aww, aren't you the gentleman? And look at that," I say, checking us out in the mirror. "Your hair perfectly matches my jumpsuit."

Nick's smile makes his round cheeks stand out. If I didn't get to see his face full of nerding-out joy at the *Star Trek* marathon, at least I can see it now. "Took you long enough to notice. You know I take our outfits seriously."

Sabrina hops behind us. "Okay, let's go already!"

She marches out of the room, pulling Cassidy behind her. But if she thinks that's all it's going to take to get us out of here, she's forgotten about my parents.

"Girls!" Dad shouts from the kitchen. "You two look famished! How about trying some of these ribs?"

"I don't think your dad gets what meals are best for formal attire." Mom steps into the room, phone in hand, but I don't need Sabrina to kill me for taking more time so my parents can grab pictures.

"Mom, I love you, but we'll take a ton of pics at the dance, I swear. Sabrina's on the verge of sending a rabid coyote after me, and I want to be able to make it to next year's Homecoming."

Mom's forehead crinkles, following my gaze to her phone. "Oh? This? No, I had this out because I was listening to something. Something I had no idea about."

She gives me a very pointed look like *You're in deep shit.* This is clearly about the podcast.

"Could you give us a second, Nicholas?" she asks.

Yep. That confirms it. Mom never asks my friends to leave unless she wants to ream me out for something, like that time I accidentally let her favorite eye shadow fall to the floor after using it. It wouldn't have been a big deal, but it was discontinued, and let's just say Shiloh Weaver does not like it when people mess with her makeup. I get it from her.

But honestly, how could she be so pissed about a podcast?

Then everything from eighth grade when she ran for mayor comes back to me. Her campaign head, Marjorie Tibbert, made it *very clear* that any sort of public media needed to be run through her first, to make sure that the whole Weaver clan was sending the right message to the world at large. And that rule was extended when she won. My femmeness never was an issue; I got blanket approval on posting anything about my looks, and the family always knew I'd be going for the Gaybutantes. But I guess this podcast goes beyond makeup and gay camaraderie; it's getting personal.

Nick gives me a sympathetic look before saying, "Sure thing, Madame Mayor," and booking it out the door.

As soon as we're alone, Mom waves her phone. "Anything you want to tell me?"

"I started a podcast!" I say it with loads of enthusiasm so Mom doesn't make a bigger deal about this than she already is.

"And when were you going to tell me?"

"I just got so caught up in it that I kind of forgot. I swear it's not a big deal."

"Not a big deal?!" Mom looms over me, which should be impossible since I'm an inch taller than her in my heels. She's got that look on her face that would make her political opponents weak in the knees, even though that's not needed since this is Mountain Pass and Mom's only opponent is now vice mayor and her best friend. But this is Mom's *No Bullshit* face, and I get ready for her to chew me out for not getting this approved beforehand, for getting too personal about dating and dick talk and what it's like to not want to live by the standards society has placed on genitals. God, how many times have I said *genitals* on my show?

But right as I think she's about to pop off, that fearsome glare fades and she's all doe-eyed and tearing up. "Honey, of course this is a big deal. That shitty boy is making you have to prove your whole identity, and I'm worried about you. Worried fucking sick. Who cares what he thinks?"

"You're not mad?"

"Mad? Why would I be mad? You've done nothing wrong. It's that guy's femmephobic, transphobic, toxic masculinity that I'm mad at!"

"So, I can keep doing the podcast?"

That one makes her pause. "Why would you? This can all stop right now. You don't have to hinge your Gaybutante status on that stupid bet. You don't have to prove yourself to anyone."

"That's just it, Mom. I do. Remember when there was that push to bring all those fast-food chains to Mountain Pass, and you ran for mayor just so you could stop it?"

Mom nods. "Those golden arches are an architectural eyesore."

"Well, you could have done nothing, and life would have gone on just fine, but the town would have been a little worse off in your opinion, right?"

"I don't see how not wanting this town to become McMountain Pass correlates."

"The world will be worse off if I let Skylar's awful, ignorant opinions go unchallenged. Will my life go on? Sure. But I'll always want to kick myself for not doing anything to stand up for my femmeness, my gayness, and all the folks who are like me."

Mom takes me in from head to toe. She's always loved my fashion sense, but I can tell she's looking deeper than that. "Okay, I see your point. But to risk your spot in the Gaybutantes? It's too much. You don't have to do this."

"I can't back out, Mom. I'm a femme of my word. It'd be like you letting Ronald McDonald move in after you won, despite saying you wouldn't."

Mom purses her lips. "Using integrity against me now, huh?"

"I learned my powers of observation from you. I just knew what would make you see my side."

She pulls me in one last time. "I love you, Riley. Just know that no matter what happens, whether or not you win this bet, your future is waiting for you, right here in Mountain Pass."

That's when this overly sappy Hallmark moment stops. While I might know what would get her to see why I'm sticking with the bet, I still don't have the stomach or the strength to tell her I want out of this town. My gut fills with dread.

"Sure," I say. "Wow, would you look at the time."

I bolt out of there before Mom can see the guilt in my eyes. I may have temporarily gotten her on my side, but I know I'll have much bigger things to worry about if she knows my end goal is to leave Mountain Pass behind.

While this town isn't big enough for my ambition, the great thing about it is there's always enough love to go around. As in, folks get just as excited about Homecoming as they do about the Gaybutante Society. Black, red, and white colors are everywhere down Main Street, Mountain Pass Eagles flags are all over the place, and whenever somebody from the football team drives through town or visits the café, everyone nearby erupts like said athlete has just won the Super Bowl. In actuality, Mountain Pass only wins about 20 percent of their games, but that doesn't matter here. It's the effort that counts.

And the Homecoming committee sure put effort into this dance. The high school gym is done up like Paris, complete with adorable fake street lamps every ten feet, and right in the center of the room, a light-up cardboard Eiffel Tower sends shimmering light across the floor. There are tables lined with macarons in every color known to humankind (most likely made by Roz), and there are even custom berets with the Mountain Pass Eagle stitched on them for everybody to grab.

"Très magnifique!" I say.

"Look at you, en française!" Cassidy says.

"Oui, mais j'ai . . . forgot how to say anything else." I haven't spoken a word of it since finishing French 2 last year. "If you don't use it, you lose it."

"Well, I know what French I'll be doing tonight," Sabrina says, making kissy faces at Cassidy as she pulls her out onto the dance floor.

Nick rolls his eyes. "Gross." But he follows right behind them, taking me along.

Normally, at any dance, or even just on the weekends in a random jam session in Sabrina's Bronco, Nick and I can shake our asses off. Like, just turn up the volume and *boom*, we're dancing. Today, we still get right into the beat, but something's off. First, Nick can't look at me. He's peering over my shoulder, checking out other couples bumping and grinding, anywhere but connecting with me. We're normally all stupid faces, making up impromptu moves—it's the only time I really see Nick be okay with looking foolish. But his lack of enthusiasm is making me feel self-conscious, and I keep picking at different spots on my outfit in this instinctual reflex like maybe I can just fix the weirdness by straightening my belt or whatever.

Second, Sabrina and Cassidy have totally ditched us. Even if they're typically all over each other, we at least all dance close, but the two of them are lost to the crowd. When I finally spot them, Sabrina is completely and totally gone in Cassidy's eyes. I can tell it's total relationship over-kill, with Sabrina being painfully obvious that Cassidy's the only one she cares about, so much so that it's starting to come across like she's laying it on too thick. But then again, I'm not the one in a relationship, and I can't even get a guy interested, so what do I know?

I glance back at Nick and find him staring at Sabrina and Cassidy too. He's got this weird look in his eyes. Like he's jealous or something. No, that's not it. Like he feels like he's missing out. And that's when it all clicks. He really *does* wish Daniel were here, even though he said he didn't mind. That's just typical Nick, always trying to make sure erratic me is okay. Why else would his eyes be dart-ing to our bestie with her girlfriend, and to all these other couples who can't stop dancing together? He's missing out on this romantic moment all because of *me*. There's got to be a way to fix this. The dance doesn't end for another two hours. If Daniel heads out right now, he could be here with at least an hour to spare.

I tap Nick on the shoulder, leaning in close so he can hear me shouting over the music. "Seriously, why don't we call Dan—"

The music switches out of nowhere, the change from an upbeat bop to some slow song cutting me off. Every couple moves in close, swaying from side to side, foreheads touching, hands on hips and—for those using the moment to get a little frisky—butts.

"What were you saying?" Nick asks, but he's whispering now. Even though this slow song isn't exactly quiet, the way everyone's paired off seems intimate. And I think if I bring up Daniel in this exact moment, it might rub it in that Nick's not getting to experience that. So, I can make the offer to call Daniel after this dance.

"Nothing," I whisper back. "Let's just grab a drink."

I try to move off to the tables of macarons and "mimosas" (which are really just Principal Ko's combination of orange juice and Sprite), but we're surrounded. Swaying hips *everywhere*. There's no way I'm going to make it off the gym floor without earning some enemies.

"If you can't beat 'em, join 'em, right?" I step toward Nick with my hands up tentatively, showing him that I'd like to place them on his shoulders. The corners of his lips quirk up and he says, "Right."

Nick wraps his hands around my waist and pulls me into him. They rest perfectly at the top of my hips, his pointer fingers touching my exposed skin. Being the most ticklish person on the planet, I let out a loud laugh that gets me glares from the couples who are milking this moment for all the romance it's got.

"Sorry!" I stage-whisper. "Ticklish!"

I look back to Nick, who's gone from a small smile to full-on teeth showing.

"Oh, I'm so glad my embarrassment amuses you."

"You just always know how to make your mark in any given moment." Nick says it through a laugh, and he's finally acting like the Nick I know and love. It feels like the right moment to make sure he's truly all right with this Homecoming arrangement.

"Hey. Are you okay?" I ask. "I know we talked about it before, but you've seemed off since we got here. I can't help but think it has to do with missing out on a real date tonight."

"I swear that's not it." Nick chews his cheek as he thinks, the two of us swaying with the music, getting caught in our comfortable silence. "I think I'm just worried about your bet. All these couples are sort of reminding me what's at stake."

My heart sinks. Mom's worried about it; Nick's worried about it. I need people cheering me on, not making me doubt myself even more than I already do.

"You think I'm going to lose?"

"We're entering the fifth week of this thing. We're nearly halfway there and you're not any closer. I just don't want you to get so caught up in this that you forget the best parts of yourself."

"That's not really an answer to my question."

"It's not that I don't think you can find a guy. It's just that I'm seeing more doubt in you than I ever have before. You're not yourself. Your radio hour was always so carefree, with you getting to know whoever you were talking to. Now on your podcast you seem . . . I don't know. Frantic. Worried."

Well, shit. That's definitely not the brand I want out there. "You think people hate it?"

He sighs. "That's not what I'm saying. It's definitely interesting listening, and there are folks who are rooting for you and others who aren't."

"Don't I know it." I think about the comments I read the other day, still feeling that sting from femme doubt and the indignation at #TeamJock supporters.

"If you're feeling too much pressure," Nick says, "if the podcast is making you feel like you honestly have to put the future of your career or gay camaraderie on the line, I can delete it all. You don't have to go through with this."

But I do. The convo with Mom is still lingering in my mind, and I need my podcast audience as my ticket out of here. So, I squeeze Nick's shoulders and try to sound as confident as I'm trying to convince the world I feel, only I guess according to Nick, it's not working out so great. "I can do this. For femmes everywhere. For me, dammit!"

Nick's smile is more of a worried grimace, but he nods anyway and says, "Okay."

The song ends and Nick drops his hands from my waist. It's only when the contact is gone that I realize he was gently stroking the spots where my skin is exposed. And it didn't tickle. It was grounding, and now I feel like I've been let loose from my mooring. I've got too many jitters this deep into the bet.

"I need a drink," I say. "A real one. Let me go grab my clutch."

I push through the crowd to find my bag and the tiny little flask that's got a couple drinks' worth of vodka in it. Then it's time to grab a "mimosa" to spike. I grab one for me and one for Nick, but as soon as I pour in my little addition, I come face-to-face with Cassidy, a light sheen of sweat over her face from all the dancing.

She points to my plastic champagne flute. "That's not just a mockmosa, is it?"

I give her a guilty grin. "You guessed it."

She motions with her fingers. "Give one here." I pass it over and she downs it in two gulps.

"It's been a weird month, huh?" I say.

Cassidy nods. "I'm trying to be cool with it—I just can't help getting jealous every time a new girl says she's into Sabrina."

She sighs, and if there's one look I know for sure, it's the look of someone who's bottling something in. "It's always best to just let it out. You can trust me, lady."

The words rush out of Cassidy like she's had them on the tip of her tongue for weeks. "I'm just a forward on a Seattle high school soccer team. And I'm nowhere near the best on the team, and it's like, how unimpressive is that? I haven't *done* anything. And all these Gaybutante followers are, like, pushy and talented and interesting, and what am I?"

"You're Sabrina's girlfriend. She doesn't take that lightly. And she chose you for a reason, just like you chose her."

"I even started volunteering at this dog shelter so I could say I've been spending time with animals while she's off doing her Gaybutante stuff, thinking she might like me more because of it. But I hate it. Dogs are not my thing. They're so slobbery and smelly and *loud*. I quit yesterday, but I haven't had the heart to tell Sabrina yet. Don't tell her, okay?"

My first thought is to tell Cassidy that I don't keep secrets from my friends. But my second thought smacks me so hard that it knocks all other info right out of my head.

"So, there's an opening?"

"What?" Cassidy asks.

"At the dog shelter. There's an opening for someone to watch over the dogs. To volunteer."

"I guess so, yeah."

"Text me all the info. It's a dog-eat-dog world and it's time to . . . eat some dogs."

Cassidy makes a barf face and I don't blame her.

"Okay, yeah. I heard it too, but just . . . give me the number of that shelter, all right?" I'm mentally filling up the Service hours in my Gaybutante journal. I'm for sure going to lose this bet and get stuck in this town if I don't accomplish all my pillars, and Cassidy's handing me one on a silver platter. I am going to volunteer at this shelter, get my Service hours in, and who knows, maybe I'll find some dog adopter to date. Skylar will rue the day he ever tried to push this femme out of the gay family.

It's time for some puppy love.

Chapter 9

Cassidy wasn't wrong when she said this place was *loud.* The second I open the door to the Cascades Animal Shelter, I'm blasted by barks and yips and howls. And that's even with a wall separating me and all the dogs, who I can see through a window behind the front desk, the biggest with their paws on the glass trying to see who just came in. It'd be sweet and adorable if it weren't for an unwavering distraction sitting at said front desk.

A cute guy.

A very, very cute guy.

Using a laptop with a rainbow-flag sticker on the front.

Jackpot.

Cutie hasn't looked up from his computer, apparently so used to the dogs that their barking doesn't signal to him that somebody's arrived. He's white, has floppy brown hair that is extremely disheveled but also extremely hot, and isn't really that much bigger than me muscles-wise. He's got these round glasses that he keeps tapping while he thinks before his long, thin fingers fall to his laptop and fly across the keyboard.

I saunter up to the desk, the dogs calm enough now that I can hear my booties clack against the cement floor, but Cutie's typing so hard and fast that I don't think he hears them. It's not until I'm right in front of him and ring the service bell that he finally looks up. Well, jolts up actually, like I've scared him, and he slams his laptop shut.

"Wow, sorry. I didn't see you there." His name tag reads Connery.

"Connery? As in, Sean? As in, the original James Bond?" Nick is a fan and has made me sit through all the movies.

Connery face-palms. "I know, I know—it's the worst name, isn't it? And no, my parents aren't Bond or Sean fans. They're just outrageously pretentious."

This self-deprecating humor is just the right amount and it's unreasonably charming. "I like it."

"Well, wait until you hear my full name." He takes a deep breath before launching into it. "Connery Tyler St. James *the fifth*."

"Wow."

He nods. "I know. I warned you."

I laugh and Connery smiles sheepishly, like he didn't expect to be funny and is soaking it up. It's so cute and unassuming the way he looks pleased with himself, but not in that Skylar way that's all gloating and assholery. It's just simple, endearing surprise.

"So, what are you working on?" I ask, pointing at his computer, and Connery guiltily bites his lip, drawing my attention to his mouth.

Thankfully, he doesn't give me enough time to stare and come across like a creep who's thinking about kissing him (even though I totally am), because he glances over both shoulders before leaning in to whisper, "It's my novel. I'm really not supposed to be working on it when volunteering, but"—he shrugs—"Darla isn't around, so I sneak it in before she can yell at me about not paying enough attention to the dogs." He grimaces then and stands up, his hands clasped in front of him, suddenly all business. "Which is probably why you're here. To see the dogs. What kind of pet are you looking for?"

God, he's so awkward and fumble-y and I can't get enough of it. "No, no, I'm not here to adopt. I actually spoke to Darla this morning. I'm the new volunteer. Cassidy's replacement."

Connery's shoulders instantly relax and his hands fall to his sides. "Phew. Don't tell Darla about this, okay?"

I mime zipping my mouth shut. "My lips are sealed."

He smiles and pushes his glasses up his nose, and how can a nose be so cute? It's all buttony and freckly and wow.

"So, um." Connery scuffs his shoe on the floor, which I'm seeing now is a nice suede loafer. He's got khaki tailored slacks on that hug his skinny legs perfectly, and he's wearing a thin maroon sweater. He's totally got the author look down. "Let me show you to the puppies."

He opens the door to the dog play area, a space that reaches even farther than what I could see from the front office. Dogs of every shape and size bounce around, sniffing each other, playing with balls, sleeping in the corner. A very slobbery Muppet-looking creature with curly blond hair, one of the big ones who had their paws on the glass earlier, bounds over to Connery and jumps up, putting their massive paws on his chest. If that were me, I'd have toppled right over, but Connery plants his feet and laughs. He scratches the Muppet behind the ears and says, "Who's a good girl? Goldie, that's who! Aren't you? Aren't you?"

It's baby talk and it's ridiculous, but it's ridiculously cute. I mean, an author *and* an animal lover? We're checking all kinds of great escort/boyfriend boxes.

But whoa whoa whoa. I'm getting ahead of myself. The whole point of this next stage in the escort search was to find a guy I liked *for him,* not because of how he looks on paper. And the best way to get to know someone is to rely on my interviewer instincts and just ask questions.

"So, what's your novel about?"

Connery gets that sheepish look again and keeps scratching Goldie behind the ears. "Don't laugh, okay?"

"Why would I? I bet it's—"

"Vampires."

That's the last thing I expected him to say. He looks so serious and studious that vampires didn't register as something he'd want to write about. But I guess that just goes to show you shouldn't judge a book by its cover. Not to use a cliché, but it fits.

Connery looks like he thinks I'm going to make fun of him, and he rushes to explain. "I know that vampires have been done before, but have we really seen all that vampires have to offer? And don't you think there's something . . . sexy about them? People who say there are too many vampire stories out there are ridiculous. They'd never say that about political thrillers, or murder mysteries, or romances, but vampires are the thing that has just *too* much? It doesn't make any sense."

He's a nervous rambler and I'm here for it.

"I'd love to read it sometime," I say.

"You would? We just met."

"Well, I like vampires. And reading."

"What's your favorite book?"

Crap. I didn't really think this through. I wanted to make a connection with him and now I've gone and lied in the first three minutes of talking.

"Um . . ." Now it's my turn to give a sheepish look. "Let's preemptively say yours. I guess I don't read all that much outside of whatever's assigned at school. And I'm not about to say *The Great Gatsby* or whatever because, honestly? I deleted that book from my brain the second after I turned in some essay where I bullshitted the whole time. I don't usually see myself in many books, so I kind of just gave them up. But I promise I'll pay attention to yours. I liked the *Twilight* movies—does that count?"

Connery grimaces again, but this time it's playful. "No, it doesn't. But depending on how long you volunteer here, I can get you reading some good books that I promise you'll like."

"That sounds nice," I say, and I really mean it. I don't spend most of my free time reading. Usually, it's experimenting with new eye shadow palettes or scrolling through beauty influencers' social media, but I know if Connery gives me a book recommendation, I'll actually read it. And I don't think it's only because he's cute. I can actually feel that he puts thought into this kind of thing, and I want to connect that way instead of just glomming on to any cute guy who's in my vicinity.

Connery gently takes Goldie by the paws and sets her down. "Good girl." His hands now free, he reaches over for mine and gently pulls me behind him. Hand-to-hand contact has got to be a good sign, right? "Okay, I guess we'd better get you to the real work. Follow me."

We walk to the back of the dog play area and end up outside. It's a large, fenced-in grassy section, half of which is covered by a wooden overhang. With how much it rains here, I'm sure this is so the pups can get some outdoor time and not instantly smell like wet dog. But today, it's not raining a drop despite the consistent cloud cover, and frolicking right in the middle of the grass in their own little pen are—

"Puppies!" I squeal.

I hop into the pen and scoop up one of the buggers in no time flat. It's black and white and is barely bigger than my hand.

"Is this what Cassidy had to do all day?" I ask from inside the soft, smooshy folds of the puppy when Connery makes his way over.

He nods. "She was on puppy patrol, four hours a week."

"What kind of coldhearted monster would hate this?" Sure, the other six puppies take constant breaks to sniff each other's butts and a little long-haired brown one keeps trying to gnaw on my bootie, but they're cute, so who cares?

"All I have to do is play with them?" I ask.

"Pretty much," Connery says. "Plus make sure their food and water bowls are full and answer any questions adopters might have. Darla lets me do write-ups on each of them. There's a binder at the front desk that I can show you." He starts walking back inside and motions for me to follow. "Come on. I'll give you the lay of the land and point you toward the kibble and treats."

"Can I bring this love muffin?" I ask, seconds before the little shmoop in my hands sticks their tongue in my mouth.

"We call him Frisky for a reason."

"Not the kind of kiss I've been hoping for, but it'll tide me over."

I stop dead in my tracks. Did I just say that out loud? But Connery laughs, and it's kind of high-pitched and maniacal, but you can feel his whole heart in it. It wasn't *that* funny, but maybe these are overzealous laughs because he likes me. And I'm not against it.

"Okay, no offense to her," Connery finally says once he's caught his breath, "but you're already a million times better than Cassidy. She just wasn't that into it, always screaming when the puppies charged her. I mean, they're puppies. She did not fall for Frisky's advances."

As if on cue, the puppy yips and licks my fingers like he thinks they're Popsicles.

"I'll show you where the sink is too so you can wash all the slobber off. But if you let Frisky run wild, you'll need a full bath. Follow me."

With that, Connery gives me the rundown of the place, and the longer we talk the more we slip into a sort of ease. I ask him about his writing, when his love of vampires started, how long he's been working here. He asks me about what brought me to volunteer, leading to a whole lot of talk about the Gaybutantes and my podcasting dreams, taking extra care to avoid mentioning that I have one airing right now, to which he replies with the magic words.

"I don't really listen to podcasts," he says. "Ever. I have too many audiobooks to keep up with my TBR when I can't physically sit down and read."

"So, you've, like, never listened to a podcast?" I ask.

He shakes his head.

"And you don't have any plans to?"

"Nope." His smile wavers. "That doesn't instantly make you hate me or something, does it?"

I beam so wide, I'm shocked my lips don't crack. "Not at all. It makes me like you better, if that were even possible."

He laughs. "Okay, good. Close call."

I spend the next couple hours poring over the puppies' backstories while playing with them until they're so tuckered out, we take them back inside to sleep. As if the universe was helping this along, not a single potential new dog parent comes in, meaning Connery and I have had three uninterrupted hours of getting to know each other.

"Okay, then," I say at five o'clock. "I guess I'll see you next week. I need to do fifteen hours of community service for the Gaybutantes, so you're stuck with me for a few more weekends."

Connery pushes his glasses up his adorable nose and asks, "Actually, would you maybe want to grab coffee sometime this week? If it wasn't painfully obvious yet, I love to talk about books and I want to bring you a few." He fidgets with the side of his specks nervously. "If you were serious about wanting to read some, that is. But I know we just met, so if this is more of a Work-Friends-Only thing, I totally get it."

Fuck yes! Just one afternoon hanging out together and he's already asking me out on a date. "I'd love to."

"Great!" Connery reaches into his bag, and I peek at least five hardcover books crammed in there. Lifting that bag has got to be a chore. "Here," he says, and he hands me a book that has a redhead with a hairstyle an awful lot like mine on the cover over a baby blue and lilac background. "It's *Can't Take That Away* by Steven Salvatore. My best friend gave it to me and it's amazing. You mentioned not having really seen yourself in books? Well, your story might be fairly different from Carey's, the main character, but I think you'll find some similarities there. It's about a genderqueer teen who's faced with all kinds of backlash when they try out for the role of Elphaba in *Wicked*, and how they literally and figuratively find their voice in the process. It's gorgeous. And the Mariah-filled playlist that goes along with it is amazing."

I take the book and I swear Connery positions his long fingers so that our hands can't help but touch. "Thanks," I breathe.

"Don't mention it," he says, beaming. "Can't wait to hear what you think about it. Does Wednesday work?"

"Absolutely."

The high from setting up our book date immediately gets thrown back down that night at an epic Lego-labyrinth escape party at Hopeful Archibald Rumner's house. He's gay, white, and a Lego-building wizard, obviously. He harnessed the power of the Lego community to build this *fifty-by-fifty-foot* maze in his mom's garage. It must have taken hundreds of hours. No, thousands! It's full of arches and spires and little nooks where those who want to partake can grab a Jell-O shot. Sabrina and me seem to be the only two not up for drinking today, because we both got anxious just before starting the maze. Cliff announced he was going to be doing a tally on where everyone stands in their pillars, and that empty page of Mentorship in my journal is starting to glare up at me. Sabrina's freaking out because she's got one glaring absent pillar of her own.

"We haven't even started talking about my hosting gig yet," she whisper-shouts as we make our way through the Lego labyrinth.

"I'm down to talk about it whenever you want," I say. But the accusatory tone in her voice is rubbing me the wrong way. "It's not like I've been the one avoiding the subject. You've been the one avoiding me."

"I haven't been avoiding you," she snaps. Well, maybe it's not a snap, but she definitely sounds frustrated. "I've just needed some alone time with Cassidy, and you know how you and I get when we're together."

It's been a week since Homecoming, but so much has changed with my best friend in just seven days. She decided I needed to send her step-by-step instructions for her makeup looks so that she can have the bonding time with Cassidy, instead of me coming over and the two of us dominating all the talk with Gaybutantes. Then outside of her clinic hours and filming her BTS shots for her socials, she just spends alone time with her girlfriend.

"I'm not saying I mind all this time you want to spend with Cassidy—just don't make it seem like it's my fault we haven't been able to plan your party."

I got the date for my hosting gig settled with Dad for next weekend, so now all I've got to do is just wait until I can pull it off. I've been ready and waiting to help get Sabrina's solidified since day one.

"I'm not—" Sabrina stops herself, taking a deep breath in for four, out for five. "Sorry. Cassidy's kind of got me on edge."

Any pissed-off vibes instantly leave my body. "It's okay, lady. But it does seem like Cassidy's becoming a little *too* jealous. She's like, taking over your life. And maybe ruining your Gaybutante season just a little bit."

"No, no, I'm still having a lot of fun, I just need to find a way to balance all this. I'll figure it out."

"I know you will." I say it to be the supportive bestie, but honestly? I'm not so sure. I've never seen Sabrina so stressed out in my life. Normally she's all chipper and like that Disney princess who can just sing a tune and get all the forest animals to come frolicking to her side. I've got to help her turn back into that before Cassidy turns her into the villain. "Hey, why don't we brainstorm party ideas at my birthday dinner?"

"What, no." Sabrina grabs my arm and pulls me in to her side, just as we exit the maze. "We should be celebrating you."

"It'd be a gift, because it'll lead to us both becoming Gaybutantes, just like we always wanted."

"HOPEFULS!" Lonny screams, reemphasizing the point that while we want to be Gaybutantes, we aren't there yet. And we won't be if Sabrina can't get her shit together, and if I can't find a date to the Ball. "Gather round, my sweet little ones."

She beckons us forward, the motion making it look like the deep orange, furry monster face on the front of her Lonny-made sweater is actually moving. She says it's "Ludo inspired," who's apparently some creature from this movie *Labyrinth*, which is very on theme for the night.

Cliff steps next to her, a Jell-O shot raised. "First and foremost, huzzah to Archibald for a hosting gig well done!"

The room erupts in cheers, followed by muffled slurps as people shoot down Jell-O. Yeah, Sabrina and I are definitely going to be the only ones not partaking in the Gaybutante-provided, DD-driven Sprinter vans waiting out front like at every Gaybutante party. It's not mandatory to drink or provide booze at any hosting gig, and there's never peer pressure, but at today's bash, it seems like folks are ready to celebrate.

Lonny quickly explains why. "Y'all are doing so well on your pillars. We're five weeks into this thing and we've already had nearly half our parties"—Sabrina gives me another worried glance—"everyone has their Service approved, and we've had basically all of you find mentees."

I nudge Sabrina. "I don't have mine yet. Do you?"

She shakes her head. "All the out kids at school have already been taken!" she says, turning green. "And I don't want to go digging into some underclassmen's lives and unearth their sexualities before they're ready to talk about it."

Crap. I'm getting so distracted by dates that I'm letting this pillar fly out of reach. I'm going to have to figure something out ASAP to find a mentee.

"Not to mention your General Gay Chaos has been truly chaotic," Cliff says. "We've had podcasts challenging gender stereotypes, lesbian leaders giving us insight into wildlife, rose-petal realness through the school halls, you name it."

I've been so busy rushing to and from date opportunities and recording podcast episodes that I've missed out on a lot of the chaotic fun. Apparently, Adam showed some CGI short he made with a bunch of hot, gay centaurs of all body types at the theater last week, and Theo Qualls literally parachuted into school out of a helicopter their dads piloted. It was all anybody could talk about the whole day and I was so bummed to miss it, but I was obsessing over *RWNADTTGB* listener numbers in the parking lot before school. I was *right there* and missed everything. But then the next day, Rosie Macabee repurposed a bunch of wilted flower petals by coating them in red glitter and created a shimmering red carpet for folks to walk down before getting photos taken for Picture Day. At least I got to witness *that*.

All in all, ever since I made this bet, there's just been a ton more anxiety involved in becoming a Gaybutante than I expected. It's definitely not helped by all the folks who come up after Lonny and Cliff's "pep talk" to ask about the podcast. Like, I knew it would make this whole bet public, but I thought the publicity would be more about uplifting femmes everywhere. What I should have seen coming was all the focus on *me*. Everyone's all "When's the next date, Riley?" or "I wish I could help, but then that sort of goes against the bet" or "Just tell us the word and we'll decimate whoever made you do this." But I can't tell them Skylar's name because it would just give him the satisfaction of knowing he's right. That I was so unconfident about finding an escort that I had to resort to getting others to bully him into letting me out of the bet. I can't do that because even if he'd let the bet go, he'd still *feel like he won* and go on in his belief that gay guys don't like femme guys.

So now my head is just a jumble of worries. Worries that I'll be stuck in this town forever, that I'll never have a boyfriend, that my best friend is losing herself because of her girlfriend's jealousy, that Skylar is right and nobody will ever find me attractive.

My season was supposed to be all about gay camaraderie, connection, making a mark.

But right now, I just feel alone.

Chapter 10

The thing about Mountain Pass Pizza is that it has the best pizza on the planet. And that's not just some overembellished hometown pride or anything. It's literally the best in the world. It's outrageously addictive too, which is why whenever you come inside, the place is always packed and everyone's in a good mood.

Nick and I sure are when we find a table, which is a gift from god because it's next to impossible to just walk in and sit right down. You're usually awkwardly standing around the sides of the restaurant waiting to pounce. But a little four-top is empty, and it'll be a squeeze, but we can fit the five of us who are joining.

"Okay, wait. We've got to buy a lottery ticket or something—this is our lucky day," I say.

"We're sixteen, Riley. Well, seventeen now for you. Happy Birthday."

Nick pulls me in for a hug and I say into his shoulder, "It's a golden birthday miracle! Seventeen on the seventeenth. Do you think this good luck will last the rest of the year?"

"I wouldn't count on it."

"At least the rest of the *day*?" I pull back so I can look him in the eye. So I can see that reassuring look he always gives when I'm worked up and can't talk myself down from these jitters. I need some good luck right now. "I really need this hangout with Connery to work out tomorrow. Like, I don't even know if it's technically a date."

"Everything's going to be fine," Nick says. "Just be yourself and he'll love you."

"It's got to be a good sign that Connery already has such a great read on me he can recommend books that I'd like and be *right* about it."

Nick slumps in his chair.

"Okay, what's that about?" I ask.

"It's just that I've been recommending movies to you for years and you never get this excited about them. But then some guy you just met gives you a recommendation for a book and you can't put it down? I'm a little offended."

"But it's always, like, superhero or action movies, which are great, but not really *me*, you know? Don't take this the wrong way, but you were always recommending stuff *you* loved as opposed to tailoring your suggestions to fit my personality."

Nick's mouth drops open. "Wow. I guess I never thought of it that way."

"Seriously, don't worry about it. I know I yak on and on about my favorite makeup brands and stuff. It's natural to want to share what you love with your best friends. But it's also okay if they don't want to partake in those things."

"I started painting my nails after you busted out that OPI kit freshman year."

"Yeah, but that was because you liked it. You said you liked the way the darker tones looked on your nails. You do like it, right?"

Nick gets his small smile and says, "Right." He even looks at the maroon shade on his hands right now, running his pointer finger over his thumbnail. "I do."

The bell on the door jingles and it's shrill enough to be heard over the hustle and bustle of the restaurant and the eighties female rock ballads blaring from the speakers. Right now, it's some pop-rock gal screaming "love is a battlefield." There's nothing that could be more appropriate for this stage of my life. Or for Cassidy and Sabrina, who've been going through it. But today, as they walk inside, they're all giggles and hand-holding and soft touches to each other's faces. Daniel pops in right behind them. When he locks eyes with Nick, he breaks out a huge grin.

Sabrina and Cassidy take the seats across from Nick and me, and when Daniel makes his way to the seat at the end of the table, I realize I'm the fifth wheel. Two couples and me. I guess I should move and let Nick and Daniel be couple-y. I was the one who told Nick to invite Daniel to my birthday dinner, but it never occurred to me how awkward it would be as the odd one out.

"Oh, here!" I shoot up, my chair smacking into the back of the person's seat behind me. "God, sorry! It's packed in here, right? Trying to make room for the couples, you know? I'll just . . ." I motion to move, but I'm boxed in by the guy I knocked into. He scoots forward, but there's still not enough room for me to get around without my butt smooshing against either this stranger or Nick.

"Hey, don't worry about it," Daniel says. "It's a tight squeeze. I can sit here."

"But the legs of the table," I say. "They'll get in the way of you playing footsie. Or holding hands."

Daniel's cheeks turn pink. "Oh, we don't have to . . . we'll be fine without . . ."

Sabrina bursts out laughing. "This is just too good." She places her hands under her chin and looks at us with wide eyes. "What a deliciously awkward show." She fumbles around for a menu. "We've got to order quick because I always like eating while watching a movie."

Cassidy playfully punches her shoulder. "Cut it out. Don't make the new couple uncomfortable." Then in a stage whisper, "But be sure to DVR it so we can watch it again."

Nick snatches the menu from Sabrina's hand and covers his face while he wipes at his cheeks. "Okay, get it out now."

"Nick has a new booooooyfriend," Sabrina singsongs. "Ooooooh."

Daniel plops into the open seat at the head of the table, so I take his lead and plop back into mine.

"Is that what we're calling me now?" Daniel asks.

"Oh shit!" Sabrina says, and her hands instantly go up to fidget with her ponytail. "I just thought . . . I mean, you've been seeing each other for a while. Are you not official?"

I gently tap the menu down until we can see Nick's eyes. He recently shaved his head while I touched up my silver because sometimes he likes to start fresh on his dye journey. The lights reflect off his scalp like a spotlight while we wait for him to tell us his relationship status right this very second.

His eyes dart from me, to Sabrina, to Daniel, over and over. The silence stretches on too long. Then finally, he puts the menu flat on the table and says, "Yes. I think we are."

Daniel beams again and Cassidy can't help herself. She literally applauds and squeals, grabbing the attention of the entire restaurant. Everyone stops talking, and some rock goddess screams, "HOW DO I GET YOU ALOOOOOONE" over the sound system.

Sabrina points up at the speakers and says, "That's what Daniel's thinking right about now," which makes him guffaw and breaks the awkward tension. Everyone goes back to their own business and we order a couple pizzas.

"So, Daniel, what's the latest with your music?" I ask.

"Yeah," Sabrina adds. "I'm so bummed to have missed your performance at the café, but I'm hoping now that you're in, we'll get some private concerts from time to time." She's good like that. Having been the person who brought the most significant others into our small circle, she does a good job of making the newbie not feel like the odd one out by specifically stating from the jump that they're a part of our crew.

Daniel gives Nick his own version of a small smile. It's not quite a *knowing* smile, but more like he feels accepted and at ease by Sabrina's comment, instead of having to be on edge to impress us and make his way into the group.

"Actually, I got a few new gigs from that show. Your principal hired me to play halftime at your home game next week, and I got a spot on Halloween at The Triple Door."

"We'll be your ultimate fangirls!" Sabrina says, and I nod along, but I kind of tune out because I can't help but notice Daniel's hand move to Nick's knee. He absent-mindedly circles his finger around Nick's kneecap, and it just seems so natural and smooth and comforting. Nick's even put his hand gently on top of Daniel's wrist, all the while listening to Daniel talk about his music. They already seem so in sync.

I glance across the table, and it's the same thing. Cassidy and Sabrina are tuned-in to Daniel, but Cassidy is twirling Sabrina's hair between her fingers, and Sabrina is sort of subtly leaning into Cassidy.

All this couple behavior. All this second nature movement like they're meant to be together. And then there's just me. Alone.

What if things don't work with Connery? I'm solidly at the point where if this doesn't pan out, I'm screwed. I have a month and a half until the Ball, but with the plan to really get to know Connery, if a few weeks go by and there's no spark, I'm totally fucked. And then there's also the possibility that Connery isn't into me at all. I don't even really know if he's single or not, or if this book talk is even a date. Or what if he thinks more like Skylar? Although, he did size up my femme energy and knew just what books to recommend with characters I'd relate to. So that's got to be a good sign, right?

"Here we go! One Veggie and one Peak with eight sides of ranch."

Our server is back and she's balancing a large pizza in each hand, doing an impressive job squeezing through the packed tables. In the center of each is a little roundup of ranch ramekins. It's the life force in this group. Pizza without ranch is like a lip kit without liner.

With the pizzas on the table, Cassidy reaches for a slice, but Sabrina knocks her hand out of the way.

"Wait!" Sabrina cries, while Cassidy looks a little ticked, rubbing her wrist.

"Okay, ow," Cassidy says with a very pointed glare.

"Sorry, it's just—" Sabrina reaches into her purse and pulls out an orange birthday candle. She puts it in the middle of the Peak Pizza, nestled in the center of a black olive slice, then grabs a lighter from her bag. She flicks it on and sets the candle ablaze. "Riley needs to make a wish first." Then she grabs a hand fan that she passes over to me. "To blow it out without spitting all over our dinner."

All eyes turn to me, and mine can't help but dart back to Daniel's hand on Nick's knee. I want that. I don't want to be the odd one out anymore. I want to find a guy who likes me for all my femme fierceness, who can meld seamlessly into my life and into this group, and who doesn't make me feel like I need to constantly explain myself and my fashion and my feminine energy. I want somebody who just gets it. And if I find that guy, it'd be the key to everything. To me winning this bet and proving that femmes can be with any person out there, to my podcast ending in success, to getting into the Gaybutantes and having their following boost my audience and opportunities so I can get out of this town.

I flick open the fan (which is purple and says QUEEN on it in neon-pink letters), close my eyes, and wish for love. Soon. Very, *very* soon. I flap the fan back and forth until the little flame goes out.

"Yay! Happy Birthday!" Sabrina says.

Nick bumps my shoulder with his. "Happy Bday, Ri."

"Thanks for including me in the festivities," Daniel says. He dishes up himself and Nick, with Sabrina getting slices for herself and Cassidy, and I just sort of sit there.

"What are you most looking forward to this year?" Cassidy asks.

"Honestly?"

Cassidy nods. "Of course."

"Um . . ." I don't want to be that person who messes up his friend's relationship, so I look at Sabrina and say, "It's about the Gaybutante Ball."

Cassidy smiles, the last reaction I expected. "Don't worry about bringing that up. You can totally talk about it. I've learned to laugh about it now. Sabrina and I have made up this game called Thirst Blockers where she shows me every DM and we block that shit together."

"I think it's very cathartic for her to press that big Block button," Sabrina says. "It's all out in the open. We're good." She puts her arm over Cassidy's shoulder while shoveling down a massive bite of pizza.

"Well, I really want to win this bet. I want a boyfriend. And I think it goes beyond the Society now too. Yes, I'm going to stick to my word and if I lose this bet and a chance at joining the Gaybutantes, I'm going to be devastated. The amount of downloads for my podcast is totally because of them at this point, and it'd suck to lose that. I know I've got some people vocally against me, but I'd hate to lose the group that had my back from the jump without even knowing anything about me. Especially considering how there are gays like Skylar out there who'd rather see me crash and burn than succeed. But also, I want what you all have. I mean, look at you. You can't keep your hands off each other, and I don't think you even notice."

Everyone goes still. Sabrina's eyes wander to her arm around Cassidy's shoulders while Daniel's and Nick's eyes float down to their hands over Nick's knee. They all, slowly but surely, move until their hands are in front of their own plates. It's so serious and solemn that it makes me laugh.

"I'm not saying you can't be couple-y. But I am saying that's what I want. I want someone to serve me pizza." I hold up my plate. "Empty. No boyfriend to be all cute and dish me up."

Nick snatches the plate out of my hand faster than I've ever seen him move. He plops the biggest slice of Peak Pizza on it and gives me my own ranch. "Sorry. We should have noticed."

"It's not that big a deal," I say. "I just want to turn this five-dom into a six-dom."

"We're still getting used to you even wanting a boy-friend," Sabrina says.

"I'll definitely help," Daniel adds. "I meet all kinds of guys on the road." He instantly looks guilty and puts his hand on Nick's shoulder. "But none who compare to you."

I know he's trying to make it better, but the affection is making this jealousy monster even bigger. I've been worried about Cassidy's jealousy all this time, but maybe I need to check my own.

Sabrina sighs into her pizza, poised in front of her mouth just before a bite.

"What is it?" I ask.

"Not to change the subject, but . . ." She looks tentatively at Cassidy, sets her pizza down, and dives in. "We gotta start thinking about our parties. And definitely our mentees. We're getting so caught up in our relationship drama that I'm straggling at the back of the pack." Cassidy stiffens, but Sabrina doesn't seem to notice. "Where are we going to even find somebody to mentor with everyone at school already taken?"

"I mean, you do have this big resource at your disposal," Nick says.

Sabrina and I turn to him with blank stares. "We do?"

Nick grabs his phone out of his pocket and scrolls through it. He flashes a Gmail inbox at us, message upon message of people writing in to the podcast. "People have a lot to say to you, Riley. You could put out a call for anybody who needs help." He nods to Sabrina. "And you could ask folks on your social media. See if anybody has been looking to get into vet sciences or anything like that and show them around your clinic, right?"

Sabrina bounces in her chair. "Nick, you're a genius. It's so obvious!"

Now it's Cassidy's turn to sigh, and she punctuates it by crossing her arms over her chest.

"Babe?" Sabrina asks tentatively, leaning her head against Cassidy's shoulder. "What is it?"

"Now you're going to start telling people *to purposely* slide into your DMs? That's just asking for trouble."

"Well, what else am I supposed to do? Just give up the Gaybutantes entirely?"

Cassidy is silent for way too long. I guess the group still bothers her more than she let on.

"I, um, think I'll go grab some more ranch," Daniel says, and he scoots away from the table as fast as the packed restaurant will allow. It doesn't matter that we already have three unclaimed ramekins of the stuff on the table; I want to do the same thing and let Sabrina and Cassidy hash it out on their own. But there's no way I'll be able to get out of this seat.

"I'm not giving up the Gaybutantes, C," Sabrina says softly, gently, trying to make her girlfriend see reason. "This means too much to me. Think of all the animals I'm already helping with my growing following. People are showing me displaced pets they've found and helped get medical care and new homes. They're changing their everyday behavior because I've shown them how it negatively impacts wildlife. I'm doing so much good."

Cassidy's body sags. "You can do all that by yourself."

"But don't you see how much harder it will be without them? One reshare on my first post from Lonny on the Mountain Pass Gaybutante account, and here we are. This isn't about whether I can do it on my own or not. I just don't *want* to do it on my own."

Cassidy's hand flies out to grab a napkin that she dabs at her eyes. "I just want to be included, I guess. There's not a whole lot of stuff on your socials about *us* together."

"What are you talking about? All my lives are of us doing makeup together from Riley's instructions. And what about our Homecoming pics? I've included you in every way I can. And in my defense, we don't go to the same school. It's hard to get constant content together when we've been apart for the majority of the past few weeks."

"Because of the Gaybutantes!" Cassidy shouts.

The table next to us stop their conversation, and Sabrina's eyes dart over to them with an apologetic smile. We're on the verge of causing a scene. I've got to change the subject fast.

"So, um, what are those red flags in the inbox, Nick?" I ask, motioning back to his open phone. There are a few messages with little red symbols by them, dotted here and there along his screen.

Now it's Nick's turn to deflate. "You're not going to like the answer, and it's your birthday. Are you sure you really want to know?"

Cassidy still looks like she could blow up or cry her eyes out at any second, so I nod quickly. "Yeah, it can't be that bad."

Nick gives me a look that's a combo of *Don't say I didn't warn you* and *I'm here for you*. "These are all the messages from trolls who have not-so-nice things to say."

"What?" My hand snatches out to grab Nick's phone before he can keep it from me. "Let me see."

It's one thing to have people write comments on my posts, but another entirely for them to actually take the time to write in. That kind of devotion takes serious hatred, and my morbid curiosity wins out. It's a lot of the same thoughts I saw on social media, just in more drawn-out sentences.

You're a DUDE! Start acting like one, pervert. If you were in my school when I was a kid, I would have kicked your ass.

God loves you but can't welcome you into Heaven for your sins. Come back to Jesus, sweetheart! He'll welcome you with open arms. You just have to repent!

As a gay man, I can't say enough how effeminate guys are setting our cause BACKWARDS. All you're doing is trying to tell the world that all gay men want to be women. I DON'T WANT TO BE A WOMAN! Riley, you do not represent me!

You are such a disgrace to femme people. Look, date whoever you want, but you don't have the right to say who we should date. I'm happily with my enby partner and we both think this whole podcast is trash. Cis is not superior!

I hand Nick's phone back and push my plate as far away as this crowded table will allow. I don't have an appetite anymore.

"Hand it over." Sabrina grabs the phone, her face turning whiter with each message. "Assholes. Complete and total assholes."

"I've preemptively blocked the ones I could find on social media before they drop hate there too," Nick says. "And deleted some of the comments on your posts that were even worse."

It turns my stomach to know these aren't the most awful thoughts about me out there. I'm grateful I didn't have to read them, but part of me needs to know exactly what we're dealing with.

"How bad were they?"

"Some are just . . ." His eyes wander. "There aren't words to describe that level of hate. They'd be besties with the racist trolls in fandoms. But truly, most people have been amazing. There's just always those few, you know?"

He pulls up RWNeedsADatePodcast on Insta and scrolls through the comments.

You are stunning!

Give me eyeshadow tips!

I'd date you in a heartbeat, beautiful ♥

I've seen this support before and lately started peeping at it when I need a boost or to see just how much steam the podcast is gaining (we're solidly in the five-digit range of listeners *and* followers). But these little bits of support are old news and aren't enough to stop the echoes of all that hate in those emails.

"Is it really worth all this?" Cassidy asks. She's been sitting with her arms crossed this whole time. The carefree Cassidy who walked in here is totally gone. "It seems like you're both blowing up your lives to me."

"It's not all bad," I say. "The podcast just broke one hundred thousand downloads, and we've got, like, twenty thousand unique listeners. That's huge. And like Rina said, it's just from getting supported by the Gaybutante accounts. This is some real experience. Some real publicity." Which will give me my ticket out of here. There's some truth to what Cassidy said, though. But I can't back out now.

"Okay." Cassidy shrugs. "If you say so." She doesn't sound convinced. She looks at Sabrina. "At least I can come to the party you host."

Sabrina and I share a look, and Cassidy instantly knows what we've telepathically said.

"I can't even come to *your* party? What kind of an organization makes you cut off your closest friends? Your *girlfriend*?"

"C, it's not like that. It's—"

But Cassidy shoots up from her chair, bashing her knee on the table. "Son of a bitch!" she screams. Then she hobbles out of the restaurant as fast as she can. Which isn't that fast. It's a very dramatic exit.

"I should go after her," Sabrina says, but she's in no rush. She looks defeated as she makes her way out, hanging her head the entire way.

Daniel gets to the table just as she exits.

"Talk didn't go well, huh?"

My eyes can't leave Sabrina's retreating, sulking back. "I think that's an understatement."

Excerpt from Episode 6—*Riley Weaver Needs a Date to the Gaybutante Ball*: "We're in This Together"

This is so much worse than just feeling alone.

Now we've got major rifts to deal with.

Honestly, I don't think any of this is my BF's fault. She's made it clear she wanted to be a Gaybutante from the jump, she's included her girlfriend in any way she possibly can, and it's healthy to have things that are just for you, that make you an independent person outside of a relationship. I mean, it's not like my bestie is trying to join her girlfriend's soccer team. She needs to be allowed to have things that make her unique. They're the things that made her girlfriend fall for her in the first place!

Okay, enough about all this drama. What we need now is to get back to the pillars, the Gaybutante excitement that many of you allegedly came here for. So, I want to do something for somebody out there since so many of you have been supporting me through this journey (minus the

*few of you who have made it very clear that you don't,
but you're not going to rain on this parade). I know I'm
not the only person out there who feels like they don't fit
society's rules for their body. And I also know how scary it
can be to really embrace your femme self when the world
has so many expectations for what each sex should be.
So, if anyone out there wants a listening ear, or if they
want advice on how to embrace their true self, send me
an email. There's no guarantee I'll be able to get to everybody, but I'm definitely going to try my hardest to at least
respond to all of you. But full disclosure, I am looking for
one official mentee. Many of you know the mentorship
requirement for the Gaybutantes, and I'm hoping to fulfill
it here. But just because this helps me get into the group
doesn't mean that our connection will be any less real.*

*Finally, to those who may be hearing a lot of negative
input in your lives and are craving some positive, or who
might not have heard this lately but really need to: You're
perfect, just the way you are. Sure, there may be things
that need improvement, or maybe you've made mistakes
that you're growing from or need to make amends. Or
maybe you don't even really know who you are yet and
are still figuring it all out. But that's part of your perfection. The imperfections.*

*I know that's easier said than done. I used to think of
myself as an extremely confident person, but now, this is
all getting to me. I didn't think it would take this long to
find someone to date. I didn't think getting those trolls'*

feedback, even if it is just a small percentage of you, would affect me so much. And I didn't know that some of your femme takes out there could cut me to the quick. Maybe this whole thing was a mistake.

But I promised you from day one that I would give you the good, the bad, and the ugly. No making everything seem all picture-perfect, social media edited to only be sunshine and rainbows when it isn't.

All that to say, if you're doubting yourself, you're not alone.

We're in this together.

Chapter 11

Not that I know from experience, but the place a person picks for their first date says a lot about them. Connery lives closer to Seattle, and so we picked a spot that was kind of in between for both of us. And by *we*, I mean Connery. And Connery picked a Starbucks.

A freaking Starbucks.

The Pacific Northwest is known for its coffee, for having an extensive selection of gorgeously hand-picked beans that were sustainably grown all over the planet, and he picks the home of mass-produced beans, of blended drinks that are so syrupy, there's no way you could ever taste the coffee in them, of bland cake pops. Even if S-Bucks did start in Seattle, it lost its PNW flair. If Roz ever finds out, she'll kill me.

But I'm not going to let this mess up my chance to get to know Connery. And when he walks through the front door in slim black jeans, black loafers, and a gray turtleneck, his hair outrageously and adorably disheveled like he did nothing to it when his head popped out of that neck-covering tube, I definitely want to get to know him.

"Hi," he says, kind of out of breath, like either I'm making him nervous or he jogged here. Or maybe it has to do with the Queen Anne Book Company tote bag slung over his shoulder packed with books.

"Okay, wow. There's no way you can expect me to read all those," I say. "I mean, I'm just getting into this reading thing. Don't push me into the deep end."

Connery smiles, and it's lopsided and so cute and makes his glasses inch down his nose just a bit. "No, no, these are for me. Well, minus one I have for you. I can't go anywhere without something to read."

"Some*thing*? That's more like an entire bookstore."

"What can I say, I like to jump around. One second I want a chapter of sci-fi, the next I pore through a romance, or maybe a biography. I just finished André Leon Talley's *The Chiffon Trenches* and it was amazing."

"You're speaking the name of one of the gods," I say. "He was such a fashion visionary." I may have learned about André by binging old episodes of *America's Next Top Model* (which inspired many a makeup look), but I deep dove into Google searches and interviews with him.

"He's totally brilliant," Connery agrees. "Probably the most important fashion journalist of our time, and to do it all in so many instances where he was the only Black or queer person in the room. Trailblazer."

"Are you into fashion?"

He gives me an up-down, taking in my brown booties, tight jeans, oversize off-the-shoulder cream sweater, and ending with my eyes, done today in muted neutral tones with a touch of gold shimmer. His cheeks get pinker the longer he gazes into my eyes before he finally looks away, down at the table, and says, "I think learning about anyone's passions is cool, especially when they're a genius at it. But I'm not good at fashion." And then he finishes it all with the most perfect cherry on top. "Not like you."

"Oh, come on, you've got a great look going for you," I say. "Your style is all chic academic. Like, if you were a teacher in any TV show, you're the one all the students want to bone." I instantly suck in a breath. *I really just said that.* "Not that I, like, *want to bone you*, or anything. And not that I wouldn't either. You're totally attractive, is what I'm trying to say, and oh god, just make this stop."

Connery looks up from the table, and rather than grabbing his books and running for the door, he lets out that loud, high laugh. "Ha! I definitely know what you meant. And thank you. That's what I aspire to be, a hot teacher."

"Well, it's absolutely the vibe you're giving off." I bite my lip. I don't know if I'm making it better or worse. I've got to change the subject, fast, so I reach into my bag and pull out *Can't Take That Away*. "Here's your book back. I really loved it. Carey for the win."

"I'm so glad you like it," Connery says. "I just learned so much from them, and I think Steven Salvatore does such

a great job showing how gender doesn't have to be either/
or, you know?"

"Definitely. That's like, my whole life, explaining that to
people. Most of the time it's fun to just be my femme self,
but other times, people can be major dicks."

"Tell me about it." Connery nods and sort of looks into
the distance. Like he's thinking of something from his
own life where someone was a serious asshole. I want to
know what he's thinking, but I don't want to force him
to talk about something before he's ready. I wonder if
he's had his own obstacles when it comes to gender, or
maybe his parents weren't so supportive when he came
out. Finally, he shakes his head and says, "But it's nice
that there's more of a conversation going now. And to
that end . . ." He reaches into his tote and pulls out a
new book.

"*The Prince and the Dressmaker*," I read.

"It's a graphic novel, and it so perfectly shows how
clothes have no gender. I think you'll love it."

The way he looks into my eyes makes me feel like
Connery really does see me. I mean, sure, he sees me
in terms of my fashion and looks and has complimented
that, but it's like he sees my heart too. How else could he
have known I'd love that book? And now *The Prince and
the Dressmaker*? He's looking inside and makes me think
he likes all of what he sees—and wants to know more.
But if this is going to go anywhere, I've also got to get to
know him.

"Why don't you work in a bookstore? Why dogs?"

Connery opens his mouth to speak when a barista behind the register claps his hands. "Hey, you two!" Our heads snap over in surprise. "Yeah, you. These tables are for *paying customers*. Either order a drink or get out."

I'm instantly in defense mode, wanting to clap back. This guy is *not* going to ruin our moment. But Connery just shoulders his tote bag and says, "Actually, there's a park not too far from here. Want to go for a walk?"

He even keeps his cool when confronted with righteous jerks. That's got to count for something when looking for qualities that could make a good boyfriend, right? I'd learn how to be a better person in tense situations.

"Yeah," I say, and he leads the way out of Starbucks, even holding the door open for me.

Swoon.

"So, dogs," he says. "It all started when my best friend Dylan was going through some stuff and starting her transition. She was understandably feeling down about all the anti-trans legislation that's been happening the past few years, and she said she wanted to go somewhere where we'd find nothing but love. So, we showed up at Darla's and she let us play with the puppies. Did it erase all the hate from the world? Definitely not. But it stuck, and I realized it's a nice break from all the heaviness, being around them for a few hours a week."

"I'm so sorry she went through all that," I say. "Keeps having to go through all that."

Connery shrugs. "I wish there was something more *actionable* I could do about it. Not to overstep, but I bet you go through your own shit from hypercis people too."

Skylar's face flashes through my mind. Now could be a good time to vent about him and maybe bring Connery and me closer. But if I talk too much about Skylar, I'm not sure I won't let slip about the bet, and then I'll be fucked. Instead, I say, "Definitely. It happens the most in bathrooms, weirdly. Like, outside of Mountain Pass, men *freak out* if they see me in heels walking through the restroom door. They insist I'm in the wrong place, or they're in the wrong place, and I have to have this conversation basically pointing out my genitals to them. It's all, 'I have a penis; I'm allowed to be in here,' and it's so embarrassing. Most of the time I'll go into women's rooms, but then there are moments where ladies freak out if I'm in there too, like they think I'm trying to attack them or something. And if they've had a history of trauma, I feel so bad for them; I really do. But it makes me feel like I don't belong anywhere. It's the whole reason I wish people would focus on hearts over parts."

"That sounds awful. Dylan's gone through a lot of the same stuff. I know she'd love to meet you someday. I mean, not that I'm an expert since we've only known each other for a few days. But it's just a vibe."

I smile at Connery, and he grins back, our eyes locked, never looking away. "I'd like that," I say.

"It'll happen. Soon. She stops by Darla's a lot."

All this talk about me meeting his friends has got to be a sign. You don't just jump into bringing someone into your world unless you really think something's there. And if Connery's already feeling it, why not extend the same invite?

"Hey, so, my best friend's boyfriend is going to be performing during this half-time show at my high school next week. And don't worry, this isn't one of those *There for moral support but they're actually a terrible singer* scenarios. Daniel is genuinely talented."

"Wait." Connery stops dead in his tracks. "Daniel Stone?"

"Yeah! You know him?"

"He played at a fundraiser for the dog shelter last year. He was fantastic!" Connery pulls out his phone and scrolls until he finds a picture with him and a girl who must be Dylan standing on either side of Daniel.

"Small world," I say. "Will you join us?"

Connery beams and runs a hand through his perfectly disheveled hair. "I'd love to."

"And then we just, like, *talked*—for hours. Two hours and fourteen minutes, to be exact. In a *park*. Where we didn't do anything but just give each other the rundown on our lives. If that's not an instant connection, I don't know what is."

"I'm happy for you, Riley," Nick says. "That's great." He looks out over the property, trees stretching miles and miles through the Lookout windows. From here, you can see the starting platforms for the five zip-lining courses before they dive into the woods. All are going to be used for today's party, which I'm finally hosting, and Dad's closed the biz so the Gaybutantes can use it exclusively. It's a pretty impressive view no matter where you sit, dark green trees as far as the eye can see, Mount Rainier in the distance. But Nick has seen this view a million times. He's not taking it all in. Instead, he's looking out all *pensive*.

"What is it?" I ask.

Nick glances over, and I can tell he's a little embarrassed by what he's about to say. "It's just that I'm a little worried you're becoming a book person now. Two books in and *boom*. You'll be turning down movie marathons."

"Hey, a couple book recommendations won't change the status of our friendship."

"You sure?"

"It could be an entire library's worth of recs and you'd still be my main man."

Nick gets that small smile but doesn't say anything or look at me. He just rubs his hand across his cheeks. Something I said embarrassed him.

"Not in, like, a weird way, or anything," I add. "I'm not trying to outdo Daniel. I don't need him to send some group of singing ruffians after me."

That gets Nick to laugh. "Singing ruffians?"

I shrug. "What? I don't know the specifics about how singer-songwriter rivalries work."

"Right." He chews his cheek a bit before saying, "It's just that we already missed out on the *Star Trek* marathon."

"But I thought you went with Daniel."

"Yeah, because I couldn't invite you since you were busy with the Gaybutantes."

"Shit, Nick!" But then again, wasn't it Nick who said he wanted to start dating? It's now nearly five months since he and Grayson broke up, and it's been weeks since Nick has needed to vent or cry about Grayson breaking it off when they left for college. "I just didn't realize my absence would be noticed. Since you were all about finding a partner again at the start of the year."

Nick gives me an *Are you kidding me?* face. "Yeah, but when have I ever not known how to balance relationships and friendships? Marathons are our thing."

He's right. Even when Nick was with Grayson, he never excluded me from anything, and I'd always be the one to let him know about marathons when I had to do commercials for them at the radio station. Recording public announcements was one of those things Wilhelmina had me do at KMPK, so I could "learn the radio industry," but I think it was more so she wouldn't have to do it herself. I'd always mention the fun things to do with the group, but with my break from the radio station, I haven't kept up with the theater schedule or much around town at all. Up until now, I've been the available best friend with no romantic prospects of my own. But as I try to juggle dating, running this podcast, and getting into the Gay-butantes, I'm really dropping the ball.

"I'll get better, Nick. I promise."

He nods once, just before an alarm goes off on his phone. It's blaring Halsey, his artist of choice, and he does this thing where he hums along for a few seconds before turning it off. I've never told him he does it because I know he'll get self-conscious and stop doing it, but it's really freaking cute. I wonder if Daniel has noticed it yet, and if not, he's missing some of the best parts of Nick.

"That's my cue to get out of here," Nick says. "All the clues are already with the Zippers, in *sealed* envelopes, so nobody thinks you're cheating."

I lean in and give Nick a kiss on the cheek. "You are the absolute best." The guilt squirms in my stomach even more, thinking about him putting all this time in for me when I've already blown off one of our rituals. "And again, I promise I'll do better. Thank you so much for all your help."

"It was actually kind of fun seeing who came before you and all they're up to. You're going to fit in great, by the way."

"I'm Venmo-ing you some money for all that time you spent on it. Maybe take Daniel out on a nice date." I'm going to make a conscious effort to bring up Nick's and Sabrina's love lives more, so it's not just me talking about mine all the time too.

"You don't have to do that," Nick says.

"Hey, I'm all about paying creators and artists and producers their worth, so this is allowance well spent."

Nick smiles again, then walks out the door, pulling out of the gravel parking lot just seconds before a whole caravan pulls in. And I do mean *caravan*. It's just the Hopefuls and current Gaybutantes, but it seems like nobody chose to carpool. In minutes, the whole lot is full and it's raining queers inside the lodge. Leading the pack are Lonny and Cliff.

Lonny whistles as she checks the place out. "I love this whole vibe. It's very log cabin modern."

"You've been here before, Lonny," I say. "Like, at least three times."

She grins. "I know. But again, I'm just seeing it with new eyes now that you're one of us."

One of us. I haven't even accomplished all four pillars of the Gaybutantes, but I love that the group assumes once you start the journey, you're going to succeed. In reality, I've only known of three people who haven't made it in Mountain Pass High's history. One was because she moved and had to change schools. The second was because their parents made them pull out (but they were inducted two years later once they went to college and were out of their awful parents' rule). But the last was because some guy dropped out since the Service portion was too much for him. He thought it would be all partying, and when he actually had to give back for a bit, he flubbed it. To each their own, I guess.

But I'd be lying if I said I'm not worried that I'll become infamous number four. I'm pretty sure I'll be able to accomplish these pillars, but if I can't find somebody to actually like me, romantically, then I'm completely screwed. And I'll go down in history as the person who failed making it because nobody actually found him attractive. Because he was *too femme*. What a legacy.

"So, what have you got in store for us, Riley?" Cliff asks. "You look like you're ready for war."

He's not wrong. Today I'm decked out in pink camo, and in addition to my normal beat, I've got pink stripes across my cheeks à la a very femme football player. I point to a table that's loaded with five different colors of paint: pink, orange, yellow, purple, and teal.

"Today's party is a little bit of a competition," I say. "Well, not a little—a straight-up competition. Follow me." I lead the group to the railing overlooking the property and point to each starting platform where Dad's hired a few of the Zippers, as he likes to call them, to get us harnessed and supervise the lines. "Five separate courses, each with four lines that total over a mile in length. You only get to leave your platform when you answer a trivia question about the Gaybutantes correctly. First team to the bottom wins."

Cliff rubs his hands together underneath that gorgeous cleft chin. "Oooh yeah. A good old-fashioned trivia night. You bitches are going to eat it."

"I better be on his team," Lonny says. "Some people get *all* the brains *and* the beauty and it's just not fair."

"I'll try not to rub it in too hard," Cliff says. Then, to me, "All right, Riley, how do we pick teams?"

I point to a coin-operated machine, one of those old ones that you see inside grocery stores with little plastic toys in them. Mom collects things like that, and being the very technical lady she is, let me know it's called a Gashapon machine. For today's purposes, it's going to decide our fate. Instead of toys, I've put ping-pong balls in the various team colors. "Give that a crank and whichever color comes out is your new family for the next couple hours."

Cliff nearly sprints over to it, and everyone else lines up behind him. Various shouts of victory or calls to see if we can switch ensue, and Lego master Archibald Rumner asks multiple times where the booze is at. But I'm not about to let anybody drink and then go zip-lining because that would be a lawsuit disaster that would tank Dad's business.

Finally, when everyone has been assigned teams, I head to the toy dispenser and see two balls are still in there. Both pink. But there should just be one left.

"Who's missing?" I ask.

"Here!" Sabrina bursts through the front door. "I'm here." Her footsteps are hurried and heavy on the wood floor. "What are we doing? Sorry I'm late."

"It's okay. You got here just in time." I crank out the last two balls, handing one to Sabrina. But she doesn't look at it or pay attention to anything I say. Instead, she's furiously typing on her phone, so I have to pull her behind me when I tell people to head to the deck. Fortunately, I don't have to worry too hard about leading the crowd because Cliff and his seriously competitive spirit lead the way with his chest all Superman-puffed, shouting, "Team Pink! Follow me!"

I let the group go ahead of us and wander near the back so I can chat with Sabrina. "Hey, everything okay?"

Sabrina sighs. It's one of those huffs of breath that has a million emotions in it: anger, sadness, frustration, confusion. But instead of venting and letting it all out, she just keeps her head in her phone and snaps, "I'm fine."

"It . . . really doesn't sound like it."

She doesn't look up, her thumbs flying furiously over her phone, and adds, "It's relationship stuff. You wouldn't understand."

Ouch. Is she really going to throw in my face that I've never had a boyfriend when I'm in the middle of the hunt for one? And that if I fail, all my dreams of Gaybutante stardom and my ticket out of Mountain Pass go with it?

"A little harsh, Sabrina, don't you think?"

She finally looks up, and she is *pissed*. "Look, I'm sorry, okay?" But she doesn't sound or look sorry in the slightest. "I would tell you, but then you might just let the whole world know about *my* relationship issues."

A fiery ball of anger flares through my stomach. "Wait, what? I told my listeners I would give them an unfiltered look at what I was thinking, and it just kind of slipped out about Cassidy getting all pissy with you. But the good news is nobody knows who I'm talking about. I didn't name you; I just said my best friend and her girlfriend. That could be anybody."

"Are you fucking stupid?"

I recoil, not used to this boiling rage coming out of Sabrina. She's not yelling—the other Gaybutantes are excitedly gathered in their groups, unaware of what's happening between us. Her rage is focused on me. But she doesn't give me time to respond because she's shoving her phone in my face. Picture after picture of us together is on both of our profiles, me doing her makeup, mugging for the camera in matching looks.

"It doesn't take a genius to figure out who you were mentioning on your show! Anybody could! And they did!" She reads through comments on a picture of her and Cassidy. "'Cassidy, you got to get your claws out of Sabrina. Sounds like you two are going to be breaking up soon. If I were with Cassidy, I'd dump her in a heartbeat. Sabrina can do so much better.'

"I didn't think I'd have to state the obvious, but *do not* talk about my life on your show! I've been calming down Cassidy *all night*." She opens up a text exchange with dozens of consoling messages to C. "I'm *still* calming her down. And this is all because of you!" She jabs her finger in my chest, hard enough that I stumble back.

"Rina, I'm so sorry. I didn't even think of how that would sound." I guess it's one of the setbacks of having only broadcast on KMPK before. We have a listenership of, like, five. I didn't think of what the repercussions would be when I'd have listeners in the thousands.

"Of course you didn't," Sabrina says. "What else do you expect when someone is so obsessed with making everything about them that they literally start a podcast about it!"

Wow. That is the most hurtful thing she's ever said to me in my life. I don't know how to handle it. My brain reels, trying to figure out the next best step, when Cliff shouts from across the room, "All right, fearless leader. Let's get this show on the road!"

He and the rest of the group leave the deck, and now *I'm* the one who's pissed. Sabrina decides to bring this up during my hosting gig? One of the most crucial moments in my Hopeful season? If she's going to act like a bitch and totally come for me, she can handle this herself. I may have messed up, but this is not the way to go about letting me know. I am *not* going to let her affect my mood when I'm finally hosting my party. What if I did that to her? She'd be livid.

I try to clear my head when I dash over to meet the rest of Team Pink. Cliff is already ascending the stairs with pink flags leading up to our starting zip-line platform. Archibald is right behind him, then senior Gaybutante Clara Ortiz (Guatemalan American, bisexual, oboist who's bound for Juilliard), me, and stomping behind one slow step at a time—head in her phone—is Sabrina.

"Come on, Team Pink!" Cliff shouts. "Let's get our head in the game." He's very pointedly looking down from our platform at Sabrina, but she's so focused on her Cassidy drama that she doesn't look up. Even when she makes it to the platform and our Zipper, Kendall, says phones must be turned in so no one can google answers, Sabrina acts like she doesn't register what's been said.

Kendall shakes her backpack in front of Sabrina's face. "Phones here, girlie." Sabrina glares at her, but Kendall is unfazed. "Give it."

Sabrina huffs and finally gives in.

"All right," Kendall says, pulling a Nick-made index card from her back pocket. He even went so far as to put the Gaybutante Society logo of a cheeky little rainbow on the back, and I can't say enough how much I love him for going the extra mile. He pays attention to the little things, which is why he's going to be a killer producer someday. It's also why he's in the lead for *best* best friend at the moment, considering Sabrina's very closed off. Her arms are crossed and she's got a pout that'd rival any seen in a cosmetic injectionist's office.

"What are the names of the Founding Fab Four Gaybutantes and in what year did they meet?"

Cliff is so jazzed, he literally jumps while he lists off at lightning speed, "Rachel Blum, Tyrell Watson, Lazarus Creek, and Daniela Mendoza! 2002! WHOO!" He even chest-bumps Archibald, who looks like he's never been chest-bumped in his entire life.

"Correct!" Kendall says. She reaches behind her and grabs one of the five harnesses waiting there. "Harness up. It's time to zip!"

"WHOO!" Cliff shouts again, and his energy is infectious. But so is Sabrina's, and it's really an emotional tug-of-war when one person seems so jazzed he could burst out of his skin and the other is sulking so hard you think you might drown in her negative vibes.

"Hey, come on," I say, trying to playfully nudge her, but she scoots away. "We're here to have fun. Let's leave our drama until after my party. The party I've been dreaming about hosting my *entire high school career*."

"Some of us have bigger things to worry about," she whisper-shouts, and I feel another verbal slap to the face. I've never seen her like this before, and I absolutely hate it. Even the exhilaration of zooming a hundred feet up in the air isn't enough to whip the bad vibes out of me. I've done this a million times before, cruising above the trees, your stomach simultaneously feeling like it's falling out of you and up in your throat, and it's so old hat for me that I can't do anything but focus on Sabrina's cold shoulder.

It's like that for the rest of the game. From *For what film did Gaybutante Chansom Murray earn their Best Supporting Actor Oscar nomination?* (Answer: *Wednesday's Desire*, named after the nearly blind racing horse that won the Kentucky Derby; Chansom played the transgender jockey who rode it to victory) to *What was Gaybutante Kelly Pham's MTV Video Music Awards red carpet dress made out of?* (Answer: Hubba Bubba Bubble Tape) and every question in between, Sabrina never once chimes in or seems excited in the slightest. It's so noticeable that Cliff finally has to shout, "Pick it up, Sabrina!"

and Archibald mumbles under his breath, "She looks like she could shit a Lego brick."

This is not at all the hosting gig I expected. I can hear the whoops and screams of the other teams across the forest, knowing they're flying through the trees even though I can't see them. I can hear them celebrate whenever they get an answer right. And when we all gather back at the Lookout to see who got through their course in the fastest time (Lonny's Team Teal), everyone has these exhilarated smiles on their faces. This should feel like a success. But Sabrina's scowl—and not getting to have fun with my best friend during *my* hosting gig like I always imagined—ruins everything.

"So, where's the victory kegger?" Archibald asks.

"There isn't one," I snap. Good ole Archie is now getting just plain old. "Not to mention the fact my dad is here, or did you not notice all the adult supervision we needed to zip-line without falling to our deaths?"

Cliff sidles up next to him. "Yeah, you got to give it a rest, bud. There's more to the Gaybutantes than getting drunk at parties."

Archibald's brow furrows like he can't fathom what Cliff is saying.

"Speaking of," Cliff continues as Archibald sulks off, "today was *epic*. Nobody makes their party a competition, and to have it so focused on the Gaybutantes?" He kisses his fingertips before throwing them out wide like a fire-work. "Chef's kiss! It was like we were in a very gay *Survivor* challenge."

"I'm glad you liked it," I say, but my heart's not in it. My eyes wander over Cliff's very broad shoulders to find Sabrina burrowed in her phone again, moping in the corner away from the rest of the group.

Cliff follows my gaze. "What's got her all worked up?"

"Her girlfriend," I say flatly. "Has it out for the Gaybutantes, I think."

Cliff sucks in a breath and grimaces. "That can happen. Sometimes it gets hard for couples when one of them isn't a part of the group."

"Can't we just, I don't know, invite significant others to these things?"

"Unless they're a member, no," Cliff says. "You wouldn't ask a straight sorority sister to invite her boyfriend to everything, right? The whole point of this group is to foster connection with other gays in a nonromantic, nonsexual way, and to boost up each of our individual strengths. It's about helping us become fully formed people. That's not to say that romance isn't important, or that we forbid relationships from forming among our own, but . . ." He shrugs and locks his apologetic eyes on mine. I would absolutely be getting lost in them right now if it wasn't for the fact that I'm so angry at my best friend for totally shitting on my party.

"Hey," Cliff says, and he sets his huge, perfectly manicured hand on my shoulder. "Go over and talk to her. That's the thing you learn about relationships, romantic or otherwise: communication is key." I know he's not trying to rub it in that I don't have the romantic experience to learn that, but still, it stings. He gives me a gentle smile, then twirls a finger over his head. "Gaybutantes, out!" he yells. "Peak Pizza on me."

The crowd hollers and leaves in a mass, people hugging me and thanking me for the thrill. The parking lot empties, Sabrina's airbrushed Bronco the only car left, the clicks of her iPhone keys echoing around the Lookout.

I march over, hovering near her shoulder, but she doesn't look up.

Click click click click click

I wait for her to notice me.

Click click click click click

Nothing.

Click click click click click

I finally clear my throat. She glances up, an angry scowl on her face, but doesn't say anything.

"Want to talk about it?" I ask.

"Talk about how you totally betrayed me by suddenly making my personal business the *world's* business?"

"Talk about how you completely shat all over my hosting gig! I've thought about having this moment with you for years, and by the grace of the luck gods, we actually got to be on the same team for a challenge Nick and I worked really hard to put together. Instead of being in the moment, you were pouting and acting like a spoiled brat the entire time!"

"*I'm* the spoiled brat? All we've done these past few weeks is talk about *your* Gaybutante season. It's always

'Sabrina, I need to find a boy' or 'Sabrina, did you listen to my podcast?' or 'Sabrina, you need to get me Service hours.' Which, Cassidy told me, she gave her dog shelter volunteering to *you*. That was supposed to be our thing! To connect! And you took it from her!"

I feel like the air has been sucked from the room. "Are you kidding me? She *hates* dogs. She practically begged me to take over for her. She even told me not to tell you that *she* was ditching."

Sabrina laughs, but it's full of disbelief. "Oh, come on, Riley. Who could hate spending time with puppies?"

"THAT'S WHAT I SAID!"

"DON'T YELL AT ME!" Sabrina yells. "Don't make up lies about my girlfriend because *you're* panicked that you won't be able to find a relationship and need to take every other couple in your vicinity down with you."

I feel like I've been punched. I can't catch my breath, so I stand there, my chest heaving, trying to make sense of anything.

"How could you say that?" I whisper.

Sabrina's angry glare wavers. Maybe she'll finally see my side of things.

But then her mouth sets into a determined line. She pockets her phone and crosses her arms again. "You need to hear this, Riley. It's a harsh truth, but it's the truth." She doesn't even know how much like Skylar she sounds right now. "That's how you're making me feel."

"You want to know how I feel? I think you have a really needy girlfriend whose jealousy is so debilitating that *you* need to take that out on *me*. Even though you're being a raging bitch, I can still see that you have done nothing wrong in your relationship, and how Cassidy can't see that is beyond me. And you're fucking delusional if you stay with someone who's so possessive and turns you into whatever monster you are right now."

Sabrina's nostrils flare. She doesn't reach for her ponytail once. That's how I know we're in *Oh shit* territory. If she's nervous, she's fidgety. If she's mad, she's full of conviction and won't budge an inch. She'll dig her heels in. And even if she's in flats, those heels can rival mine any day.

"Monster? *Raging bitch?* This is exactly what I'm talking about. You're not able to see anything any way other than yours. So, I think it's best if we don't see each other at all. Let's just get through this season by ourselves. That way you don't have to deal with my *needy girlfriend* and you can focus on your stupid podcast on your own. And I can finally finish my pillars without getting so distracted by *you*."

"Fine."

"Fine!" Sabrina marches toward the entrance and flings the door open. Even the way her engine revs sounds ticked. After one pissed burst of gravel as she flies out of the parking lot, I'm left in the Lookout.

Angry as hell.

Excerpt from Episode 7—*Riley Weaver Needs a Date to the Gaybutante Ball*: "Tantrum over the Treetops"

And that was not the feeling I was expecting when I finished my Hosting pillar. I thought this bet was going to help me find love. But somehow, I royally pissed off one of the people I love the most. I'm not going to go into details, though, because even if I'm mad as hell, I don't want to dig this hole even deeper and continue to talk about someone who doesn't want to be talked about. But, god, would it kill people in your life to recognize all the good you have done for them, and how supportive you've been from day one, and how it's not your fault if their significant other isn't as supportive as you are?

Riley. You're getting dangerously close to talking about it again.

[deep breaths]

Thanks, Producer. You're right. Anyway, I'm making a not-so-gentle request that you stop making comments on other people's posts in response to what you've heard here. And without naming names or getting into specifics, definitely do not comment on anyone's relationship dynamics from what you've formerly heard on this podcast. I shouldn't have opened my big mouth to begin with, and I certainly won't in real life either, because look at where it's gotten me!

I should be celebrating this week. I should be focusing on how I only have one and a half pillars left to accomplish before I can become a full Gaybutante. I should be excited that I'm meeting up with a dog-loving, geek-chic writer cutie again, but I can't. Because now, in addition to all my worries that I'm too femme for any guy to ever take notice of me, I wonder if there actually are things wrong with me. Deeper than gender and how I know I should present myself to the world. Am I selfish? Am I a terrible person? Am I the only Gaybutante Hopeful in existence to blow up their friendships in the process of trying to get in?

Am I the monster?

I've only got six weeks left to win this bet, and I'm feeling as unsexy and unwantable as ever. Because who's going to want a partner who tanks their friendships? I think I need to accept the fact that there's a very real possibility I will lose this bet. And if I do, what does that say about me? What does that say about femmes? That can't mean The Jock is right. It's just got to mean that while masc gay guys would date femme people, it's me personally who's undesirable.

I don't know if that's better or worse.

Chapter 12

"**C**an you believe she said that? I mean, can you? That I was distracting her from *her* pillars of gayness? Like I was the person blowing up her phone being the jealous one? Blame Cassidy, not me!"

Nick and I sit in beanbags on his bedroom floor, my MacBook in my lap. We're supposed to go through the emails from potential mentees, but I'm too busy venting about Sabrina. Again.

Nick runs a hand over his head, a solid layer of hair grown out now after his shave. "Listen, she has her side of this too. She feels like you haven't been present enough for her and Cassidy's problems."

I throw my hands up so hard that my laptop falls to the floor. "What am I supposed to do, put *everything* on hold for her? I made sure Cassidy was invited to things, including my birthday. If that's not welcoming her in, I don't know what is. I've got things I need to do too! Like, I could have just not invited anyone and used that night for a date with Connery."

Nick cringes. "I'm not saying I agree with Sabrina, necessarily, but I am saying everyone's feelings are valid."

"But sometimes people are just wrong. Sometimes there's clearly one side that's right. And if I'm not being obvious enough, the side that's clearly right is my side."

I stare at Nick long and hard, and he stares back. Neither of us says anything. I click my blush-pink nails together, like a ticking clock passing the time. I need him to say it.

Reading my mind, Nick finally says, "You get that you're not a Jedi, right? You can't mind trick me into picking a side. I'm the one who's caught in the middle here."

"Ugh, fine—you're right. I hate when you're all reasonable and levelheaded."

"You love when I'm reasonable and levelheaded."

"But not when I'm seeking vindication!" I wave a fist in the air. "I need to get this anger out somehow."

I pick up my computer, the podcast email inbox up and waiting, and see the perfect emotional punching bag right there. The red flags. Every asshole who's written in to say something awful. I click through each one and scream a response, letting all my frustration and pissiness boil over.

I'm tired of your Woke Warrior ass clogging up my airwaves.

"Ha! But he's the one who streamed it to begin with! Delete!"

> Just get a transition already and stop messing
> with what it means to be gay.

"Maybe I should give this guy Skylar's number and they can bury their faces in each other's assholery together. Delete!"

> Your a pervert and a pedaphile!

"Try spellcheck, honey! Delete!"

Every punch of the Delete key lets off a bit more steam. Five more and Nick gently holds my wrist before I smash the keyboard completely.

"I'm doing this for your laptop's own good," he says. "You're going to pop a key off, then you'll be angry *and* have to trek the hour drive to the Apple store."

"Angelique could fix it." Senior Gaybutante, Lite Brite artist who on the side can fix anything tech-wise that they put their mind to.

"Okay, well, then you'd have to wait for them to fix it, and we've got more important things to do." He gently deletes the rest of the red flags, then pulls open the much happier emails that are all labeled with bright stars. "Things like picking a mentee."

He scrolls through the emails. Well, *scroll* is generous—

there's not even one page of them, but there's a bunch of shiny stars all lined up in a column of love.

"Sixteen people reached out?" I ask.

Nick gets his small smile and nods. "And it's only been a week," he says.

"Sixteen people think I could make their lives better?" Why are my eyes leaking?

"Yes, Riley." Nick puts his hand on my knee. "I may not want to pick sides in this battle between you and Rina, but I know for sure you have a good heart. And these people can feel that, even just by hearing you speak."

I sniff and dab at my eyes. "These people are also ruining my makeup." And it's a good look too. I practiced making a smoky eye but with a royal-blue-and-gold palette that I want to perfect before I see Connery again at the football game.

Nick hops to his bedside table where a box of tissues sits and pulls a few out for me. "I think you should just say goodbye to your makeup entirely. I've read through these and they are . . . really emotional. Some sweet, some sad, and if just knowing there are emails is making you cry, you're going to be a mess when you actually look at them."

I take the fistful of Kleenex and open the first message.

Dear Riley,

  Okay. Wow. You're the first person I'm going to say this to, or write this to, I guess. Well, you're the first person I'm telling in any format whatsoever . . .

I'm gay. And I guess I'm writing in because I don't know how to tell people. Sure, I just told you in this email, but you're a stranger. I don't know how to tell my dad. I don't know how to tell my grandparents. I don't know what my friends will think. Especially my best friend because I'm in love with him and don't know how to tell him. Or if I should tell him at all. I'm in the middle of nowhere Montana and it's just not something a lot of people talk about here. I don't know if that makes me a good mentee, but it would just be nice to have a friend who I can fully talk to about this stuff, you know? And I'm writing to you because even when you have a million questions about life and if femme guys can be gay or are faced with maybe no one asking you to the Gaybutante Ball, you still just go for it. You're unafraid to share your weaknesses and your doubts and I really admire you. A lot. Thanks for your podcast, Riley. It really helps.

Sincerely,

Nate

Nick's right. I'm a complete and total mess. Nate from Montana actually took the time to write this. To thank me for my podcast. He genuinely thinks I might be able to help him solve his problems when I have so many of my own. I know I made the call looking for people who need advice, but to actually see with my own eyes that listeners out there want that advice? It's a lot. In the best way. But also, in a way that makes me feel seriously unqualified.

"How can I help Nate solve his problems when I can't even figure out my own?" Despite my best effort to hold them back, tears finally start slipping down my face.

"I don't think being a mentor is about having no problems whatsoever," Nick says, handing me another tissue even though I already have a fistful in my lap. "I think it's about the distance from somebody else's issues. Being a listening ear and saying the first ideas that pop into your head. That's what you're good at. That's why you want to be a podcaster to begin with, right?"

Exactly. This is what I love to do. And I'm letting everything get to me: Skylar's hate, Sabrina's hate, these anonymous commenters' hate. But no matter how disgusted with me or mad at me someone might be, it doesn't change the fact that I love to talk to people, and I love to get to the bottom of issues. This job was meant for me.

"Poor Nate is in love with his best friend," I say. "He doesn't know how to tell him."

Nick's eyes bounce between the computer screen and me. He's doing that hesitation where he's drafting up the perfect thing to say in his mind.

"No, no, it's okay," I say. "This advice is on me. And I haven't even read the others yet. You know what, I think we need some mood music."

I open up Spotify and start playing Daniel's songs. His voice is ethereal and sweet and heartfelt, just him and a guitar crooning about love and being who you're meant to be. It's the total right vibe for this moment.

"You listen to Daniel?" Nick asks.

"Of course!" I punch him in the arm. "Just because I've got this public-facing mission doesn't mean in normal life I'm not still a supportive best friend." Although Sabrina would argue with me on that.

Nick rubs his arm. "Okay, ow. It's just that I didn't think it was your kind of music."

I roll my eyes. "That's not the point. I wasn't into watching cross-country meets either, but that didn't stop me from going to Grayson's with you. It's what friends do. Besides, Daniel's actually really good. It's not like those meets where you just stared at a path and waited for a runner to cruise by."

Nick laughs and I see him gaze at Daniel's picture on his verified artist profile. I think his feelings are intense. But I haven't done the best job of asking about it.

So, I set my laptop to the side. Emails can wait another few minutes.

"How are things with him, by the way? Is this the relationship you'd been hoping for?"

"Daniel's great. I got to go into the studio with him and see how a single is put together. Music production is a whole other world. Like, synthesizers and laying down beats, and throwing in instruments that aren't even there in the room, but you can do it with just a press of a button. They barely even auto-tuned him. It's impressive. He's impressive."

"Sorry I haven't been able to spend that much time with him yet."

"It's okay," Nick says, and when he sees me about to object, he adds, "No, seriously. You were there for me every single time I needed you over the summer. Every tear, every angry rant about Grayson leaving or how unfair it was that they graduated early, you were there."

It's true. I was happy to do it. Besides, Nick never showed extreme emotion like that before, and he always sat by while Sabrina and I had some sort of meltdown about a palette selling out before I could get to it, or an animal Sabrina's parents couldn't save.

"I was just returning the favor," I say. "I've got you, and you've got me. And I promise when this season is over, regardless of what happens, I'll be more present in your life again. I'll really get to know Daniel. I'm excited for his show."

Nick smiles and leans over me, grabbing my laptop and flipping it back open to the podcast emails. Daniel's voice croons from the speakers. Nick stays close while I scroll through and burrow into the beanbag, even though it fucks with my hair in a way that I hate after spending so much time on it this morning. But if my face is going to be a mess of tears while reading these messages, my hair might as well be a mess too.

Besides, my hair isn't the thing to focus on right now.

It's these kids, reaching out for help.

"RILEY! You showed up!"

Daniel stands at the foot of the bleachers, Nick rubbing his cheeks by Daniel's side thanks to his boyfriend's screams grabbing everyone's attention.

I'm sitting in the bleachers of the Mountain Pass football field, folks all around me decked out in red and black and white, proudly sporting eagles on shirts and posters. Mountain Pass spirit knows no bounds. It's a typical lovey-dovey, chilly late-October evening with everybody ready to yell our asses off even if the players lose. Which they most likely will.

The only thing not typical is the fact that I'm sitting up here alone. Nick is down with Daniel, as he should be, helping his BF figure out logistics with Principal Ko. Sabrina would usually be by my side, but instead, I'm here shivering under my way-too-thin neon-blue jacket completely by myself.

As if on cue, Sabrina and Cassidy choose that moment to arrive, racing down the side of the field to wrap Nick and Daniel up in hugs. I can't hear what they're saying, but it's clear Rina and C are giving Daniel pep talks. Cassidy's even wearing the *Get Stoned* T-shirt that one guy wore during the café showcase.

Crap, I should have thought of that. Instead, I'm here all decked out in an outfit that I thought would make that new, blue smoky-eye look pop even more. The only problem is, blue is the color of the Bellingham Bulldogs, so not only am I not in best-friend's-boyfriend supportive gear, but I look like a traitor to Mountain Pass. I'm getting so caught up in impressing Connery that I'm breaking cardinal bestie and MPH rules. Mom will kill me when she shows up for her mandatory mayoral appearance and sees my color scheme.

The two slices of my bestie sandwich gab for a bit, making me feel like wet lunch meat just slopped uselessly on a table. As if he can feel the deli disaster that is my soul, Nick nods in my direction. Sabrina briefly glances up toward me, Cassidy too, but the second we lock eyes, they look away.

It's a stalemate. It's been this way all week at school too. Sabrina hasn't sat at our usual table once. Mostly probably because she's mad at me, secondly probably because she doesn't want to hear me say anything about how disappointed I am that she made her social media accounts private. Cumulatively, her videos have gotten over a million views, and she's still getting attention that I know she loves, but Cassidy must have gotten to her. Maybe it's not the worst thing, because Sabrina's clearly resorted to trying out makeup looks from YouTube tutorials, but she just can't get them as right as I could, and she doesn't need even more people seeing that.

Catty observations aside, it really hurts not to be included in her Gaybutante journey anymore. This was supposed to be our year. To pour salt in the wound, Sabrina and Cassidy march away, heading to the opposite side of the bleachers to sit by themselves. Nick looks my way and shrugs, nervously chewing his cheek.

I quickly tug out my phone and text him. *Don't worry about me. I'll be fine. Focus on Daniel.*

This is his big night, after all, and I don't want to be that friend who tells his BFF to stop focusing on his love life, especially when I know how important being a partner is to Nick.

"I'm here, I'm here! Sorry I'm late!"

I look up from my phone to see Connery standing above me, his gloriously disheveled head framed by stadium lights. He's an angel sent from above.

Or from Bellevue, but whatever.

Connery plops down, the motion extra loud thanks to his ever-present tote stuffed full of books. He's completely oblivious to my emotional rawness of getting snubbed by Sabrina, but that's exactly the energy I need. Someone who's carefree and excited and not steeped in best friend drama.

"What'd you think of *The Prince and the Dressmaker?*" Connery asks. It's like we haven't had a week since we last saw each other. He picks up our conversation as if he just stepped outside for a second instead of us being apart all this time. It's perfect, it's natural, and it totally lets my guard down.

"You've nailed me again, Connery!"

Oh. Shit.

What did I just say?

What did I just say?

"Not, you know, *nailed me*. Like sex. I'm not some horndog, I swear." Fuuuuuck. "Not that there's anything wrong with being horny." Why can't I stop talking? "Because everyone's sex life is a journey for themselves, you know?" Wow. "I can't seem to make this any less awkward, can I?"

Connery, however, looks like he's loving every last second of it. With each new word, his smile gets wider, his laugh gets louder. By the end of it, he's rolling on the bleachers, and it isn't until the speakers blare to life and the announcer welcomes the teams to the field that he finally gets himself together.

"Listen, I'm going to have to call you when I need inspiration for dialogue from awkward characters. That was priceless!"

The heat in my cheeks flares up, but not so much from embarrassment now. I like being able to make Connery laugh like this. That's got to be a good sign, right?

"Come here," he says, beckoning me toward him. "That deserves a hug. Your performance was epic."

Wait a minute. Is he for real asking to hug me right now? We've gone from Connery giving me hand-selected book recommendations to him asking if he can hug me. And what a gentleman to give me an opportunity to opt out and not just force himself on me. If we're now moving to consensual hugging, going on real dates cannot be far behind. And then it's Escort City (not the name of my new brothel).

I lean into him, and with one arm, Connery pulls me close. His other arm is occupied in his tote bag until he pulls out a blanket.

"It's freaking freezing," he says, offering me a corner. "Want some?"

I nod, unable to speak, and Connery whips out his blanket so that it covers us both. The motion makes his scent fall over me; he smells like bodywash and books. I try to get a big whiff again without coming across like some cannibal creep. Once the blanket falls gently over my lap, our body heat mingles to create the most perfect cocoon of warmth. He even leans deeper into me, his body shaking just a little. Maybe it's the cold, or maybe it's that he's just as excited as I am that we're cozying up together.

Slow and steady is totally going to win this bet. He'll be asking to be my escort in no time.

I lock eyes with Connery, and he's got this huge grin on his face.

"Still thinking about how epically cringey I am?"

Connery pulls back softly, leaving only inches between our faces.

"No, your hair was tickling my cheek," he says. "It felt nice."

We sit there, his arm around my shoulder, pressed together, looking into each other's eyes. It would just take one tiny lean forward for us to kiss. Just one little movement and our mouths—

"Hey, guys!" I snap back. Nick's standing in the aisle, next to our seats, motioning for us to scoot over. "Mind if I join you?"

Connery scoots to the side, his arm moving from around my shoulder, the moment lost. "Not at all," he says. "Get in here. We were just talking about books." Nick's soft smile drops into a frown, but Connery doesn't notice while he glances back to me. "What was your favorite part about *The Prince and the Dressmaker*?"

I give a quick apologetic look to Nick. I don't want him worrying that this book talk will encroach on our movie time once this heavy dating period is over.

"It was a perfect take on how arbitrary gender rules are," I say. "I would kill to have a designer friend like Frances. Or to raid Sebastian's closet. I mean, our tastes are so similar. I feel like he would rock this outfit. Well, if you could see it under the blanket." Underneath my jacket is a blue-and-green diamond-patterned wrap-tie blouse with matching wide-legged pants, finished off with black booties.

"You look gorgeous in everything you wear," Connery says, and it's so sincere and so sweet, followed by such a genuine smile, that it stops me cold. I don't know how to follow up a cute gay guy complimenting my femme fashion in a way that makes me feel so seen and appreciated.

Except, maybe I *do* know what to say. Connery is soft and sweet and gentle, and maybe he's so gentle that he doesn't want to be the one to push the pace too quickly. But I don't have time to wait anymore. I've got to determine once and for all if this could go down the path to dating and potential escort-dom *fast*, or I'm out of the Gaybutantes for good.

"Can I ask you something?"

Connery nods. "Shoot."

I take a deep breath—four in, five out—hoping beyond hope that my words don't come out so quickly that my brain can't catch up before it's too late again. "Would you maybe want to grab dinner sometime? I loved our coffee chat the other day, and talking here, it just feels like maybe there's a connection, you know?"

Connery smiles again and runs his hand through his already-ruffled hair, somehow tweaking it just right to make it peak messy sexy. "I'd like that. Should I bring you a new book?"

"I'd like that," I echo, and Connery nods like he's feeling all this too. Like everything really is just right.

"Great," he says, and his voice is breathless. "It's a date."

Holy shit! I guess he's not too worried about setting the pace after all. *It's a date!*

I can't stop this perma-smile from taking up my face. *This is happening!*

I beam at Nick, but his head is turned the other way, watching Daniel on the sidelines tuning his guitar. This is just perfect. It'll be Nick and Daniel, Connery and me, and Sabrina and—wait. I glance over my shoulder to find Sabrina in the crowd, and the second I spot her, her head snaps in the opposite direction. Maybe it won't be Sabrina and Cassidy with us. I've been with her through three relationships, and when I finally have one starting of my own, she can't even be there for me.

No. NO! I will not let her taint this moment. Things are *finally* going my way with this bet, and her relationship drama does not get to seep into my love life when it's actually beginning to take off.

So instead, I lean into Connery, and we talk and talk and talk, not paying attention to the game at all. He even gets Nick involved in the convo and can easily switch from his favorite books to his favorite movies based on books so that Nick doesn't feel left out. It's all so natural.

And when Daniel sings during halftime, crooning the single "Forest of Feeling" that he recorded while Nick was in the studio, no words have ever felt more appropriate for the budding relationships my best friend and I are building.

"*Forest of feeliiiiiiing.*
Growing through the pines.
Forest of feeliiiiiiiing.
Planting seeds to make you mine, oh, yeah."
Things are looking up.

Excerpt from Episode 8—*Riley Weaver Needs a Date to the Gaybutante Ball*: "A Romance for the History Books"

I never in a million years would have thought that books would spark my love story, but here we are. I was literally trying every trick in the book to get a potential love interest to not judge this book by its cover, but when I just hit the books that Bookworm recommended, things finally started happening. Not sorry about all the book clichés.

I really can't thank all you listeners enough for your advice and support. Especially you, MeetCuteMama206. When I just took a page out of your book (last one) and leaned into connecting with a specific person for what makes him him, it all just clicked into place. And what's amazing is, Bookworm's really leaned into my femmeness. I mean, he's always complimenting my looks and actually knows about books where the main characters explore their gender. And he did that on his own, before he met me. He's so clearly not one of those gays who limits their own love lives by arbitrary gender rules and definitely doesn't try to force other gays into acting and looking a certain way. His heart of gold is going to make The Jock totally eat it.

All this is to say, I feel so hopeful right now, and not just because I'm starting a romance for the history books. I'm feeling hopeful because of all the love from potential mentees. We are up to twenty-eight of you who have written in, looking for a mentor. The amount of love you pour into these messages has made me cry in the best way, and I really needed that after doubting I could ever win this bet with all the drama lately. I promise I'm going to reply to each and every one of you, and I'm going to keep the call for mentees open for another week. I know sometimes we've got to work up the nerve to reach out and begin this journey of unlocking our true selves, and I don't want anyone to feel rushed.

Except there is a hard-and-fast deadline of November fifth. I'm sorry. The reality of Gaybutante deadlines means this has to happen sooner than later, and that will give us a few weeks to make a mentor-mentee connection.

All right. Actual, real date updates coming in the next episode.

Stay tuned.

Ah!

Chapter 13

It's the morning of my date with Connery and I feel on top of the world. It's Friday, I got a B- on my chemistry midterm, which is way better than my usual C-range results, and the cute boy I've been flirting with for weeks is finally taking me out. Nothing can kill this buzz. Not even Skylar sliding into my DMs to message me Tick tock, Riley! That was one message request I deleted immediately. Skylar's profile pic is so smug too, but I'm positive one date with Connery is going to smack that cocky grin right off his face, and his baseball dreams will go crashing down.

Vindication is so sweet.

If only there was somebody I could share this with, but Nick is nowhere in sight. My eyes rove the quad; I can't find him anywhere. This is very unlike him. He's usually the first to hold down our table, but I was on such a high that I didn't even notice the spot was empty. Sabrina hasn't been sitting with us since she blew up at me, so that's the new shitty norm, but it's her choice. Which means on what could be the most monumental day of my Gaybutante season so far, I'm all alone.

This is not how I want to be psyching myself up for tonight's date. I want to get this energy out; I want pep talks from my friends. I don't want to be feeling like a complete and total loser.

That's when I finally spot a face in the crowd, headed right for me. Breathless. Like she's been running. She even has a rainbow crocheted sweatband around her head.

"Hey, I've been looking all over for you," Lonny says. It can't be to check in on my pillars. I know she listened to my most recent episode about finding a mentee because she approached me at the last Hopeful's party (Aparna Laghari's dance party, which she DJed from her own techno remixes of nineties R & B) to say she just knows I'm going to change some little femme's life out there. It was really sweet. So, this look of total distress on her face is super-throwing me off.

She wipes a stray bead of sweat falling down her forehead with a matching rainbow band around her wrist. "It's about Sabrina."

"Oh." Instead of getting to talk about my date, I'm forced to be thinking about all her negativity *even more.*

"She just came to me and had an epic breakdown," Lonny says. "Like, snot pouring, ugly crying, warped words as she tried to squeeze them out through a lump in her throat that I swear I could see bulging through her esophagus."

"And I bet she was tugging so hard on her ponytail, you thought she might rip it out."

Lonny nods heavily. "Yes! Exactly! She said she's worried about getting all her pillars done in time to join. She has zero ideas for a party and hasn't even started looking for a mentee."

"I don't see how any of that's my problem," I say, with way more bite than I mean. "She shouldn't have focused so much on the General Gay Chaos that is Cassidy. That girl is all kinds of chaotic."

Lonny waves her hand in front of my body. "So, is this why she's not talking to you? This overall snappiness?"

Her scowl of judgment makes me instantly ashamed. But it's not that black and white. I'm not the bad guy here.

"Oh, I'm sure she told you what a monster I am, right? But she's the one who told *me* we need to stop talking to each other until the end of the season."

"This is not what the Gaybutantes are about," Lonny says. "We're about friendship, connection, helping each other through hard times. And for the record, she didn't mention anything about your fight, or how you brought her up on the podcast. Which, by the way, was one of the terms of our agreement. That you wouldn't put anyone else's life on blast. The only reason we haven't pulled the plug was because Sabrina asked us not to. She *knows* it was just a slip."

She's silent, letting that all sink in. I could have had to end *RWNADTTGB*, but Sabrina came to my defense. Meanwhile, I've been over here begrudging her this whole time.

"Fuck. I really am a monster."

"I don't think you are. I think you've messed up and you've got to do right by your friend. And there's a really clear way you can do that since I had to tell her that my hands are sort of tied in terms of accomplishing her pillars. This is supposed to be a journey that Hopefuls complete on their own to prove their eligibility for the group. But there's nothing that stops Hopefuls from helping each other. When I suggested she turn to you for help, she bolted."

She looks at me expectantly, but for once I don't have the words. I feel so bad for Sabrina, I really do. And I feel even worse that I'm part of her problems. But she's not the only one who's hurting.

After way too long of an awkward silence, Lonny sighs. "This is where you're supposed to chime in with your game plan."

"I can't just force her to talk to me. I don't think you get how stubborn Sabrina is."

Lonny looks at me like Connery does, like she's really seeing me. Although, with Connery, it makes me feel liked—possibly even more. With Lonny, it makes me feel vulnerable, seen in ways I maybe don't want to be.

"Is she the stubborn one? Or are you?"

Lonny gets up and walks away without another word, leaving me squirming in my seat, feeling guilty, mad, confused.

Nick, where r u? I really need u.

Those text dots appear, erase, appear, erase.
Finally, I get:

With Sabrina. Talk soon.

What was that about date-night excitement?
I can't seem to find any of it now.

I really should have thought this date through better. At least the location. Connery said he didn't want to go up to the city because traffic on a Friday night is unreal, so I suggested we meet up here. No matter what time of day, traffic in Mountain Pass is a breeze. Even if it's a night where it feels like all of Seattle has come to see what sort of queer artistry they can partake in, you'd be fine. You can park at one end of downtown and be at the other in five minutes. Six and a half if you're wearing stilettos.

I asked Connery to meet me at Mountain Pass Café, in the heart of Main Street. The only problem with that is, I have to walk past every single other store, and on a Friday, this place is bustling. Everyone is here, from the entirety of Mountain Pass High grabbing a slice or going to see a movie, to local adults doing the Friday wine-and-cheese night at the Mountain Pass Art Gallery. I know Mom's around here somewhere, always trying to get as much face time with Mountain Passers as possible. But right now, you'd think I was mayor because it feels like everybody wants to talk to me.

"Have fun at your date tonight!"

"Good luck with the writer cutie, Riley!"

"Looking sharp, lady!"

I mean, it's nice that everybody is rooting for me, but I'm suddenly realizing how everyone in this town must be listening to the podcast. I now have a total of 31,244 unique listeners, and it seems like every last resident of Mountain Pass is one of them. How else would they know that I was headed to a date? And while I appreciate all the love and support, it could totally tank the vibe if we have people watching us with horrifying doe eyes hoping this date works out.

I want to text Nick about it right away, but he's on Sabrina watch. Lonny wasn't kidding: her meltdown was huge, and Nick let me know that he has to take supportive best friend duty to help talk her down. Normally I'd be by his side to boost her up, but, Nick was pretty clear he thought me showing up when she was this upset would only make matters worse. Which means at this crucial moment in my love life and Gaybutante-hinging bet, both of my best friends (one of whom is my producer) aren't by my side. So, there's nobody to help talk away these nervous all-eyes-on-me butterflies.

The weird thing is all eyes are on me a lot. Not in a self-centered, narcissist kind of way. But anytime I walk into a room, I'm instantly clocked by people. It's this bizarre phenomenon when you aren't gender conforming. On the best of days, you get people giving you the up-down with an approving smile, liking it when someone can step outside the box. Sometimes it's old people who aren't judgmental, necessarily, but who look at me and I can practically see the wheels turning in their heads trying to figure out what the kids are up to these days. At the funni-est, it's a straight dude who has clearly been checking me out from behind, but when I turn around, they realize I've got a dick and they don't want to cop to the fact that they were just thinking a guy's ass was attractive. At the worst, it's someone who hates me for not playing by the gender rules and wants to kick the shit out of me. Regardless, I'm used to attention.

But that's just attention for being me. Now it's attention for how my love life is going to shape up, and that's just as much pressure as everyone's hope that I succeed at getting into the Gaybutantes. What if this doesn't work out? I'll look like such an idiot, and I'll feel everyone's pity that I couldn't get someone to fall for me. Not only that, but I'll have let femmes down everywhere, and that's the biggest reason why if I don't win this bet, I'm sticking to my word.

I can't join a society about boosting queer people up if I've proven a cis asshole right that femme folks can't find masculine gays to date them. I'll be bringing my entire community *down*, not lifting them to greater heights!

Then I'll be stuck in this town forever, doing interviews at KMPK and dreaming of what could have been. But by that point, even locals probably won't want to sit down and talk with me because they'll all remember what a massive, public failure this whole bet was.

Why did I ever do this stupid podcast? And get so caught up in proving Skylar wrong that I thought I should blast our bet to the world? Maybe Lonny's right and I really am the most stubborn person on the planet, and now that's going to bite me in the ass when I humiliate myself in front of the entire town.

"Riley!"

All my worries vanish as soon as I see Connery making his way up the other side of the street. He's got this huge grin on his face, like there's nowhere else he'd rather be. His hair is mussy, as always, except now there are tiny drops of water in it from the mist we've got going on. The way they glimmer under the marquee of the Mountain Pass Cinema makes it seem like there are diamonds in his hair. He's in a pillowy cable-knit sweater, looking like a sexier, smarter, gayer version of Chris Evans. He picks up the pace and jogs until he's wrapping all that perfection around me in front of the café. There's that smell of body-wash and books again.

Shit, what was I even anxious about? This night is going to go perfectly.

"Shall we?" he asks, being that ultimate gentleman and holding the door open. I can't stop the smile that breaks across my face. I'm sure I look like the biggest dork, but when I lock eyes with Connery as I walk through the door, his smile gets wider too.

Just two lovestruck gays looking at each other like idiots.

The instant we walk in, all chatter dies down. Like, it was hustling and bustling, then *bam!* Dead silent.

"Whoa," Connery breathes, and scans the room.

Yep. All eyes are on us.

Way to play it cool, Mountain Pass.

I figure the best way to get through this awkwardness is to just call it out. "Okay, everybody, back to your own business! Can't a lady date in peace?"

Some awkward laughs, a lot of genuine ones. Sometimes Mountain Passers don't know how obnoxiously wholesome they are until their weirdness is shoved back in their faces. The chatter instantly goes back to packed-restaurant levels.

"Sorry about them," I say to Connery. "They're just excited."

We make our way to a corner table, which Roz calls the Romance Table since the lighting is low and something about the way the brick walls meet makes it so you can only hear what the person across from you is saying.

"About what?" Connery asks as we sit down.

"You," I say through a laugh.

"Me?" Connery's eyes go wide. "Why? You don't get a lot of new people here?"

"No, no, we get out-of-towners all the time. Haven't you heard of the Mountain Pass queer scene?"

Connery shakes his head. "Remember that part where I mentioned reading all the time? Yeah, if it's not in like, a five-mile radius from me, I don't know much about it. Although when I saw Yelp reviews of this place, it mentioned there being an epic open mic night."

"That's where Nick met Daniel," I say. "One moment Daniel was up on stage singing sweet love songs, and then *boom*. Fireworks!"

"That sounds straight out of a romance novel," Connery says. "I used to think romances all seemed so far-fetched. But if that kind of stuff can happen in real life?" He shrugs. "Who knows. Maybe my romance is just around the corner."

He reaches for a menu and our hands brush. That had to be intentional, right? That was too perfectly timed to wonder if his Romance Novel Come True could ever happen and then "accidentally" touch me like that.

"So, what's good here?" Connery asks.

"Roz makes the best chicken parmigiana. Like, it's legendary."

Connery looks down at his cream-colored sweater, his entire face falling in the cutest look of dread. "This was totally the wrong outfit choice for marinara sauce."

"I'm sure Roz has some bibs in the back."

Connery laughs. "It'd be a worthy fashion sacrifice if it's as good as you say."

Roz comes over and we each order the chicken parm. "You're making my life easy," she rasps. "And what to drink?"

"Just some sparkling water for me," I say.

When Roz turns to Connery, he suddenly seems really sheepish. A blush creeps up his cheeks, starting all the way down in his neck, until he's this glowing beacon of redness.

"Don't worry about it, hon; there are no wrong answers," Roz says.

Connery glances at me and ducks his eyes. "Okay, I know this is going to sound ridiculous, like a little kid in first grade. But could I have a root beer float? Please? Ma'am?"

Roz jabs her pen in Connery's direction. "As long as you never call me *ma'am* again, you can have whatever you want. One root beer float coming up."

The second she's gone, I burst out laughing. "Okay, has anyone ever told you that you're *adorable*? I mean, I haven't had a root beer float since like, Levi Welch's birthday party in fourth grade."

Connery glows even redder, and it's so refreshing to see someone so smart and talented and hot get embarrassed. "I can't help it. It's this Friday-night tradition my grandma started when I was little. Root beer floats at dinner. And

I've kept at it, even if we aren't together. She'll check in tomorrow and make sure I did it, I swear."

"Family pressure? I can relate."

Connery cocks his head to the side. "That response seems to have some layers. Want to talk about it?"

Sigh. He can sense when something bothers me and wants to talk it out. The list of Connery pros keeps growing longer.

"It's just that I get these little reminders from my mom every single day that she expects me to stay here in Mountain Pass when I get out of school," I say. "But, as much as I love this town, I want more. I know there's so much outside this little place that I want to see and people I want to talk to and grow from. But the second I say that, I know Mom is going to feel abandoned. She'll be the last remaining member of her family here, and we kind of have a legacy in Mountain Pass."

"Wow," Connery says. "That's a bit more expectation than whether or not you drink a root beer float, isn't it?"

I laugh, but it's weak. Worried. "You can say that again."

"Hey." Connery reaches over the table and grabs my hands. "You deserve to accomplish anything you set your mind to. All right?"

The way he says it, I just know he's the one to help me win this bet. I'm setting my mind to proving toxic cis views wrong, and Connery would be all about that. And it goes beyond that too. I can fully see us side by side, in a relationship post–Gaybutante Ball, supporting each other in all our dreams. Me sitting in the audience at his future book signings, him cheering me on as I create new podcasts and book new guests and talk for a living to my little femme heart's content. I can't help but grin at the thought.

"That's better," Connery says. "And in answer to your question before: no, nobody's ever called me *adorable*. At least not to my face. I'm not like you, where I'm sure you're told you're beautiful all the time."

The most amazing things happen all at once. First, my heart starts pounding in the best way. I've never had such a perfect guy call me *beautiful* before. I mean, I've heard it from my parents, or from fellow Mountain Passers who want to be supportive of my femmeness. But never from somebody I actually liked, while I'm right in front of him in all my femme glory. Connery takes in all of it, from the black high-waisted pants to the forest-green silk blouse that brings out some of the green flecks in my hazel eyes, to the neutral-gold palette I've got going on for eye shadow, even resting on my dusty-pink lipstick. Then there's the fact that when he said it and while he's taking me in, the redness in his cheeks has gone down. It's this sign from his body that he truly means what he said and isn't embarrassed to share that with me, with the whole restaurant, who—even though they're still keeping to themselves—are definitely sneaking peeks at our table.

This is what I've been hoping for all along: somebody who sees the full me and isn't afraid to let the world know that they like a person who doesn't fit the gender mold.

This wave of relief washes over me. And when it finally reaches my face, the very last thing I ever thought would happen in this moment happens. I tear up. When I blink, a single drop falls down my cheek.

"Oh my god, Riley, I'm so sorry." Connery even squeezes my hands for emphasis. "What did I say?"

"No, no, it's me. *I'm* sorry." I let go of his right hand for the briefest moment to dab away the tear. "I'm being way more dramatic than I usually am. And that's saying something."

Connery laughs and does slow circles with his thumb over the back of my hand. "Tell me what's going on. How can I help?"

"It's actually a good thing, I swear. It's just, to answer *your* question: No, I haven't been called *beautiful* before. I mean, other than from friends or well-meaning strangers who just want to give you a small little compliment, you know? I've never heard it before from someone I actually liked."

Connery's thumb stops moving. His hands get clammy. The redness blooms up his face again, there in an instant. Like a severe allergic reaction. To what *I* said.

"Oh, um." Connery clears his throat. "Riley."

He doesn't move. He doesn't make eye contact. He doesn't say anything else.

I whip my hands from Connery's and want to slap them over my eyes. "Oh no. No no no no no. Connery. You're not into me, are you?"

He bites his lip while he shakes his head. "I mean, not like that. But I definitely like you as a friend."

"God, I'm such an idiot. The first time I find a gay guy who's respectful and appreciative of the way I present myself, and *of course*, he's not into me."

"Wait. I'm not—who said I was gay? Not that there's anything wrong with that at all. I'm just not. I'm not gay. I'm straight."

I feel like the spinning color wheel of death when my MacBook freezes up. This does not compute. "Wait, what? But you have that rainbow-flag decal on your laptop. You've read all those books about queer people."

"Because I try to read outside my own experience. I've told you about my best friend, Dylan, who's trans. She's opened my eyes to so many great stories, and I just always want her to know I'm an ally."

Jesus, he really is as amazing as I thought. He's just not an option. Even though he sends *very* mixed signals. "You called me *beautiful*. You held my *hands*." It's not really an accusation, more a statement of fact. Me, blubbering around, trying to save face and explain why I thought he was so into me.

"You are beautiful." He cringes. "Fuck. Dylan's warned me about this. That I'm too open with my feelings and that my affection could send the wrong signals. And here we are, major wrong signals. Riley, please know I think you're great, but—"

I can't hear the *but*. I shoot up from my chair so hard that it clatters to the floor. The resulting *bang* gets everyone's attention, and it's my worst nightmare come true. All eyes are on me, zeroing in on the moment this whole night turns to trash, listening to my entire plan go haywire.

"You said it was a *date*," I angrily whisper.

Connery smacks a hand to his forehead. "I know. I'm so sorry. It's an expression!"

A gasp echoes through the room. Everyone instantly clocks the misunderstanding. Their shocked looks turn to pity, and I have to get out of here *now*.

The bell over the café door is more grating than it's ever been as I make my way out onto the street. I dash out of downtown as fast as my boots will take me, but it's not fast enough. People register my hurried pace, asking me what's wrong as they spot how devastated I must look.

Everywhere I turn, Mountain Passers know that this night was an epic failure.

I've always known I'd leave someday, but I've never wanted out of this town more.

Excerpt from Episode 9—*Riley Weaver Needs a Date to the Gaybutante Ball*: "You Know What They Say When You Assume"

Within a five-minute time span, every hope I had for a boyfriend-turned-escort shriveled up and died right before my eyes. Just like that!

Here's the worst part about the mix-up with Bookworm: I fell into some serious stereotype traps. Like a complete asshole. Here I am saying that not all gay people are exactly the same, yet because BW is affectionate, open with his emotions, and proudly displays and discusses his interactions with the queer community, I assume there's no way he could be straight. How terrible is that? Like, Bookworm's actually a dream version of a straight guy. But I just went right ahead and assumed that person didn't exist and went about acting like there was no way some-one straight could possibly have a rainbow-flag sticker on their computer or read about queer people in books. I was just as unfair to BW as others have been about me and femmes assigned male at birth, and just, uuuuuugh.

None of this is as easy as I thought. If I had just slowed my roll and actually taken a second to ask Bookworm what he was into, none of this would have happened.

But now, I don't have time to slow things down. I'm in the last act of this bet, and it's not looking like I'm going to get the happy ending I'd hoped for. It's less than a month until the Gaybutante Ball, there are no escort pickings at Mountain Pass High, and I can't just stand on some Seattle street corner on Capitol Hill with a sign saying DATE ME, PLEASE! I need to be asked by my non-existent suitor, remember?

Which means I have to finally face the fact that The Jock could be right. I've had a solid eight weeks of putting all the vibes out there that I'm looking for someone to date, and I've had no bites. None. Does this mean that gay guys really don't like femme guys? To be honest, I'm feeling like I'm destined to be alone, and while a future without a partner never really bothered me before . . . it does now.

I want somebody. Somebody to love me.

Chapter 14

Saturday goes by in a blur. Like, a literal blur, because I keep blurring over with tears when I think of the mess I made by entering into this stupid bet in the first place. There's now a perma redness under my eyes from how often I've dabbed at them with tissues, because no matter how much my eyes water, I refuse to shed a single tear. That just means I'm letting Skylar and his assholery get to me, and I won't let him win like that.

But it's a close call so many times. I think of how my heart soared whenever I looked at Connery, and how quickly it sank when I saw his face turn with the realization of all the strings I attached. I try to distract myself by trying out new looks with a Baby Yoda eye shadow palette Nick got me, but my heart's just not in it, which is a first for me. The only thing I can think to do instead is scroll through social media. The algorithm decides to stab me in the back by showing all the successes of the other Hopefuls, shining a bright spotlight on the epic futures they'll have as Gaybutantes while I'll be stuck watching at home like everybody else.

Archibald has a sped-up time lapse video of the Lego labyrinth he built for his hosting gig. Verity poses in front of the house they helped build with Habitat for Humanity. Gulshan holds a TikTok Live with his mentee where they talk about obstacles they have to face as openly queer athletes in club sports. It's all so fabulous, it's all so beautiful, it's all so gay. And here I am deluding myself that since I'm not letting a tear fall, I'm not crying. Dream on, Riley.

Dad stops by a few times asking if I want anything to eat, but I'm not hungry. On Sunday, his is the first voice I hear as he gently knocks on the door again.

"Okay, Riley, one day is the maximum amount I'll let go by without you sampling anything I cook." I can tell he's trying to be lighthearted, but there's real concern in his voice.

"I'm fine, Dad."

Muffled whispers come through the door. Mom has joined the chat. I hear Dad say, "Give him space" and Mom respond with, "What does he have to hide from us? We can help!" Ultimately, as always, Mom wins. She jimmies the door. As the designer of this house and the installer of the doorknobs, she knows just how to manipulate it to override the *very weak* lock.

My door swings open. "Riley Weaver, we don't keep secrets under my roof!"

My roof. That's just it. This isn't *our* house. It's her house. Just like no matter how welcome I've been here, this isn't *my* town. It's her town. But now that I've lost the bet, I'm going to be stuck here forever, dreaming of what could have been.

That's when the tears finally fall.

Mom's angry facade melts in a heartbeat. She rushes over to my bed and cradles my head in her hands.

"Riley, honey, what is it? What's wrong? Who hurt you?"

"You, Mom. You."

The room goes dead silent. Well, silent except for me sniffling, snot dribbling down my lip that I wipe away with my silk robe.

"M-me?" I've never seen Mom look so shocked in her life, and that's saying something considering the shit people comment on her social media accounts since she's an outspoken liberal woman.

"I don't want to live in Mountain Pass all my life. But every time we talk, you always bring it up. Me staying here and keeping up the family name, when technically it's not even my name. I'm Riley *Weaver*, not Hayden, and the Hayden trajectory's not enough for me, Mom. The family's not enough for me. It's not that I don't love you and Dad, or that I'm not proud of everything our family's done in Mountain Pass. But I've got to see what's out there. I need more. I feel trapped."

"I—Riley. I never—" Mom glances over her shoulder to Dad hovering in the doorway. "Chester, am I that bad?"

Dad gives her a small, knowing smile. "You do have a lot of hometown pride, honey."

"Riley, I'm so sorry." She pulls my face back a bit so she can look me right in the eye. "I love this town; I'm so proud of everything we've done to make it what it is. But I love you more. If you need out of here to spread your wings, I'll always support you."

"Why didn't you ever say that? Why can you only ever talk about me *here*, running the radio station with a whopping listenership of like, nobody?"

Mom's silent for a long time, not looking away, even with my slightly angry glare. I didn't realize until this moment that I don't just feel pressure from her, I'm mad at her too. She's put all her expectations on me without asking about mine, and I need to know why.

"Oh, Riley," she finally says. "I guess I only ever told you about the visions that I hoped for. Consider it a side effect of being mayor, telling your constituents what you see for the future and then making it a plan."

"But as mayor you also walked door-to-door and asked everybody what they wanted. You never did that for me."

Mom sighs. "I guess, after your grandparents died and my cousins moved away, I put undue pressure on you as my sole remaining relative here. Not to mention, it's every parent's dream to get to live near their children. I think I got a little overzealous about what the Weaver future could look like."

"You do that sometimes," Dad says. "Get overzealous."

Mom gives him an *Are you kidding me?* look that makes me snort.

"Riley, deep down, would I like you to stay here in Mountain Pass forever? Yes. I'd be lying if I said that wasn't the case. But what I want more than anything in the world, even more than you staying here, is for you to be happy. Got it?"

She has this look like she's disappointed in herself, sad that I ever thought she'd work against my dreams, and confused as to how we both let this misunderstanding get so far. I can tell that she means what she's saying. But, regardless of whether or not Mom is cool with me moving away, there's one cold, hard reality that's going to make the odds of me ever leaving slim to none.

"Well, I don't think you'll have to worry about me going anywhere," I say. "I've lost the bet. No one is going to ask me to the Ball. It's less than a month away, and if my track record from the last two months proves anything, I do not know how to find a man."

"What do you mean, kiddo?" Dad asks. "What does one date have anything to do with your future?"

"I'm not getting into the Gaybutantes!" I say it way louder than I mean. "I can't back down on the bet, and even if I did, there's no way I can join a group about celebrating queer voices when all I've done is broadcast to the world what a femme failure I am. And without the Gaybutantes backing up my work, I'll never have a following big enough to get me any opportunities outside of Mountain Pass. I guess it's just KMPK after all. Yahoo."

Now Mom's giving *me* the *Are you kidding me?* look. "Riley, don't take this the wrong way, but that's the dumbest thing I've ever heard."

"Wow." I scoff. "So, the supportive-mom thing's gone out the window, huh?"

"No, no, what I'm saying is, you can succeed whether or not the Gaybutantes are with you. I mean, look at everyone out there who's accomplished their dreams that you know of, famous or otherwise. Only something like point-oh-oh-oh-oh-oh-oh-oh-oh-one percent of them are Gaybutantes."

I fall back onto my bed. "But it will be so much harder without them."

"Yeah. That could be true. But anything worth having is worth working your ass off for." She pulls me back up, never one to let someone mope in their feelings, always wanting them to hop to action and get things done. "It doesn't matter whether you have one listener or one million. As long as you've got one heart to connect to, that's a job well done. How many people have listened to your podcast to date?"

"I don't know . . . Thirty thousand something?"

Dad's eyes bug out of his skull. "Thirty fucking thousand?! Riley, that's huge!"

He says it with awe and suddenly I'm feeling very bashful. "That's only because the Gaybutantes posted about it."

Mom shrugs. "So what? Don't you think that whether or not you end up joining the Society, at least *some* of those listeners will follow you to whatever you do next? Your start is already here, Riley. People are already interested in what you have to say. So quit sulking around and start saying something."

"I don't think it's going to be that easy." I've thought of the Gaybutantes as this major stepping stone since I knew they existed. I can't just *say something*. I need to make a whole new plan, and I don't know where to start.

I should just be able to call Nick or Sabrina and get out all these feelings, start brainstorming what life will be like without my goal of Gaybutante status. It's what my hands itch to do, wanting to pull up my favorite contacts right now. But Nick's on Sabrina duty, and even if she's being completely unreasonable, I don't want to be the one who ruins her breakdown recovery by calling Nick in the middle of some heartfelt confession or big breakthrough. He said I could call after I sent him the audio of my post-"date" episode (that I had to record alone), but I know it'd just set Sabrina off since she's the one who demanded space in the first place. She's just as stubborn as I am, and I know she'll go on and on about breaking her very clear boundaries if I try to call her or interrupt her time with our shared BFF.

"It's a lot to think abo—" I'm cut off by some serious stomach rumbling, which Dad instantly jumps on.

"AHA!" he shouts. "I knew you were hungry! Come on,

let's go to the kitchen. No good plan was ever made on an empty stomach."

Even full of waffles and parental support, I'm not any closer to figuring out what the last few weeks of my Hopeful season are going to look like. My mind races with possibilities until Monday morning, when I get way more pitying looks than I ever have before in the MPH hallways. All those supportive comments from Friday have suddenly turned into those *sorry for your loss* comments where no one knows quite what to say but has to shove it in your face that they feel bad for you.

"Oh, Riley. You doing okay?"

"Keep your chin up, lady."

"Hang in there, bud."

After that last one I put my earbuds in and my head down. Mom might be right that I can make it without the Gaybutantes, but that doesn't take away how humiliating my very public failure is. I sulk with my eyes on the floor all the way to my locker. My heart nearly falls out of my butt when I finally get within inches of it and see *two* sets of feet, one of which I've been trying my hardest to avoid. I glance up to find Nick, wide-eyed and horrified, his gaze bouncing back and forth between Sabrina's and my red-rimmed stares. I wasn't the only one crying this weekend.

"Sabrina," I breathe.

She opens her mouth like she's about to speak, but instead a hiccup comes out, and she slams her locker shut before shouldering around me and racing down the hall.

"I take it the weekend didn't go well?" I ask.

Nick shakes his head. "She and Cassidy are in another huge fight. Sabrina deleted all her social media, but it still wasn't enough. Daniel and I tried everything. We went to the movies with Sabrina, visited her at the clinic. We invited Cassidy to come along, but she's ghosting all of us. It's bad. Really bad."

"Why doesn't Sabrina just dump her already? I mean, honestly. Cassidy is blowing this way out of proportion."

"I know." Nick shrugs. "But I can't force that down Sabrina's throat. If I do, then she'll cut me off like she did y—" He clamps his lips shut. We stare at each other in silence, and while I want to be angry, all I am right now is sad. I could use Sabrina in my life, the other slice of bread that used to keep this bestie sandwich together.

"Sorry," Nick finally says. "I didn't mean to bring it up."

"It's fine," I say. "It's not your fault. How's Daniel?"

Nick's face switches to a scowl, probably from my extremely clear attempt at a subject change. But then the warning bell rings, and Nick's never been late to a class in his entire life. He glances up at the bell and says, "Everything's good." I can't tell if his answer's short because he wants to get to class, or if his small smile being a little crooked means there's something he's not telling me. But honestly, ever since Sabrina, I'm kind of hesitant to push too deep into relationship issues before I'm pushed away by the only true friend I have left.

"See you at lunch?" I ask instead, and Nick nods.

"Definitely."

He dashes off, and I quickly do a mirror check in my locker to make sure I was able to cover the tissue tenderness under my eyes. It's covered, all right, by a hideously caked-on amount of concealer, but here we are.

Head down again, I make my way to homeroom, blaring my music to block out any potential *Hang in there*s that are sure to keep bombarding me today. I plop into a seat and pull up my social media accounts, scrolling through the good, the bad, and the ugly comments on my posts, hoping I'll be struck with some idea on how to move forward.

That's when I get a DM from the last person to give any sort of inspiration.

Skylar.

And because I'm a walking poster child for self-betrayal, I can't stop myself from opening the message.

I just wanted to come over here and give you an out.

My heart skips. If Skylar is about to drop the bet, then this whole thing can be done. I don't have to worry about giving up my Gaybutante dreams. I can just go on and try to forget any of this ever happened. Try to forget the fact that I can't get anyone to date femme, formerly-thought-of-as-fabulous me.

You can just give up, Skylar goes on. There's no reason we have to prolong the inevitable. Just drop out of the Gaybutantes now. We both know you're not going to find a date in time.

Ms. Jennings enters the room before I can get out an eviscerating reply. She goes over the latest announcements, including reminding us that our workloads will pick up the week after Thanksgiving break as we near the end of the semester, that juniors will have a college fair to attend next week, and reminding everybody to cheer on the Gaybutante Hopefuls as we near the finish line of our season. The finish line that's apparently going to be full of studying and holiday breaks so no one will be available to date.

Once again, all eyes turn to me with that *poor Riley* look, while Ms. Jennings clearly thinks she's given me a nice little pep talk. Meanwhile, I can't wait for the minutes to ooze by so I can get out of here. With each passing second, Skylar's message won't quit blaring through my head.

He's right. I won't find a date in time. So why go on humiliating myself?

When homeroom ends, I burst out the door and text Nick the only thing that can get this to stop, once and for all.

I'm calling it. I'm dropping out of the Gaybutantes.

I can hear Nick climb up to the zip-lining platform before I see him. Not just his footsteps, which anyone would hear, but him mumbling to himself, like he's practicing something. But the second his head pops above the stairs— his newly dyed, bright bubblegum-pink hair totally at odds with the deep scowl on his face—he seals his lips shut.

It doesn't take a mind reader to know what he was doing.

"You're going to try to convince me not to leave the Gaybu-tantes, aren't you?"

Nick's scowl only furrows deeper before he gives a weak "No."

We stare at each other awkwardly until the words finally fly out of me. "How did I get here? How? Am I really that undat—" My throat closes, clogged with emotion. "Fuck." I swallow, but it feels like trying to get a pair of Crocs down my windpipe. "That undatable?"

"Riley." Nick takes the last step onto the platform and flops down to wrap me in his arms. He doesn't say anything, just breathes in for four, out for five. My head rises and falls with his chest, and before long my breaths are in sync with his. My throat relaxes, the Crocs slide down, but I can't help the handful of tears that drip on top of his Mr. Freeze T-shirt, the vintage one I got him for Christmas last year.

"Why did I start that stupid podcast? Why did I make it so easy for thousands of people to see me fail?"

"Because you're not wrong," Nick says. "Femme people deserve love just as much as anyone else. It's amazing that you wanted to stick up for any other femmes out there who have heard and internalized shit like what Skylar told you. You did this for them, and I love that about you."

"But it's going to send the exact opposite message when I can't get a date for the Ball. When I admit to everyone out there that Skylar was right. I'm *not* able to make a guy fall for me."

Nick stares at me again, but the scowl isn't there this time. He's back to his usual small-smile self.

"What is it?"

"You *have* made people fall in love with you." He reaches into his pocket and pulls out his phone. A few clicks later, he's opened up the hashtag WeaverFever. "Take a look."

There's picture after picture, video after video, of people sharing their love and support for me and the podcast. I scroll farther and farther, each new post about some form of femme connection. About their dating escapades, about how I boost them up, about how people wanting to deny femmes their lives and happiness and say we're just weird sexless beings can go shove it. People saying things like "I finally bought my first pair of heels because of Riley and I've never felt more POWERFUL" and "I'll get to be my femme self someday, but for now, I'm living through Riley. His podcast makes me feel like I'm not alone."

"These are amazing, but I've seen supportive comments before," I say. "It doesn't change how many people out there still hate me because they don't like the kind of gay I am or they think I'm a backstabber to all femmes."

Nick gives me his pensive nod. "I get that. But you know no matter what you do, people are going to hate you, right? It's a sad world, but there'll be folks out there who hate you just for existing. There will be people who disagree with you so strongly that they make it personal. Even on things as inconsequential as a fandom forum." He gets quiet, and I know he's thinking of the instances of online hate that made him leave social media altogether. He's had his own battles because of his race and sexuality that I know have hurt him just as much, if not more. "The key is finding ways to do the things you love while protecting your heart. Your mental health." He scrolls through posts and pulls up one more video. "I think this person says it best about your specific situation."

Nick turns his phone around so I can see a fabulous femme who I'm going to have to get liquid eyeliner tips from because *damn they're good*. Their handle is DreamWeaver613, and when Nick presses Play, they say, "I hope Riley knows it doesn't even matter if he wins this bet. It matters that he's put himself out there, that he's opened up this convo for all of us to talk. That he's showing what it's like to be femme in this world that STILL is so boxed in by gender rules. Riley is a superhero. WEAVER FEVER FOREVER!"

That's when I lose it again, a real face-warped, ugly cry. The kind of cry that I'd only let Nick see. And he lets me. He doesn't say a word, just keeps a hand on my knee while I let it all out.

Finally, I stand up, brace myself against the platform rail, and let out the most guttural scream of my life. We call it the Break Up Banshee move, something Sabrina's done twice up here, Nick once. It's the first time for me. And while I might not be breaking up with someone, I'm getting out all the negative emotion that I can. All the insecurity from Skylar, all the self-doubt and shame, all the worry that I'm somehow unworthy of any love or attention.

When I finally turn back to Nick, that small smile is full-on beaming. "Feel better?"

"I needed to see that."

"I just wanted you to understand all sides of this before you make any decisions. It's ultimately up to you to choose what the best thing to do is. But before you pick your fate in the Society, there's something else you need to do." Nick swipes a few times, then shows me the emails from listeners who've written in asking to be my Gaybutante mentee. "You've known all along the GS isn't about finding a date for the Ball. It's about queer connection. Don't let Skylar take that away from you. Don't give up on these kids who look up to you."

"But I'm a femme of my word. If I don't meet the rules of the bet, I'm still going to drop out."

Nick clearly doesn't like what I've said, but he goes on anyway. "That's fine. But you've got to follow through with what you've promised your listeners. People want to hear from you whether or not you join the Gaybutantes. You see that, right?"

I think back to DreamWeaver613's video. Nick's right. All these people are right. And it's a definite no for the Gaybutantes if I don't follow through on all my pillars of gayness. Whether or not it ends in me being introduced at the Ball with an escort by my side, I owe it to my nameless mentee out there to do this.

I take a deep breath. "Okay," I say. "I'm ready."

Excerpt from Episode 10—*Riley Weaver Needs a Date to the Gaybutante Ball*: "An Inconvenient Truth"

So, based on my last episode, I think none of you will be surprised by what I'm about to say . . .

Deep breath, Riley.

[long inhale, longer exhale]

Right. Um, I'm not going to win this bet. There's three weeks left to go until the Ball, one of which is Thanksgiving, when eligible bachelors are at home with their families. The others are full of cram sessions and college counseling, and it would just be the real cherry on top of a wild season if I flunk out in addition to tanking my love life. So, I don't know if there's enough time anymore to have a guy fall for me and ask to be my escort.

I want everyone to be prepared for that now. I'd be lying if I said I've one hundred percent accepted this myself, but I'm getting there.

Okay, enough of the depressing stuff.

What I've realized in this journey is there are so many more important things at hand than whether or not I get a date. So many more important people.

You.

This isn't about me finding a date—it's about femmes sticking together, about allies learning more of what we go through and how they can help when we come across assholes who say we aren't deserving of love. To that end, I'd like to introduce you all to my mentee. Whether or not I get into the Gaybutantes, this part of the Hopeful journey is important to me, and I think all of us older femmes should help those coming into their own fabulous selves.

Here's what my new mentee had to say, shared with their permission:

"Dear Riley,

First, I just want to say that I'm really nervous. You're like, such an inspiration, and to get a chance to talk to you, even in a letter, is wild."

Oh, wow. I probably should have skipped over that part because it seems pretty narcissistic to broadcast a letter about someone gushing over me. But I swear this isn't why I picked them. Okay, here we go for real.

"Second, and probably more why I'm so nervous, is because I've never told anyone that I'm femme before. Ever. I live in a pretty rural part of Washington state,

and it's just not normal for people assigned male at birth to do anything that could be described as girly. I shouldn't say *normal*—that's not what I mean. Because what is normal, right? I just mean: it's not done here. But I've always known from the very first moment I can remember my mom putting on makeup that I want to wear it too. Not just makeup. Heels and skirts, everything. When I get home from school and my parents are at work, I've tried on some of her stuff and it just feels . . . right. Perfect.

Me.

But I can only do that when no one else is around. I know we're in the 2020s, but sometimes you'd think we're in 1920 based on the way people talk about queer folks here. Not to mention how so many parents got on board that messed-up bandwagon of trying to ban books from our library and my school that had anything to do with LGBTQIA+ characters or people of color. You don't need someone to say to your face that they don't want you to know that they don't, you know?

Sorry if I'm rambling. But what I'm trying to say is, I'm really tired of being this person other people want me to be. I want to finally get to outwardly express who I am. I want to know how to put on a face, I want to know what type of heels I like best, I want to try it all. I'm not sure how it's going to be received, I don't know if I'll just have to do this in secret until I graduate in two and a half years and move out, but I know without a doubt that I want someone to show me these things, even if it's just us. Or, I don't know, I've been thinking about maybe wearing the kind of shoes I like to Winter Formal, seeing how people take that. But whether I do that or not, I'd just love some tips? On how to be me?

Even if you don't choose me, thank you for taking the time to read this. It really felt nice to get this all out.

With so much love,

Your Mentee Hopeful"

Well, Mentee, I can't say I know exactly what it's like to be in your shoes, having grown up in a spot that's pretty queer-friendly. But I do get the nerves that go along with becoming the true you for the first time, or those weird glances from folks sizing you up. I've got your back. And your face and your feet when it comes to showing them off in the way that you want. I'm honored you've asked me to be a part of your journey.

With so much love right back to you,

Riley

Chapter 15

I t took me three days to finally pick a mentee. Poring over all the submissions filled with so much heart and hope and looking forward to a femme future made me feel better than that time I was able to actually get my Telfar bag before it sold out. But knowing I couldn't spend time with each and every person was hard. The one I finally picked, Josiah, seemed the best for so many reasons. For starters, they live in the same state, so I can easily take the two-hour drive to pick them up and bring them to the queer paradise that is Mountain Pass. Most importantly, though, I remember being exactly where they're at, not knowing how to put together any of the femme looks that I knew could outwardly express my heart. It's the weirdest feeling walking into a Sephora and asking for makeup. Not because the makeup artists are judgy, but there's always that mom shopping with her daughter and looking over her shoulder at you every five seconds to make you feel like you don't belong. It's mind-boggling to me that gender nonconforming beauty influencers can have millions of followers, but in real life, it can seem like people have no idea what they're looking at when they see me and other femmes that they assume are male. I want Josiah to feel support and like they've got a sister in me throughout this whole thing.

I can't concentrate in any of my classes, sketching out ideas for looks we could do based on the phone call we had last night where they told me all their favorite colors and style inspirations. It felt so good to just gush over the feminine stuff I love again after more than two months desperately trying to find a boyfriend. It made me feel the most me I've felt in a long time.

So much so that when I make it to the quad for lunch a few days later, I'm expecting everything to be normal. For Nick and Sabrina to be waiting for me at our usual table. But when I look up from my notebook, and Nick is waiting all alone, my heart drops. Things aren't normal.

But they should be.

I look around the area hoping that for once Sabrina might decide to eat here instead of wherever she's been hiding out, but I can't find her anywhere. Everyone's doing their own thing, acting like everything hasn't drastically shifted in such a short amount of time. Most of the other Hopefuls sit together, having all completed their pillars and floating on a high until they're inducted into the

Society. But for me, I'm not at all where I expected to be just a couple weeks out from the Ball.

The other not-normal thing? Nick is reading instead of looking up behind-the-scenes film footage on his phone.

I sit across from him. "*The Prince and the Dressmaker!* You're reading it."

Nick smiles and nods. "It's pretty good. I guess Connery knew what he was talking about." My gut squirms with guilt. Connery. I need to find some way to apologize for pulling him into this whole mess with my assumptions.

Nick looks like he's about to say something, but just before words come out, his mouth falls way open. Like, I-could-shove-my-bootie-inside-his-mouth open.

"What is it?" A shadow passes over me. I instinctively turn, and I'm face-to-face with the only other person I need right now.

"Sabrina," I breathe.

She stares down at me, her face blank, tugging on that ponytail like she always does. I've missed being able to be the one to gently pull her hand away from her hair. Based on what Nick's said, I'm sure he's had to do it a lot.

I don't know what comes over me. My body just reacts on its own, knowing this is exactly what I need. I fling myself up and wrap my arms around her, hugging her tighter than I've ever hugged someone in my life.

"I've missed you so much."

I'm bawling before I can stop it. In front of a crowd. And they are for sure watching. But I don't care.

I can't catch my breath. At first, I think it's because I'm crying too hard. But as I try to inhale, I feel this pressure around my ribs, and I realize it's because Sabrina is hugging me back. Just as hard as I'm squeezing her.

The quad erupts in applause. Echoing, boisterous almost-pop-your-eardrums claps and whistles that reverberate past the school and into the forest.

Sabrina finally pulls away, her cheeks blooming with pink. "God, this place is so cheesy."

That makes me choke out a laugh that turns into a hiccup that turns into happy tears. "I guess everyone knows you're fighting when you talk about it on your podcast. God, Sabrina, I can't believe I did that. I'm so sorry. You didn't have to have my back with Lonny like you did. I wouldn't have blamed you if you wanted this all shut down."

"Yeah, you really should have kept your mouth shut. But I know when you're venting and something accidentally slips out. Just don't let it happen again."

I mark an X over my chest. "I swear on my favorite discontinued Moschino x Sephora Collection brush set."

Sabrina laughs. "Wow, you really mean business."

The applause dies down as soon as we take a seat. Well, except for one last shout from an extremely happy Lonny who cries, "That's what I'm talking about, you two!" Even though Sabrina and I have sat side by side literally thousands of times, this feels like the first time. And my heart is pounding just as hard as when I thought

Connery was going to ask to be my boyfriend, or when Antoine kissed me.

"I never thought we'd get here again," Nick says. "You're both so fucking stubborn."

That sucks the air out of both Sabrina and me. Nick is always so cool, calm, and collected, and really only swears when he's ultrapissed. It was f-bomb city when he was venting about Grayson, but other than that, he's chill.

"We really put you through it, didn't we?" I say.

"We're the literal worst," Sabrina adds. "What sort of selfish assholes force one corner of their bestie triangle to be in the middle? It defies all rules of friendship and geometry."

"I don't know what any of that technical stuff means, but *that*." I put my hand out, and Nick puts his in mine. His blue-painted nails are chipped. It hits me that he hasn't asked for me to freshen them up like he always does. He's probably been too focused on making things fine for *us* that he stopped thinking about himself.

"It's fine," Nick says.

"It's not," Sabrina and I say together.

"You guys were going through it," Nick adds.

"And making you go through shit too," I say. "That's not right. We were, like, the overflowing septic tank of emotional garbage."

Sabrina places her own hand on top of ours, nails cut short, no polish, her hands dry from all the times she washes them at the vet clinic.

"I listened to your podcast," she says. "All along. Because I missed you. I was still so pissed. But I missed you. And then you go and make that whole episode about it not mattering if you get into the Gaybutantes, but how you want to boost up femmes everywhere, and it just made me remember why I love you so much."

I know I should be happy that she sees this shift in the podcast mission and that we've finally ended the rift between us. But right now, the only thing I'm feeling is gut-turning guilt.

"I really appreciate that, but I shouldn't have given all my attention to helping strangers. I mean, do they deserve community and support too? Absolutely. But I should have listened more to your problems with Cassidy. I should have done both."

Sabrina nods, quiet. Then, "Well, now you don't have to worry because I've got no more relationship for you to hear about." Sabrina's eyes fall, and Nick puts his other hand out to cover hers.

"It's okay," he says. "We've got you."

"Sabrina, I'm so sorry," I say.

She purses her lips. "Isn't this what you wanted all along?"

Ouch. But maybe I wasn't getting my concern out to her well enough.

"That's never what I wanted. In the perfect world, Cassidy would have stood by you and understood that all the attention you were getting wasn't your fault. Well, it was your fault in that you *are* fabulous and of course everyone would fall in love with you, but it wasn't what you were asking for. I wish she could have seen that, and all I was trying to say was that her jealousy seemed suffocating. Like, stuff you in a garment bag, weigh it down with bricks, throw you in Peak Lake kind of suffocating. And you don't deserve that."

"I think that's drowning, but I get the morbid metaphor," Sabrina says. "And you were right. No matter how much I tried to tell her nothing was going on, it was never enough. It *was* suffocating, especially when I loved that my mission was *working*. I've seen so many pics from followers volunteering at shelters and animal clinics. But when I tried to tell her how upset our fight was making me, she couldn't hear it. Even after deleting all my apps, she was convinced I'd downloaded them somewhere else. She was so suspicious. Thank god for Nick, or I really would have lost it. But it still felt off without you there."

"If y'all ever put me in the middle again, I'm going to stuff you in those garment bags myself," Nick says. "Is it nice to be a friend you can rely on? Sure. But sometimes I just need the two of you to say exactly how you feel about what's going on in your lives *to each other* so I don't have to spend so much mental energy trying to think of exactly the right thing to say. Do you know how exhausting it is to be a soundboard for everybody's feelings? That's what you two usually do for each other, and I get to be the brains of the operation and actually move us forward instead of just cussing out folks until we're out of breath. I can't do both. I need you two."

This whole time I thought it was Nick and Sabrina keeping *me* together, but apparently, we do that for each other.

"We're all the bread to our bestie sandwiches," I say.

Nick frowns. "What?"

"It means we hold each other steady," Sabrina says. "Sandwiched in the middle."

I hook my thumb toward her. "That!" God, I missed her.

We stare at each other like morons, stupid grins on our faces, holding hands, just soaking up the fact that we're finally together again.

"So, what do we do now?" I ask.

Nick looks at me like I've just said the most idiotic thing in the world.

"What do you mean, what do we do?" Nick says. "Isn't it obvious?"

Sabrina and I share a look, and even though we don't say a word, I know exactly what she's thinking. At the same time, we turn back to Nick and say, "No!"

Nick throws his hands in the air, knocking ours askew as he hollers, "You get your shit together and finally take the Gaybutantes by storm like you've always freaking planned! Jesus, I can't with you two sometimes."

"What was that part about you not saying what you're thinking as you're thinking it?" Sabrina asks with a smirk.

"Yeah, dude, I agree. Guess we rubbed off a little, huh?"

Nick wipes his hand across his cheek. I want to tell him how adorable he is when he's embarrassed, but I know that'll only make it worse for him.

"Well, now that I've called out the obvious, you two can make all the plans," Nick says, propping up *The Prince and the Dressmaker* against his bag. "I'll be over here if you need me."

"You're not seriously going to drop out of the Gaybutantes, are you?" Sabrina asks. "All because of Skylar?"

Mentioning his name brings his last DM to mind. Who am I kidding—he's *always* in the back of my mind. I can feel his presence, like I have this entire semester even though I barely saw him, knowing he's judging me, his messed-up views spurring me on to prove him wrong. Except now that probably won't happen.

"I can't go back on the bet," I say for the millionth time. Nick clears his throat with disapproval, but he doesn't look up from reading so I know he's not going to fight me on it again. "Just imagine what all the Team Jock people will say. That not only are femmes repellent to gay guys, but that we don't stick to our word either. That we're fragile *snowflakes* who melt under the reality of the world."

Sabrina looks pissed, but for the first time in weeks I know it's not at me. "You know that's all bullshit, right? None of that is true."

I nod, but I can't get myself to say anything. While in theory I know somebody who's right for me exists, I'd be lying if I said it didn't sting that I couldn't find them when I set my mind to it. And I'd be super lying if I said I didn't think it maybe has something to do with what Skylar insists it does.

"You know what I think will snap you out of it and remind you just how femme and fierce you are?" Sabrina asks.

"Sending a video to Robin Antin as an audition tape to become the next Pussycat Doll?" In addition to being a Melissa Joan Hart lover, Sabrina's mom listens exclusively to pop music from the mid-2000s, which is the only way I'd ever know who the hell those ladies are to begin with.

Sabrina laughs. "I actually think that'd be counterintuitive because we all know that while you love it, you would never grasp the hairography." Watching music videos of the Dolls may also have been what made Sabrina realize she's a lesbian. "I can't say I think you dropping out is a good idea, but I'll support you. And if that's the route you go, it doesn't mean you can't still go to the Ball and drop out in blazing femme glory. Maybe we can pick fabrics for outfits together? Mitzy says she still has time to create our looks, if you're interested."

She's right. Nothing about dropping out says I can't at least savor every last second of my Hopeful season. And I'm going to show the world just how fabulous femmes can be. That it doesn't matter whether I have some random guy's love, or Skylar's approval.

I've just got to be me.

I clutch my right hand over my heart and pull Sabrina into me with my left.

"I thought you'd never ask."

Chapter 16

There's only one place in town to go to for fabrics: Mountain Pass Crafts. Don't let the wholesome name fool you. Mitzy Hilton owns the place, and her eye for finding one-of-a-kind textiles is so good that even Joann or Michael or whoever else has a craft store chain named after them would be jealous.

MPC lies on the opposite end of town from school, and for the first time in forever, Sabrina and I walk out the front doors together. We're instantly in step, getting back into the groove of things like we never had time apart to begin with.

"So, wait, what about you?" I ask. "What's left for your pillars? If you held a party and didn't invite me, so help me!"

Sabrina looks like she might throw up. "I found a mentee, but yeah, definitely no party, and that's what I'm routinely stumbling on now. Everyone else has held theirs, and I don't want mine to just be, like, having people over for pop in my basement. That'd be so embarrassing. But the only other place I have access to is my parents' clinic, and a skunk with a distended anus does not scream *party*."

"That is the most horrifying animal anecdote I've ever heard you talk about."

"Imagine what it was like in the office. Every time Dad tried to push it back in, the thing sprayed!"

She looks at me, eyes wide, nostrils flared, like she'll forever be haunted by the experience. And who wouldn't be? But after a moment of her reliving it in her mind and me imagining it, we both lose it. Like, have to move to the side of the street so other people can walk by while we howl, holding our ribs. I'm crying so hard from laughing, I even lose a lash.

People give us weird looks, but it doesn't matter. Not when we haven't laughed like this in forever. I really have my best friend back.

"I can't breathe," I wheeze. "I can't breathe!"

"Riley?"

Dirty sneakers enter my line of sight as I'm bent over double trying to catch my breath. I follow them up past track pants, a Crestview Carnivores T-shirt, and then— holy shit—Skylar's face. Totally unsmug. Totally confused, worried, concerned, lost.

I thought I couldn't breathe before, but now I really can't. So much so that I can't speak. It's so jarring seeing him in real life, when throughout all this, it's only the third time I've seen him in the flesh. But even still, it's like he's been right beside me all along, taunting me, hating me. Making me so unsure of myself.

Sabrina, however, has got me covered. "What do you want?" she demands, arms crossed, stepping in front of me to become my human shield.

I assume Skylar will get combative, will smile all cockily and make fun of Sabrina for thinking she could take him (which she totally could, by the way; you don't spend all that time around vicious mountain cats and not learn some tricks). But instead, he actually takes a step back, puts his hands up, palms out—the tentative *I come in peace* stance.

"Hey, I swear I'm not here to start anything," he says. "I just thought, maybe, um." He takes a deep breath; his eyes dart to the ground. Like he's nervous. Then, finally, he cranes his neck, stretching past Sabrina's shoulder so he can look me in the eye. "Maybe we could talk. I promise I won't be a prick."

Sabrina turns around and gives me a look. We're both thinking the same thing. Neither of us expected him to call himself a prick. Maybe he's seeing the light.

"Oookay," I say. "You came all this way to talk, so . . . what do you have to say?"

Skylar glances at Sabrina. "I was hoping maybe we could have this talk in private."

Her ponytail whips back and forth as Sabrina shakes her head. "No way in hell I'm leaving you alone with him."

"Whoa, down, girl," I say. Her territorial instincts are kicking in. See what I mean about learning a lot from feral felines? "We can talk alone, but maybe we could go somewhere with nearby witnesses. Just in case. The café?"

Skylar shrugs. "Sure."

"I'll meet you at Mitzy's," I tell Sabrina. "Give me five minutes."

Sabrina glares at Skylar one more time before hugging me and saying, "If I don't hear from you in five minutes and one second, I'm calling the cops." Then she walks down the street, backward, giving Skylar the evil eye the whole time.

"She's a good best friend," Skylar says as we pass a few storefronts before he opens the door into the café. And holds it open. Like a gentleman. My heart aches for a second, thinking back to the last time this happened and I was sure I was going to be told that Connery couldn't stop thinking about me. There's no way Skylar is going to tell me that now, but I've got to admit that his weird, sullen-yet-polite demeanor has me curious, so I walk inside.

"Where should we sit?" I ask.

"How 'bout back there?" He points to the corner table, the romantic one, the one where Connery (rightfully) shot me down. I guess it makes sense to taint just one table with bad memories here, so why not.

I lead the way, my heart hammering against my chest. I don't know what's going to happen, and my body isn't sure how to take it.

I sit in the spot that keeps my back to the rest of the restaurant because if I get any more terrible news, I don't need tables full of studying students and the lesbian moms book club to see me have a meltdown again.

Skylar pulls the chair out across from me and it scrapes against the floor, setting my nerves on edge. Skylar cringes too, and I swear he whispers something to himself. Something like, "Keep it cool, dumbass."

He plops into the seat but doesn't say anything. He folds his hands on top of the table, twiddles his thumbs, unfolds his hands, wipes them on his jeans, awkwardly taps his fingers. All the while he's tentatively making eye contact, then glancing away. It's just way too damn awkward.

"What the hell is going on?!" I know it's loud—I'm sure other people heard—but I have to get to the bottom of why Skylar is acting like this.

"Okay, look, Riley. I, um, I need to tell you something. Something really personal." His eyes get all wonky. Like, super round, and this soft smile comes over his face an awful lot like Nick's, and I can't stop myself from thinking that he's actually kind of cute. Looking unsure of himself and innocent, almost. But if there's one thing I know about Skylar, it's that he's not. That. Innocent.

"Yes, and?" I prod.

"I like you."

"You do not." This is just ridiculous. This guy who says he could never like a femme person because he's gay doesn't like me.

"*Yes*, I do."

"*No*, you don't!"

"Riley!" His hands suddenly aren't so nervous and fidgety anymore. They're confident and sure in their trajectory to grab mine over the table. I hate that there's nothing to nitpick about his. They're not clammy; they're not shaky. He just uses all that hand-eye coordination from baseball to snatch my hands right up, staring at my neon-orange acrylics, his smile getting bigger when he takes them in. "These are nice."

"Who are you? Weren't you the person who said he could never like somebody like me?"

I try to pull my hands back, but his grip only gets tighter.

"Just hear me out. I like you. A lot. Ever since we made this bet, I couldn't stop thinking about you. At first, I thought it was because I just wanted to win. I have this competitive streak, you know, and I don't like losing. But I was talking about you all the time. I was listening to your podcast all the time. Lunch, weekends, postgames—I was constantly thinking about you. So, then I was telling Adam about that last message I sent you and Adam was like, 'Dude. If you say Riley's name one more time, I'm gonna have to assume you have a crush.' And that's when it hit me. I *didn't* have a crush. I have so much more than that. I really, really like you, Riley. I don't want to say *love*, because how can you love somebody before you really get to know them, but I need you to know. This has been so much fun. This big challenge between us. And I love a competition, and you were just so game from the start. We have so much in common. We're both stubborn, hotheaded guys who love the limelight. Why else would you want your own show? Why else would I want all this baseball stardom?"

"This is your idea of a romantic speech? You just called me a stubborn hothead." Although, maybe his assessment isn't entirely wrong.

"What I'm trying to say is, I can't stop thinking about you and maybe we should explore what we've got between us."

He stares at me expectantly, like he hopes I'm going to say yes. I mean, the truth is, I have been thinking about him nonstop. But not at all because I started to crush on him. Because I wanted *to crush* him and make him rue the day he ever made this bet and doubted femme people everywhere. But here he is, saying the exact opposite of what he insisted back in September. None of this is making sense.

"What? How? I haven't changed. I'm still as makeup loving, sports hating, nails doing, heels wearing as I've ever been."

Skylar nods frantically, his smile getting so wide, it makes him look demonic. "Don't you get it, Riley? I can look past all that."

Hold up.

I fling Skylar's hands off mine and they *thunk* on the table.

"Oh, how *good* of you, Skylar. You can look past the things that make me *me*? You get how fucked up that is, right?"

"No, no, no. I'm saying this wrong." Skylar wipes a hand across his sweaty forehead and looks me square in the eyes. "Riley, I want to date you. I want to take you to the Gaybutante Ball. Will you go out with me?"

"No!" There's not a single question in my mind, not for a second. This was the guy who got me to question myself and put me on the defensive for the past two and a half months. This was the guy who insisted someone like him could never like someone like me. This was the guy who went out of his way to shit all over femmes everywhere just because *he* thought he could never be into someone who presented themself femininely. *Incorrectly*, though, I should add, since now he's here taking it all back.

"Wow, that's, um." Skylar takes a deep, shaky breath. "That's the first time anyone has turned me down before. Ever."

"For the record, this isn't because of any stupid superficial thing like how you look or the way you're constantly showing your lack of fashion creativity by always donning Crestview Carnivore gear," I say. "This is because of who you are inside. Are you really that surprised? How could you possibly think that after all you've put me through I would have developed feelings for you?"

Skylar's lost his confident edge again, staring at his hands while he says, "I guess I just thought that after all this time thinking about me, you might have seen the good in me too. Riley, you made an entire podcast around *me*. And I thought maybe this could be one of those enemies-to-lovers things you always hear about. Adam seemed to think so. I always teased him for falling for that shit, but he ended up giving me a bit of hope."

I want to say I feel sorry for him, turning him down like this. But honestly, I don't. Do I want to rub it in? No. But I'm not about to sit here and suddenly let him be the victim in all this.

"Adam doesn't get any points either. He went along with all this. There's no way in hell this is getting flipped."

For the first time, finally, after all these weeks, Skylar looks a bit ashamed. "I was kind of terrible, wasn't I?"

"*KIND OF?!*" I don't mean to yell it, but I can't help myself. All eyes turn to our table. Some MPH kids with interest, the lesbian book club moms looking a tad affronted that I've interrupted their conversation, and Roz glancing up from the espresso machine to gravelly shout, "You kids are cool to sit there, but don't go disturbing my whole shop!"

"Sorry, everybody. Sorry, Roz. I'll take two strawberry crème Italian sodas to go." They're Sabrina's favorite, and I've got to get back to my life. But first, I have one more thing I need to say to Skylar.

"Look, you were *awful*. You went out of your way to shit all over an entire group of people just because you don't like them." I pause, anticipating Skylar to fight back or deny it, but he actually listens for once. "I get that attraction just happens, and a lot of the time we don't have control over it. I see somebody taller than me and get tingles in my gut. A shaved head can be really hot. Hell, queer people exist because we can't help who we're attracted to or not attracted to, despite all the input about what's 'normal.'

"The first thing you got to do when there's just that *something* that makes you go wild in the best way is make sure you're not fetishizing the people who push your buttons. These are people; there's consent. Remember that this is a two-way street and whoever does it for you might not feel the same way. Then the thing you can't do, shouldn't do—or else make people hate every ounce of your being when you do—is make a point to let others know when you're *not* into them, when you've never been asked in the first place. That's when we get into femmephobia, transphobia, fatphobia, racism, you name it. What did you gain when you told me that gay guys don't like femme people? Or when you told Adam that one guy was too feminine to be his escort to the Ball? Anything?"

Skylar sits there and chews his cheek. But at least he looks up at me and shakes his head.

"That's right. Nothing. Other than gaining the very accurate label of *asshole*. You know what I gained? A semester's worth of self-doubt. And to be honest, it wasn't just this semester. It's all the time when I get looks because I'm not the run-of-the-mill definition of *boy*. How society treats me isn't your fault, but your declaration that I could never get a gay cis boyfriend definitely heaped another load of shit onto an already-steaming shit pile.

I don't deserve that. I'm better than that. And honestly, with behavior like yours, I'm way better than you."

I get up from my chair, Skylar following me with his eyes. "You're right," he says. "You *are* better than me. I didn't think. And I didn't deserve you hiding my identity like that on your podcast. A lot of other people would have hung me out to dry."

I nod. "Probably. But this whole thing wasn't for revenge toward you. It was vindication for me."

"I get that. Like I said, you're competitive, man. Or, uh, lady? I don't really know what to call you."

I let him sit in all his awkwardness.

"Anyway," he goes on, "I wanted to say I'm sorry. I was wrong. And I won't put that out there again."

"Put what out there?" I need him to say it. I need him to truly understand how his opinions were so fucked up.

Skylar swallows. "I, um, I won't say what gay guys can and can't be interested in. I won't tell people that they can't be seen as attractive by others just because of, like, their labels and shit. Or just because of what I like."

It's a start. A little unrefined, but a start.

"Good," I say, then turn around and don't look back, even though there's a solid sixty seconds where I have to grab my drinks and pay for them. I can feel Skylar's stare burning into my back the entire time. It isn't until I'm on the street, hustling out of sight of the café windows, that I squeal. Loudly.

"God, that felt good!" I don't say it to anybody; I just get it out into the universe. All this time having to deal with Skylar's judgment, with trolls who were #TeamJock online, and I finally got to say how I feel about it in real, coherent sentences that don't get parsed apart by stupid emojis or comments about how I should just put on a pair of guys' jeans and shut up.

I swear, even the way my heels clack on the sidewalk sounds lighter, happier. And that's saying something because I got these silver-toed purple booties at 83 percent off, and nothing makes me happier than a deal.

I literally frolic into Mountain Pass Crafts, the bell jangling over the door as bright and cheery as I am. I (horribly) dance over to Sabrina, who's poring over fabrics with Mitzy.

"Wow, you're in a surprisingly good mood," Sabrina says. She looks worried, a concerned crinkle in her eyes like she thinks I might break down from having to spend even a minute alone with my former archnemesis. "I guess that means your talk went well."

"Better than well. It went spectacu—"

My crossbody jangles with buzz after buzz. I'm getting so many notifications, it practically shakes with the force of an earthquake. The only person who messages like this is Nick, and only in an extreme emergency, like that time his knees gave out after Grayson broke up with him. And in case he needs me to lift him up again, or for any other reason at all, I set our drinks on the front counter and open my phone.

It's not Nick, though. I have a string of DMs, all from Skylar.

You know what this means right?

You won the bet.

You had a masculine guy ask you out.

Me.

I asked you to the Ball.

I never said you had to accept to win.

And yeah I knew about the bet but I kind of created it with you so it's not like you could cheat and tell me about it later or anything.

So you won dude.

I'll drop out of baseball.

"Holy shit," I breathe.

"Oh my god, Riley, what is it?" When I don't answer, Sabrina shakes me by the shoulders, panicked. "What is it?! Mitzy, call an ambulance!"

Mitzy whips around so fast, her silver wig almost flies off. Her panic is enough to snap me out of it.

"Mitzy, wait, stop. Everything's fine." I look at Sabrina. "More than fine. I won." The word feels funny on my lips. Funny, but fantastic. "I won the bet!"

I show her the string of messages, her mouth dropping wider as she reads each one.

"I get to be a Gaybutante," I say. "I GET TO BE A GAYBUTANTE!"

I'm screaming, I'm crying, I'm grabbing Sabrina's hand and jumping. This is really happening. The wave of relief that washes over me is so strong, it almost makes *my* knees give out. I get to have that huge queer community I've always dreamed of. I get to show femmes everywhere that we can be belittled and ridiculed and still come out on top. I get to start next semester ready to share that femme fire and have the entire Gaybutantes backing me up as I launch my podcasting and interviewing dreams. It's all going to happen.

"Riley! Riley, that's great!" I know she means what she's saying, but there's a bit of sadness there too.

"Don't for a minute think you're getting left out of this," I say. "I've got a plan for your party. We're not letting anything get us off track."

Because Riley Weaver is going to take the world by storm.

And that wouldn't be possible without my friends.

Excerpt from Episode 11—*Riley Weaver Needs a Date to the Gaybutante Ball*: "Road to Redemption?"

And that's how I'm here, sitting in Producer's basement, recording words that I stopped believing I would get to say.

I won.

Before we move on to the next steps of the Ball process, I want to talk a minute about redemption. Because, no matter what you've done, I think there's always a road to it. If there wasn't, no human could make any mistake ever. If you're living, if you're taking the chances that are out there for you, you're going to make at least one. Most likely thousands. Most probably insignificant. But some huge ones too.

The Jock made, in the grand scheme of things, probably a moderate mistake. It felt huge to me because he was in my head all the time, but when compared to the world and what's going on in it, I don't know that the universe sees it as gigantic. And that's kind of a lousy thing for us femmes out there, because while one person's negative opinions might not seem like a lot to some, it all adds up when you have to confront multiple Jocks every week. But, in the end, The Jock seemed to understand that what he'd said was wrong, that his opinions were gross and hurtful and led to a whole culture that keeps gender nonconforming people scared to be themselves. Maybe I'm being too hopeful about his change of heart. Maybe a few days not focused on the bet and he'll go back to being exactly how he was before. But he did say he was going to be a man of his word and leave his teams even when I told him later he didn't have to follow through on that. More importantly though, he said sorry, and at the time, I think he meant it.

But here's the kicker when you're making amends for your screwups. One sorry doesn't cut it. Just saying you've seen the light isn't enough. Not when you've gone out of your way to take away the light for so many people, so many times. It doesn't mean you can't get better, but you're definitely not there with one apology. Still, that apology is the first step toward becoming a better person. It takes follow-up, not necessarily directly to the person or people you've harmed because they don't owe you anything anymore unless they want to give it, but in the world at large. When you see folks belittling femmes, say something. When you notice someone doesn't fit the gender mold and might have some anxiety because of it, welcome them in.

Maybe some of you listening to this podcast were always Team Jock, and maybe you still are. But I hope now, after all these episodes, you see that there isn't a single ounce of good your opinions have done for the world. Like I told The Jock, go ahead and have those things you're attracted to, but if I'm not it, keep it to yourself. Because what's the point trying to tear someone down? I'm not asking to date you, you're not asking to date me, so let's just support each other's love lives in harmony, right? And if somebody you're not attracted to does respectfully ask you out, don't make them feel like shit if you don't recip-rocate those feelings. Let them down gently, and just go about your life.

And for those of us who are femme, who are nonbinary, who are genderqueer, who are different and don't quite know how to label it: If you've got the space in your heart to help lift others up with you, do it. I know it's hard some-times. But if you can, fight the battles you need to fight, then focus on building others up who the world has tried to break. You're going to see way more good in you and around you.

Trust me.

It's so much better than letting the assholes get you down.

Chapter 17

"This is the spot," I say to Nick as I pull into the Denny's parking lot. This was the space that Josiah said would be safest, with their parents at work for the day, and the majority of the kids from their school at some weekend soccer game.

As soon as we drive up, a figure dashes across the asphalt. They duck behind cars, a duffel bag in their hands, until they make it to the back passenger's side door and pop it open.

"Riley!" For someone who came into this car very incognito, they are surprisingly upbeat now. "It's so good to meet you." They reach over the backrest to squeeze my shoulder. "And you must be Nick!" they say, hugging Nick's side. "I can't believe this is actually happening!"

"Well, you'd better believe it, babe!" I say, putting the

car in reverse. "It's time to treat you like the queen you are."

The entire two-hour drive back to Mountain Pass, and the whole afternoon shopping and trying makeup and letting Josiah have their way with my closet, Josiah will not stop talking. It's an endless stream of words, which is saying something because I sure know how to talk. A lot. But it's the best sound I've ever heard in my life. Like Josiah has felt bottled up all this time and is finally able to just be themself. And now that they've had a taste of it, they don't want it to stop.

It isn't until about hour five, sitting in front of my vanity while I show them the perfect eye shadow tricks, that Josiah finally notices. "Oh my god, I've been talking about myself this entire time."

"Yeah, don't worry about it," Nick says from my bed. "We're used to one person hogging all the airtime."

"Hey!" I throw a makeup sponge at him, and he laughs as it bounces off his nose. "Anyway, that was the whole point of today, Josiah. For you to just be you. It's a lot to keep that inside."

Josiah bites the side of their cheek, and for the first time today, they frown. But it's so much more than just a downward tilt of their lips. I can practically feel the weight of the pain they've been through all these years, not being themself.

"Want to talk about it?" I ask.

"That's all I've been doing," Josiah says, their eyes downcast.

I slowly, tentatively—so they see my fingers coming and can stop me if they want—tilt their chin up and meet Josiah's eyes. "That's what having a mentor is all about. You finally have someone to let it out with. So go ahead. Let it all out. If you feel comfortable."

Josiah gives one last chew to their cheek, then looks at themself in the mirror. They take in their foundation, their perfect highlighting, the slightly smudged eyeliner that they'll get better at in time.

"You look great," I say. "I know we just met, but you look like you. I can feel it."

Josiah nods. "I just wish I could be this way all the time. Especially with my parents."

Their tone says so much. "Do you think they'd ever be supportive?"

"No. Not at all. I've never been able to share my pronouns with them because they're constantly complaining about how there should only be *he* and *she*. And my dad just hates any time I express anything even remotely feminine. He caught me wearing my mom's heels once, and he went ballistic. Screamed so hard at me, I'm surprised he didn't pass out. And I just stood there and took it while he pushed me out of her shoes. I wasn't used to wearing them yet and I completely lost my balance and twisted my ankle. He didn't check to see if I was okay. He didn't react when I cried out in pain. He just left." Josiah reaches for a

Kleenex and dabs at the corner of their eyes. "Dammit, I will not let him ruin this moment too. I did a pretty good job at my eyes for a first-timer, don't you think?"

I smile, trying to put my all in it despite the visions of Josiah alone and in pain flying through my head. "You did! You've got this innate talent. It took me forever to figure out blending and all that, but in, like, a week, you're going to be better than all of us."

Josiah gives me a weak grin and we sit there in silence, both of us lost in our own thoughts. I see Nick out of the corner of my eye, and his head isn't buried in his phone. We're both just listening to Josiah, and I know Nick's feeling the same way I am. Helpless. Helpless that we can't change Josiah's living situation, even if they are my mentee.

Josiah finally says, "The worst part isn't that he pushed me or screamed at me. The worst part is that he can't stand my femininity but adores it in my mom. I've heard him say countless times how much he loves her in heels, or how amazing she looks in her favorite shade of lipstick. But the second I put that on, he's disgusted. How can he love femininity in her, but hate it so much in me?"

We both know the answer to that, and when our eyes lock, Josiah names it. "He hates it because I have a dick. He'd never say that out loud because he knows it'd say a lot more about him than it does about me, but he can't stop thinking about the fact that I have a penis when I'm wearing things he thinks should be for women only. It's so messed up."

I nod. "*Society* is so messed up. There are a lot of people out there who think beyond those arbitrary gender rules, but it doesn't make it hurt any less when we come across people who don't. And you don't owe an explanation to anyone about presenting your body in the way that you want."

"Hearts over parts, right?" Josiah says.

"Hearts over parts."

Josiah gives one last dab to their eyes, then heaves a deep sigh. "Okay, whew. Enough of that. I've maxed out on heaviness for my *life*. And I could be a decent human and ask you, like, *one* question about yourself." Josiah snaps. "Oh, wait! I need to know what you're going to do about the Ball. Since The Jock is so obviously out, who's going to be your escort?"

The exact question that I was trying to find the right time to ask myself.

"Well, um, funny you should mention it," I say. "So, originally, Nick offered to escort both me and Sabrina."

"We're basically a throuple anyway," Nick says.

"Okay, wow, let's stick with bestie sandwich." Now it's Nick's turn to throw the sponge back. "But then I thought, there's still so much good that can come from this Ball too. And I remembered how you mentioned in your letter that you've always wanted to be able to go to a dance dressed exactly how you want to be dressed. There's no better accepting place than the Gaybutantes. So, what do you say? Want to make our debuts to the world together?

We can even make sure that no one posts any pictures with you on social media if you're not ready, but at least you can have this one glorious moment in person."

Josiah is completely silent, not at all the chatterbox they've been most of the day. It makes me oddly nervous.

"Hey, don't feel any sort of pressure at all. I know it's a lot to spring on you and—"

Josiah throws themself around my neck and bursts into tears, makeup be damned. I'm not able to make out much of what they say, except for two words. "R-Riley! Yes!"

It doesn't take long for me to burst into tears too. This was the point of the podcast: To build connection. I'm so thankful for every last listener, but this moment right here, this is my absolute favorite. There's this shared bond knowing some of what Josiah is going through, knowing all that worry and anxiety from being different than other gays, knowing that the world doesn't perceive you as man enough, whether that world is gay or straight. But even with that, there's this relief when you finally get to be yourself, and I know that's what Josiah is feeling right now. I can feel it radiating off them, and it's reminding me of the first day of freshman year when I wore my first pair of heels in public. I tottered all over Main Street, and it took me about twenty times longer to get anywhere than it would have in flats, but even that bit of drunk-toddler-walking embarrassment was worth it to finally get to be me.

"You've just made my entire Gaybutante season, Josiah," I say into their shoulder. "Thank you."

Josiah pulls away, snot trailing down their lip that they perfectly lined all by themself. "Are you kidding me? You've just made my life." Josiah sighs one of those deep satisfied sighs where you can feel some of the weight leave them with each passing second. Then they catch sight of themself in my vanity mirror and squeal. "Oh shit! I'm smearing everything. Give me one second and I'll be right out."

They dash into my bathroom, and without them in the room, I realize how exhausted I am. Emotionally filled up, for sure, but exhausted. I collapse onto my bed next to Nick.

"I don't think today could have gone be—"

My words are cut off suddenly, dramatically, tenderly, as Nick takes my face in his hands and kisses me. It's so shocking that it takes my breath away, my lips parting as the air escapes, and Nick takes that slight opening to briefly dart his tongue against mine. It makes every single part of me snap awake, exhaustion long forgotten.

I'm more alert than I've ever been in my entire life. I can feel his fingers alternate between pressing deeper and easing up, and I can practically hear Nick's thoughts wanting to make sure he's not pressing too hard. I love the way our knees touch and how every time I lean into him, he leans back. I can't get over how well our lips fit together, and how there's not any sort of awkwardness in our rhythm. It's as if we've been doing this our whole lives, but like, I know we haven't, and now I feel like the biggest idiot on the planet. How have we never done this before?

Why have we never done this before? Has he wanted to do this before?

"Okay, I'm—oh, wow." Josiah comes out of my bathroom, and Nick and I float apart. Not snap apart—float, like we're both hesitant to drift away, like if we just stay within centimeters of each other, we could get back to that.

Josiah opens my bedroom door and gives a little wave. "I'll just go downstairs and take your dad up on all those snack offers. Take your time. It seems like you two have some *talking* to do."

When the door gently clicks shut, we drift back together. One. Two. Three more kisses. Until that constant chatterbox in me finally rears his head.

"Wait. What are we doing? And why haven't we ever done this until now?"

Nick laughs, and it's full of so much emotion. Disbelief, probably, that we're actually doing this. And relief, I think, that suddenly going from best friends who didn't kiss to best friends who perfectly kiss hasn't made things weird.

"I've been thinking the same thing. The past few months."

"The past *what*?" I can't believe it. I put Nick through this for *months*? "All this time, when I've been making a show about dating other guys! When *you've* been dating another guy?"

Nick gets quiet, no small smile on his face. He starts inspecting himself, beginning with the nails that he let me do for him this afternoon, a deep purple this time. I know he's taking time to gather his thoughts before he says, "First, Daniel and I aren't a thing anymore. We broke up. Weeks ago, actually. Honestly, a few days after we made it official at your birthday."

"Nick! Why didn't you say anything? I would have been there for you!"

"I know," he says. "Like you were with Grayson. But once Daniel broke up with me, I couldn't go to you. Because you were the reason we broke up." My eyes bulge out of my head and Nick rushes to explain. "Not in any intentional way. I, um, like you, and after talking about you nonstop on my dates with Daniel, he helped me realize that I was talking about you in ways more than a friend. In fact, he said that 'Forest of Feeling' wasn't about his feelings for me. It was about how I talked about you, describing all those hours we've spent above the treetops on your zip-lining platforms."

My mouth drops open. "I've, um . . . huh, I've never been more speechless in my life."

Nick laughs, soft, gentle, perfect. "That's a first."

"But in all this time talking about it with Daniel, why didn't you mention it to me?"

Nick's eyes wander while he explains. "I don't know, it's just, when you set out on your show, you had a very specific guy in mind. Like, the most masculine of guys. From Antoine to Connery to that Ricky guy, it was somebody who seemed to fit a very specific mold. None of them were really out of the box, you know? Nobody dyed their hair, nobody who was into certain types of makeup, no pan-sexuals who would rather sit at home and geekily obsess over movie production than, I don't know, chisel some sculpture out of wood or go work out or something. I know it was part of the parameters Skylar set for your bet, but . . . I didn't think I was what you wanted."

"Holy. Shit." I'm smacked by a realization so hard that I actually bolt from the bed. Hit by what a profound dumbass I've been. "I did to you exactly what Skylar did to me. I made you feel like how you presented yourself wasn't it. Nick, I'm so sorry. I'm so, so sorry."

"Well, it's not like you went out of your way to be an ass to me about it."

"Yeah, but I got so caught up in proving a point, I didn't realize how this could be interpreted. I didn't think how *you* might interpret it, and you're my best friend." I start pacing now, the points of my heels making imprints in my rug. "This must have been what some of those folks were trying to say in the comments, the other femmes who said I was an embarrassment. Their delivery was a little harsh, and I just got defensive instead of really figuring out what they were trying to say. I need to clarify this in the next episode. I need to not be a part of this gender-shitting-on-gender crap. I need to—"

Stop. I need to stop what I'm doing right now and focus on the moment at hand. I need to directly make right the biggest miscommunication of all.

"I need to do this." I sit next to Nick, grab his hands and

place them so he's touching the small of my back, then lean in for a kiss. And another. And another.

"You were always more than enough," I say.

"It doesn't make things weird, does it?"

"Yeah, it does." Nick's forehead bunches into a scowl in a nanosecond. "But weird in a good way. In the best way. In the how-did-I-not-see-this-from-the-start way. You've always had my back. You've always been there for me. I just never thought you felt like this."

"It started back in June, right after my breakup. You instantly knew what to say and how to make me feel better, and you were there literally every single time I needed you. You always came to bat, and it's not like I didn't think it before, but I realized just how big your heart is. At first, I didn't want to say anything because I thought it might be rebound feelings, right? And I didn't want to make my best friend a rebound. But then the feelings stayed, throughout the whole summer, and getting to spend so much time with you one-on-one while Sabrina was at the clinic or with Cassidy just made the feelings stronger. Things are easy with you. You get me."

"And I fucked that up with this podcast."

Nick's small smile is back now. "You nearly fucked it all up, yes. I tried to distract myself with Daniel and accept that best friends don't usually end up together, but I couldn't. Daniel noticed. He was so nice about it too."

"I should reach out and apologize to him. I never meant for there to be so much collateral damage in this bet."

Nick laces my fingers in his, caressing my squoval-shaped neon-orange nails with his short purple ones. We've been hand in hand so many times before, but it's never felt like this. I can't believe it took me so long to realize that we could be a thing.

But I'm so glad I finally did.

Excerpt from Episode 12—*Riley Weaver Needs a Date to the Gaybutante Ball*: "A Clarification"

First off, big news: not only do I now have a date to the Gaybutante Ball, but I do, in fact, have a boyfriend. Wow, it still feels so weird calling him that when he's always just been known as my best friend since forever. And you just so happen to know him. Say hi, Boyfriend.

Hey, everybody. Boyfriend here, formerly known as Producer, but, uh . . . I like this new name. A lot.

Oh my god, we're insufferable. But you're gonna have to suffer through it at least a couple more episodes, folks.

Anyway, no, my boyfriend will not be my date to the Ball, if that's what you're thinking. And that's already been cleared with him, so we don't need comments trying to start drama.

But, speaking of drama, I think I may have been the cause of some of it. Or maybe some turmoil, for some of you, during the course of this podcast. It all began in order to create some General Gay Chaos—and to document my time dating cis masculine guys to see if femme gays could, in fact, be found attractive by them. But in that single-minded focus, I worry I may have sent the message, at times, that this traditionally masculine type of guy is the ultimate-get.

Ugh, I hate that word. Traditional. Nothing is traditional about it. It's just the type of masc guy who's been of the moment the past hundred years or whatever. Sky-high curly wigs and cute little heels replaced in today's media with the most ripped guys, the ones who look like they didn't spend a second on getting ready but just woke up sexy, the ones who have no idea what an eyelash curler is or couldn't name a nail shape at the manicurist if they tried.

But who's to say that's sexy? Or not sexy? Can't we all just agree that every type of person, regardless of how they present their gender or label themself, is the right person to press all the buttons for somebody out there? I know that, at times, it may have come across like I was saying that new traditional cis guy is the only thing that's it, but what I want to make clear here and now is that we're all it. You are beautiful. You are hot. Inside and out. Yes, you, the person listening to this right now. And while not everyone may think that of me or you or the person listening next to you in your car, or of your siblings or best friends, there is a person—there are people—out there, who can't wait to get to know you and them more. People who want to learn your good sides and bad ones, who want to lift you up when you're feeling down and celebrate with you in all your successes. Because that's what we all deserve. We need to understand that not everyone is going to get those feelings for us, but we can correct them when they make declarative statements that no one will ever feel that. And we should correct them.

I'm glad it was pointed out to me when my words could have been taken a certain way, and I'm sorry that I didn't understand that sooner. Some of you were trying to point this out to me before, but I didn't get it at first. I got so caught up in people working against me and telling me I was wrong that I didn't stop to think about what parts of this podcast you were examining and why. But I'm so freaking happy I realize it now. One, so I can check myself in the future, and two, because I get to have this moment with you to say I'm sorry and to tell you that you are beautiful. Femme, trans, cis, gay, straight, pan—any and all genders and sexualities. You are gorgeous.

Now get out there, beautiful, and go find your person, or people, or escort, or best friend, or whoever the hell you want, romantically or otherwise, because I can guarantee you one thing:

They're waiting for you.

Chapter 18

The yips and woofs and staccato barks start the second I open the door. Per usual, Connery doesn't look up. It's all just background noise to him while he slams away at his keyboard, his disheveled hair jiggling as his fingers pound the keys.

"How far away are you from finishing the next great vampire novel?"

Connery shoots up at the sound of my voice, slamming his laptop shut. "Sorry, Darla, sorry, I—" He finally meets my eyes, and his whole being slumps. "Oh. Sorry, Riley. I didn't realize it was you."

There's that word. *Sorry.* The whole reason I'm here. My last two podcasts about redemption and making amends made me realize there was still some apologizing left to do on my end.

"No, Connery, *I'm* the one who's sorry. I never should have put you in such a weird situation. I never should have just assumed you were gay and made our hangouts a date when that wasn't your plan to begin with."

Connery absentmindedly taps the cover of his laptop, right over the rainbow sticker that still shines out and proud.

"You really are such a great ally, and it wasn't fair of me to jump to conclusions just because you're versed in queer culture. Dylan's so lucky to have a best friend like you."

At the mention of her name, Connery smiles. "I'm the lucky one. She's great. I meant it when I said that she'd love you. We should all hang out together sometime."

"Really? You'd want to do that?"

"Definitely." Then his face gets all mock serious. "But just to make sure we're on the same page, we're hanging out *as friends*."

I roll my eyes. "All right, all right, I get it. Besides, I have a boyfriend now."

"Wow, moved on from me pretty quickly, huh?"

"Actually, it was a relationship quite a few years in the making."

"Slow-burn romances are my favorite," Connery says. "I'm happy for you. I hope to meet him."

I know he means it. Connery's one of those great guys who can truly move on from any awkwardness. He'll make a girl really happy someday.

"Well, I didn't just drop by to disturb your writing time. I wanted to run an idea by Darla. Trying to help a friend with her last Gaybutante pillar, and this place is a key part of the plan."

Connery cocks his head to the side like the adorable little buggers that I know are yipping in their playpen. "Plan?" he asks.

"That's right. A puppy plan."

"Wait, the Gaybutantes are supposed to be, like, the most glamorous organization in the country for queer teens, and here we are changing in the tiniest bathroom I've ever been in."

Josiah has a point, as we're perched over the sink in this ferry restroom with terrible, splotchy gray lighting. Thank god for the portable vanity I brought in case of just such an emergency.

"We could have changed before we got here, but then everyone would have seen exactly how we look as soon as we arrived. That sort of contradicts a debut, don't you think?"

Not to mention that somehow, every year, the location of the Gaybutante Ball is known by avid GS fans who will snap pictures of us and leak them to the internet before we get a chance to put them out there first. There's a picture with me arriving in a pink tracksuit, with Josiah next to me but unrecognizable in a giant sun hat and bug-eye sunglasses. There's a picture of everybody arriving, so the secret's already out that every Hopeful who signed up in all four cities has made it through. Which just makes everyone on board even more psyched about tonight. That's truly the best part about the Gaybutantes: anybody who wants in, gets in. We just have to make sure we don't get in our own way.

"We are so lucky this thing has four floors or else there's no way everyone would be ready in time," Josiah says, which gets an "Amen" from Adam and an "Asexual men!" from Adam's asexual boyfriend, Ethan, who are both getting ready in matching tuxes. Adam's apologized—several times—about not being more vocal against Skylar, and while that doesn't make us besties, I can see that he's trying.

Each floor of the ferry has been assigned to one Gaybutante-represented city, and we'll all meet in approximately five minutes to reveal ourselves to the current Society members and alumni who could make it, and to our resident photographers—including an Annie Leibovitz–protégé alum—who are going to take our pictures and share them on all our socials.

The stall door behind me slams open. Nick is practically strangling Sabrina with her dress. I've never seen Nick this sweaty in his life. He's tugging on her zipper so hard that the baby-pink fabric of her gown is cutting off her air supply. "Why the hell won't this thing close?" Nick grunts. "It's stuck."

"Need. Air!" Sabrina gasps. Nick lets up and she takes in two heaving gulps. "Of course this would happen. *Of course it would!* I finally accomplish all my pillars just yesterday, but now I won't have a fucking outfit for my debut. I should have adopted one of those puppies. You can't be stressed around a puppy!"

Her party came together perfectly. Sabrina knew everyone was going to have predebut jitters, and I knew where to find critters that could help everybody forget their nerves for just a little bit. Darla loved the idea, and so did all of Sabrina's followers on her reinstated social media accounts where she gets to bask in her much-deserved attention again. People went wild for the Sabrina-hosted Puppy Party, where the anxiety was licked and yapped right out of us.

Until this moment.

"I think you all need puppies," Josiah says. "You're so nervous, it's making *me* nervous. And really, we should all just be excited. I mean look at me." They motion to their outfit, from head to toe, and damn, they look good. Their hair is swooped back in this gorgeous wet look, and they're wearing a deep purple halter-top jumpsuit, with just the right amount of bedazzling, complete with a detachable train with even *more* jewels. To top it all off, they wear the most gloriously strappy high-heeled sandals. Josiah sparkles over every inch of themself, and they deserve all the attention. But like the amazing soul they are, they really meant that self-appreciating comment to open the door to compliment everyone else.

"And look at all of you," they say. "We are freaking gorgeous, and this moment is about soaking that in. The good you're doing for gays everywhere. You're fucking Gaybutantes, and you've got to say it like you mean it."

We all stand or precariously perch over toilets and sinks in stunned silence. I don't think any of us was expecting this pep talk.

"SAY IT!" Josiah shrieks, and as one we let out a frantic, anxious, and excited, "WE ARE FUCKING GAY-BUTANTES!"

The moment we scream it, we crack up. People (cough, me) bat at eyes so tears of laughter don't ruin their makeup. Sabrina's no longer all tense and Nick is able to slide her zipper up, smooth as butter. I know in that moment that although they can't be in the organization with us, we will all count Josiah as an honorary member forever.

"Okay, people, it's time!" Lonny's voice comes from the other side of the door, and we all immediately do last looks in the mirror.

"How is it time already?" I ask. "It can't be time already!"

"What did I just say?" Josiah shouts, before sashaying out the door.

"We. Are. Fucking. Gaybutantes!" Sabrina chants as she follows.

Everyone streams out—everyone except Nick, who sidles up next to me, his hands caressing my lilac jump-suit, his thumbs stroking back and forth over the jewel-embellished corset belt around my waist. One of my favorite things about him in the couple weeks since we decided to give our relationship a chance is how he strikes that perfect balance between taking in my look and then looking me right in the eyes. Like he's trying to see all of me, inside and out, and loves both sides.

"You're beautiful," he breathes before pulling me in for a kiss. It's soft, it's perfect, it's confidence boosting, it's romantic. It's everything I never knew I wanted.

"You're beautiful," I say. "Save a dance for me after the introductions?"

"Okay, but just one," he says, that small smile so irresistible that I can't help but kiss it.

Nick slides his hands down from my waist, lacing his fingers through mine.

"You ready?" he asks.

"I'm ready."

"Introducing Riley Weaver," Cliff announces from the side of the viewing deck, "podcaster extraordinaire, gay, femme, and fabulous!" I don't know if anyone screams or not, because I just get this unreal moment of, like, an out-of-body experience. I'm floating over me and Josiah as we walk across the deck, Gaybutantes surrounding us on all sides, mouths open and smiling and supposedly cheering, Josiah's teeth sparkling with their deliriously happy grin, and they don't miss a single step as we clack next to each other. It's their laughter that finally pulls me back to reality, that love-filled, relief-saturated, joyous bark that escapes their throat.

"This is the moment I've been waiting for!" they say, squeezing my arm.

As if on cue, Lonny—in the most fabulous crocheted ball gown made to look like couture rain clouds—adds, "Riley is escorted by his mentee and third slice of bread in his new-and-improved best-friend double-decker sandwich, Josiah. Give it up for Riley and Josiah!"

The crowd truly does go wild. The way the lights of the Seattle skyline reflect off Puget Sound makes it look like the whole city is applauding for us.

After our second lap, the photographers snap a couple solo pictures of me so Josiah doesn't have to deal with the wrath of their parents, and then we're pulled to the side to see the very last Gaybutante get announced. Out of four cities, I was the only *W* last name, and after me, Atlanta had just one Z. The whole alphabet made me shake with jitters while forty-six other kids were called before me.

But now, cradled against Nick's side with Josiah holding my hand on the other, and Sabrina's gown big enough to swoop behind us and brush against my legs, all feels right in the universe. I know that no matter what else happens as I make my Gaybutante journey—whether I ever reach my goal of leaving Mountain Pass, seeing the world, and becoming one of the top interviewers in the country—I have just the right people to weather anything that gets thrown our way.

I started this process looking for that queer camaraderie and connection to make all my dreams come true.

Turns out, I already had it.

Excerpt from Episode 13—*Riley Weaver Needs a Date to the Gaybutante Ball*: "The Last Dance"

And that was that. It was the most magical night of the Gaybutante season thus far, and even though it's just the beginning of my Gaybutante story, it still felt like an ending. An ending to an older version of me, the Riley who didn't know how important love was to him, who wasn't really sure about all the deep-rooted insecurities that were in him until he had to bare his femme soul to the whole world. But through this process, I've learned that I truly love myself. And I truly have loved doing this.

But this podcast needs to end. I no longer need a date since I've got the best forever-date now, and I think I've done enough talking about myself to last me quite a while. We've had thirteen episodes and 37,122 unique listeners—which I'd say isn't bad for a first go at a podcast. Although, that number isn't because of me. It's because of you out there who've followed the Gaybutantes or shared these podcasts and wanted to build a community. All I did was sit in a room, press Record, and talk. But what you did was listen. What you did was post. What you did was write in and tell me the insecurities that you've had in your own dating lives, which made me realize so many of us are looking for love. Some romantic, some platonic, some not at all—and how that makes you feel like people see you as different too. So, I think it's time to launch a new podcast where you'll do the talking.

This is the introduction of our new show, Riley Weaver Wants to Help You Find Love (Or Not). I know, I know—another ridiculously long title, but we can all agree I'm a long-winded gasbag, so it feels on-brand. What I need from you is to write in, call in, share with me and the world—but only when you feel comfortable—the struggles that you go through in your own little corner of the gender spectrum, and let's discuss how all of us can help. Whether you're trans or cis or gay or aromantic or femme or any sexuality or gender or unsure of how to label yourself, all are welcome. I'll ask you about the love you're looking for, give the advice that I have, and look to our listeners to beef that up because, let's face it, I'm new to love and not the most experienced gal to ever host a podcast.

But that's the best part. There's no pressure here. Because we're all learning together. And if there's ever any sort of fun new kissing techniques you need Boyfriend and me to try out and give feedback on, we're more than happy to.

Riley!

What? Aren't we?

Okay, yes. Yes, we are.

See? What did I tell you? We'll be here for all of it, and I can't wait to talk with each and every one of you.

Until then, I'm Riley Weaver, and you are beautiful.

Acknowledgments

While my readership is not nearly as vast as Riley's listener-ship, it is the wildest thing to go from someone hoping to make art for people to actually consume to being someone who gets to do that for a living. I am honored to get to write books for the queer community, and I wouldn't be here without the love and support of many people who turned me from an unknown writer to a still mostly unknown author but with real published books out there. The biggest thanks to:

Brent Taylor. Thank you for championing my books from Day One, confident that someday writing novels would go from a dream to a career, and for giving me the best guidance whenever I text with *Got five minutes to chat?* knowing full well the call is going to go longer than five minutes.

Megan Ilnitzki. I mean every last word in that dedication, and no amount of words will ever be enough to truly thank you for your time, your encouragement, your perfect editorial eye, your ushering me into the world as a Gaybutante and telling folks they should read my work. You're stuck with me now!

Parrish Turner. Your insights, your thoughtful notes, and everything you did behind the scenes was so helpful, and I hope we get to work together on many more projects!

Sarah Mondello, Laura Harshberger, and Mark Rifkin, thank you for all the copy edits. I . . . don't know the English language, apparently, and it really means a lot that you never hold that against me. Al Pal, thanks for giving this another look-through when I was shaking in my grammatical boots.

Ricardo Bessa and David DeWitt. Thank you for once again illustrating and designing the absolute best cover. It is 100% Gaybutante-worthy!

Big thanks to these authors who have spent time with me either in person or online and boosted me up, especially this past year: Aaron H. Aceves, Cate Berry, Gene Brenek, Erik J. Brown, Kat Cho, Robbie Couch, Melissa de la Cruz, Antwan Eady, Debbi Michiko Florence, Jonny Garza Villa, Eric Geron, Bayne Gibby, Brian D. Kennedy, Emery Lee, Lyla Lee, Mackenzi Lee, Stephan Lee, Julie Murphy, Abdi Nazemian, Kelis Rowe, Steven Salvatore, Adam Sass, Melissa See, Lori R. Snyder, Christina Soontornvat, and Robby Weber.

So many folks who gave so much of their time and effort to help make *Out of the Blue* a success. Nina West, the entire mer community, Claire Davey and Andrea Swanson at Auntie's Bookstore, Shelby Devitt at BookPeople, Kathy Burnette at Brain Lair Books, and Laura Graveline and Joy Preble at Brazos Bookstore. All of your enthusiasm for getting *OOTB* out into the world meant so much to me, and the book literally wouldn't be a bestseller without y'all. Thank you so much!

Jonathan Unger, Benjamin O'Keefe, Adam Wescott, and McKenna Marshall. Y'all make me feel like a real creator. I'm so glad we're framily now!

My friends and family and friends who are family. You know who you are, and I'm so thankful to all of you for boosting me up on this ride, asking about my works in progress, and making sure I don't forget to celebrate along the way.

Teachers, librarians, and booksellers. You are on the front-lines of the most disheartening battle of book banning. Thank you for getting books into the hands of teens who need them. Thank you for letting those readers know they are seen, even when you face threats from hateful community members. You are heroes.

Readers! You make this writing life truly so special. I hope you know that the Gaybutantes are a love letter to you. I can tell that you are all ready to make your mark on the world, and I know that you will. All of you reading this right here, right now, are inducted into the Gaybutante Society. I can't wait to see how you change the world.

Jerry, for standing by my side while I transformed into my true femme self over these years. I literally look like an entirely different person than when we first met, and through it all, you've always seen my heart. I love you.